YOUR DAUGHTER
WILL DIE!

YOUR DAUGHTER WILL DIE!

PETER ROHRBACH
WRITING AS "JAMES P. CODY"

BRASH
BOOKS

For Sarah, who watched me write this.

ISBN-13: 978-1-954841-93-2

Published by
Brash Books
PO Box 8212
Calabasas, CA 91372
www.brash-books.com

PUBLISHER'S NOTE

James P. Cody was the pseudonym of Peter T. Rohrbach, a former Catholic priest of the Carmelite Order who lived, prayed and served in a Washington D.C. rectory until he left the priesthood in 1966. Rohrbach wrote the first book in the *D.C. Man* series, *Top Secret Kill*, as a side project while he was a priest. He wrote the next three novels in the series after he left the priesthood.

To further confuse things, the name that Rohrbach was given at birth was actually James Cody. During his childhood, his parents died and he was adopted by the Rohrbach family and took their last name. But when he joined the priesthood, he changed first name from "James" to "Peter Thomas."

Your Daughter Will Die was originally published in 1975. The details about Rohrback / Cody and the series were first revealed by Tom Simon on the *Paperback Warrior* blog in 2018. The popular article had the unintended effect of making copies of the original paperbacks scarce and expensive… until the publication of these new editions on the 50th Anniversary of the original series publication.

CHAPTER ONE

"They've abducted her, Petersen."

"What do you mean, Senator?" I asked. "Who have they abducted?"

"My daughter! Damnit, Petersen, they've kidnapped my daughter."

As he told me that, his face was seared with anguish, an emotion I had never before associated with the usually controlled Senator Lester Rankin. Listening to him now, I couldn't help recalling those many poised performances of the veteran senator from the southwest on the Senate floor, as he resolutely pushed for the conservative legislation which had become his trademark. Some Washington commentators said he had a patrician air, but others, less kindly, called it arrogance. However, there was none of that right now. He was a deeply troubled man, and his voice was cracking as he talked to me in the study of his posh Kenwood home in suburban Washington.

"They've sent me this cassette recording," Rankin was saying to me. "And half of Ellen's driver's license." He handed me the cassette and the driver's license. The D.C. license had been torn crudely in half, leaving the part with the photograph on it. The picture showed a pleasant-faced girl with long, straight, blonde hair, and the date of birth next to her picture told me she was twenty-two years old. Ellen Rankin, the senator's daughter.

"My God, what is the country coming to," Rankin said. "Another kidnapping! They want three hundred thousand dollars. And they've threatened to kill her if I inform the police."

"They?" I asked. "Who are they?"

"That lunatic on the tape identifies himself as General Camillo, and he says he is speaking for the National Federation Army."

I shook my head. "I never heard of it, Senator."

"Neither have I," Rankin said. "I made some cautious inquiries after I received the tape this morning, but I couldn't find anything about any such animal as the National Federation Army. I suppose it's another one of these fanatic groups that are trying to destroy the country we know."

"Perhaps," I said thoughtfully, turning the cassette over in my hand. I didn't like the smell of this thing, and I now regretted that I had agreed to meet with Lester Rankin here at his home this afternoon. God knows I had tried to avoid this meeting.

The first indication that Senator Lester Rankin had a problem of some magnitude occurred about ten-thirty this morning when I arrived at my Connecticut Avenue office. My secretary, Annie, handed me the morning mail and four or five phone messages which had come in before my arrival. One of the messages was from Lester Rankin, and he had placed the call himself directly to my office. I raised my eyebrows at that. Not only is it highly unusual for a senator to place his own phone calls, but it is doubly unusual that Rankin would call old Brian Petersen. Although I had met the man at a few cocktail parties around town and shaken hands with him a few times, I could hardly say that I knew him. Furthermore, I doubted very much if Rankin would be particularly interested in cultivating my friendship. And that didn't bother me at all because Rankin wasn't my kind of senator.

It wasn't his politics which disturbed me (after all, when you get to know the congressmen in Washington you find out that there's not a hell of a lot of difference in the political stances most of them adopt publicly), but I just didn't care for his self-righteous posturing. There are too many nice guys in this town to waste time on a stuffed shirt. And I wasn't about to waste any time on this one now.

I went into my office and Annie brought me some coffee while I flipped through the mail. I returned some of the phone calls but I tossed away the slip with the message from Lester Rankin. If the old bastard had stooped to calling me I knew that he must have some sticky business which he wanted me to handle in a discreet way. The hell with him. Let him stew in his own juices for a change and see how the rest of the world lives.

I had a luncheon engagement at the Monocle on Capitol Hill with Congressman Jack McKiernan, a ruddy-faced Irishman from Ohio. Jack had agreed to meet with me for lunch and listen to my little spiel about import quotas on farm products, a little lobbying job I was doing for one of my clients in the Far West, a farmers' group. We had some drinks and a pleasant lunch and Jack listened patiently while I made a short pitch for tighter restrictions on farm imports and then gave him some mimeographed data which had been prepared for a PR firm in Chicago. I don't think Jack was much interested in, or convinced by, my presentation, but he did do me the courtesy of listening. He figured, I suppose, that I was just doing my job as a lobbyist, and furthermore he was an old friend of mine. I could at least report back to my client that I had made this astonishingly persuasive presentation to Congressman McKiernan, overwhelming him with facts and dazzling him with my brilliant logic.

After lunch, Jack went back to his office in the Rayburn Building on the other side of the Hill, and I stopped at a public phone booth to check back with my office. Actually, I was planning to call it a day and drive out to Burning Tree and shoot eighteen holes of golf, but I wanted to touch base with Annie once more before folding it up. She told me that Rankin had called again, and this time he had told her it was quite urgent and would I please call him at his home.

"Sure, it's always urgent when they want a favor of some kind," I said to Annie over the phone. "But if it were the other way around I could call Rankin's office daily for six months and never get by his secretary."

Annie ignored my remark. "And you've got another phone call, from another senator. And this one is urgent, too. It must be your day, Brian."

"Who's that?"

"Senator Harold Phillips. He's in his office, and will wait there for your call."

That was a phone call I would indeed return. Harold— or Hank, as intimates called him—Phillips was also a rather conservative senator, but one that I liked and admired. (See, I don't have any ideological hangups about a congressman's political posture.) He had been a good friend of Zach's when my father-in-law had been in the Senate, and I had gotten to know him rather well: a large, gregarious, warm person. Hank also had had a serious drinking problem some years back, but he had beaten the booze and today he speaks and lectures quite candidly about his earlier problem. You've got to admire honesty and candor like that in Washington, where so many people are trying to sweep any of their former misadventures under the rug.

I also knew that Hank and Lester Rankin had joined forces on a number of pieces of legislation and were considered to be friends, and as I put the coin into the telephone slot to call

Phillips' office I wondered idly if there was any connection between the two urgent calls.

Harold Phillips came right on the line and his voice sounded unusually agitated. He said he had to see me right away, and if I preferred, he would come to my office himself. I told him I was in a pay-phone booth about three minutes away from the Old Senate Office Building, and I'd be right up.

I took the elevator up to the second floor of the SOB (that's an acronym that never fails to amuse visitors to Washington), and walked down to Phillips' office. His secretary ushered me right into his private office, where I found Hank sitting behind his desk, drumming his fingers on the wooden surface. He didn't waste any time getting into it, and I knew immediately that my suspicion had been correct.

"Lester Rankin has been trying to get ahold of you," he said.

"So I hear, Hank. However, I don't think that there's anything Rankin and I have to discuss."

"But there *is*, Brian. He's in a very difficult situation, and he needs your help."

"My, how the mighty have fallen."

"Brian, please. I recommended you to Lester."

"I appreciate the recommendation, Hank, but no thanks."

"What have you got against Lester Rankin?"

"I don't like his vibes."

"Oh, I know Lester can be a little ... shall we say ..."

"Stuffy," I interjected.

"All right, stuffy, then. But he's not a bad sort. And he's really in trouble."

"I don't like to see anybody in trouble. But I'm not the man to help Rankin."

We tossed it around for about fifteen minutes, and I kept telling Hank politely that I wasn't interested. But he kept insisting quite strongly that I simply had to help old Lester Rankin. I was quite surprised by Hank's insistence, and the note of desperation that was creeping into his voice.

Finally, Phillips came around the desk and stood inches away from where I was sitting. "Please, Brian, do this as a special favor to me."

I took a deep breath, and with the greatest amount of reluctance said: "All right, Hank. At least I'll listen to his story. I don't promise you any more than that." I was frankly embarrassed by the pleading look in Hank's eyes.

"Thanks, Brian. I won't forget," he said.

In Washington terminology that meant that Senator Harold Phillips had just given me a big IOU for a large favor I could redeem at any time of my choosing. And in this city of wheeler-dealing, that's a valuable thing to have stored away in your hip pocket. But I don't think that was the reason I agreed to meet with Lester Rankin. It was, I suppose, that pleading expression on Hank's face and his appeal for help. You didn't want to turn down a good guy like Hank Phillips. I also thought for a moment that maybe Hank himself might even be mutually involved in some problem with Rankin.

"Want to tell me the problem?" I asked gently.

"I think I'd better let Lester tell it to you himself. He's at home right now, and I can drive you out there myself."

And so now the three of us were sitting in Rankin's study. Harold Phillips was seated in a leather armchair a few feet away, while I was on a low couch, holding in my hand the tape cassette Rankin had given me. And Rankin himself was standing in the middle of the room, telling me about his daughter's kidnapping.

"When was she abducted?" I asked.

"I don't really know," Rankin said. He ran his hand nervously across his forehead. He was a tall man, probably about six or six one, but I doubt if he weighed 160 pounds soaking wet. His full head of silver hair was carefully brushed, and he wore rimless glasses. Rankin's appearance was usually a stern one, but his face appeared to be breaking up now. "You see, Petersen, Ellen doesn't live at home. She's my youngest child, the last one to leave home. My wife died three years ago, and then about a year ago Ellen decided to get an apartment for herself in town near Dupont Circle. You know how young people are these days." He waved his hand around the elaborately furnished study, as if to indicate wonderment why anyone would not prefer to live here.

"Yeah, I know how they are," I said, a little touch of irony in my voice.

"Well, this morning I received the cassette at home here in the mail just as I was about to leave for the office. They simply say that they have Ellen, but they don't say when they took her. I haven't spoken to Ellen for about a week, so it could have been any time in the last few days. I called my office, and had my Administrative Assistant go right over to Ellen's apartment near Dupont Circle, and there was no sign of her there. And, of course, her voice is on the tape. Here, let me play it for you, Petersen." There was a tape-player on the coffee table in front of me, and he took the cassette from my hand and started to insert it in the machine.

"Just a minute, Senator," I said. "Why are you telling me all this, instead of the police?"

Rankin glanced over at Phillips. "Didn't you explain it to him, Harold?"

Phillips shook his head. "I thought I'd let you tell him the whole story."

"I called Senator Phillips this morning almost immediately after I received the tape," Rankin said. "He's an old colleague and a trusted advisor, and he came right out here and we discussed the problem and how to handle it. In the course of our discussions he suggested that we employ you to advise us during this crisis; to make sure we were doing everything properly to insure Ellen's safe return. Senator Phillips says that you have been acquiring a reputation around town, Petersen, for excellent service in situations which require discreet but efficient action. You're supposed to be able to keep confidences inviolably, and of course you have no connection of any kind with any law enforcement agency. Furthermore, as you will hear when you listen to the tape, these maniacs want the three hundred thousand in small, unmarked, unserialed bills. I can get the money from various accounts all right, but the small unmarked bills are a problem. I understand that if banks receive requests for large amounts of monies in small unmarked bills they are instructed to inform the police about the transaction. And we don't want that. Therefore, the money will have to be ..."

He paused, and I offered: "Laundered?"

"Yes, laundered. We thought you could perform that service for us." He started to fiddle with the tape machine again, apparently quite satisfied that he had told me all I had to know.

"Don't bother playing that tape for me, Senator. We can all save ourselves a lot of time. I'm going to give you the advice you asked for. It's free and it's easy. Call the FBI immediately."

Rankin looked at me incredulously. "My God, man, weren't you listening to me? They explicitly told me not to call the police."

"They usually say that in kidnappings."

"But, God, they threatened to kill her instantly if we call the police."

"They often say that, too. But it's usually a bluff."

"Bluff or not, I simply can't take that chance. They said not to call the police, and that's precisely what I'm going to do."

"It's too risky, Senator. You can't just play this by yourself, and hope against hope these people will return your daughter. You need the large resources and manpower of an organization like the FBI."

"It's more risky to play it the other way," Rankin said, and he glanced over at Phillips for support.

"I'm afraid I have to agree with Lester," said Phillips, shifting his rather massive weight in the leather chair. "We went over this again and again this morning, exploring all the possible alternatives, and all things considered, this seemed the safest way to proceed. After all, we don't even know what this group is, the so-called National Federation Army. And we don't know what irresponsible thing they might do to Ellen if we don't go along with them. It's not an easy decision to make, Brian, and I understand perfectly how you feel about turning it over to the authorities. But we'd never forgive ourselves if Ellen got killed in some police shootout or something. I realize that we're walking on very treacherous ground, and that's why I counseled Lester to get you to advise us as we go along."

"You're both wrong," I said. "Turn it over to the FBI. They have an excellent record in kidnap cases."

"Excellent but not perfect," Rankin said. "Remember the Greenlease boy in Kansas City. The FBI captured the kidnappers, but the boy was killed. And, more recently, some of those diplomats who had been captured by terrorists in South America were killed before their release could be obtained. And, Petersen, if you'd kindly listen to the tape I think you'd find we're dealing with some kind of terrorists here. No, I can't take a chance with Ellen's life. I'm going to get the money, I'm *not* going to inform the police or the media, and I'm going to deliver the money to them. Then we'll get Ellen back. Quickly, and with no complications."

"There might be plenty of complications," I said, but Rankin ignored the remark. The old fire was back in his eyes, and I could see that he was absolutely determined to do it his way. We continued to argue about it for the next twenty minutes or so, but it was useless, the man was totally adamant. And I couldn't help but marvel at this notorious law-and-order type and his refusal to notify the proper authorities. If it had been some other person's problem, I felt quite sure Rankin would have advised him immediately to contact his dear friends, the police. But maybe I shouldn't have been so rough on the poor bastard, maybe he was right. Perhaps the safest way to get his daughter back would be to quietly surrender the ransom and hope against hope he got his daughter back from the kidnappers. Perhaps.

But then another disturbing thought struck me. We'd be working in the dark, all by ourselves and without the resources of the FBI and the police, and we wouldn't have a broad-scale investigation going for us during the time we were trying to obtain the release of Ellen Rankin. And a full investigation of the situation is invaluable, perhaps essential. Suppose this wasn't a kidnapping at all, but some kind of hoax or rip-off. I picked up the driver's license from the coffee table and studied the girl's face in the photograph. It was a poor picture, one of those quickies they snap when you are applying for a license, and it didn't tell me much. Was Ellen Rankin possibly involved in some kind of gigantic and cruel hoax? Or had she perhaps become radicalized and joined this National Federation Army, and was now trying to bilk her own father out of some money for the movement? It certainly wasn't beyond the realm of possibility. Nothing was. But perhaps it was only my own curious mind which made me think like that. Or maybe it came from too many years of living in Washington, where you almost automatically find yourself beginning to look for sinister implications in every situation, no matter how simple and uncomplicated it initially appears.

I didn't know. And for the moment I didn't care, because I didn't think I wanted any part of this Rankin affair.

Lester Rankin must have been reading my thoughts, because he said: "You will help us, won't you, Petersen?"

I took a deep breath. "I don't know," I said quietly, still gazing at the picture on the driver's license.

"I'll pay your fee, of course. I understand that you get five hundred a day, plus expenses, for this type of special service. Petersen, I'll even double it. A thousand dollars a day."

I threw the driver's license angrily on the desk. "Damnit, Senator, I'm not trying to make money out of your troubles. If I came in, it would be for my usual fee, and no more."

"All right, then. But I haven't got any more time to waste haggling, Petersen. My daughter's been abducted, and every moment is precious now. And I need help in getting her back. Are you in or are you out?"

I looked up at Rankin, and then across at Harold Phillips. Hank's eyes were trained intently on me. "Brian," he said. "Whatever else ... the Senator does need help now. And you can help him." His voice was even and unemotional, but he had that pleading look in his eyes again. Damn you, Hank, you owe me another IOU for this.

I returned my gaze to Rankin. "Okay, Senator, I'm in. Play the tape for me."

CHAPTER TWO

It was a small half-hour tape with fifteen minutes' time available on each side, and the recording Rankin played for me occupied almost the whole of one side.

After a short delay at the beginning of the tape, a man's voice came on in flat, unaccented tones:

> *Lester Rankin. This is to inform you that your daughter, Ellen Lynn Rankin, is being held in custody by the National Federation Army. My name is General Camillo, and I am the leader and spokesman for the NFA. The high tribunal of the NFA has decided that your daughter should be held in this protective custody as an act of retribution for your capitalistic and fascist crimes against the people during your years of public service. The people of this country, and other countries, have been exploited for centuries by capitalistic people like you, and as a result the vast majority of average people live in poverty, hunger, discrimination, and slave employment. The NFA will change all that. We are the vanguard of a new wave of hope for the people. We will terminate the capitalistic system, and return the power to the people. We will eliminate ...*

I listened as the voice droned on, reciting a melange of Mao theories with a touch of Tupamaro rhetoric. And my mind was making notes about the performance on the tape. The voice was obviously a male, caucasian, probably somewhere in his late twenties. No particular identifying speech patterns. And nothing in the rhetoric which could place him. It was old-hat stuff, which you could hear spouted off at Dupont Circle from a soapbox any summer evening. And then I suddenly remembered that Rankin had told me that his daughter had moved into an apartment near Dupont Circle. That was an interesting association, and I mulled it over as I listened to the claptrap on the tape.

Rankin had taken a seat on the opposite side of the room, and his lips were tightly clamped as he stared at the slowly rotating tape on the machine with something near hatred in his eyes. Hank Phillips had leaned back in his chair, his eyes closed, but he was now smoking a cigarette. They had both heard the tape earlier, of course, and listening to it again must have been like rubbing sandpaper across an open wound for them.

The voice on the tape kept reciting the woes of the people and the liberating force of the National Federation Army, and it was only near the end of the tape that my ears perked up. General Camillo started to get into the mechanics of the kidnapping, or the protective custody, as he called it:

Rankin, your daughter will be released from our custody if you pay a restitution sum of three hundred thousand dollars. You have one week to prepare this money. And note carefully, the money must be prepared in small bills, no higher than twenty dollars each. And they must be old bills, and not in serialized sequence. If the money is not ready in that form in one week, the high council will meet again to decide on a time and place for the execution of Ellen Rankin in retribution for your capitalistic crimes. And also note, this is most important. Your daughter will be executed immediately if you inform the police or the

FBI about any of this. The arrangement for the transfer of your daughter is strictly a private deal between you and the NFA. And your daughter will also be executed if you inform the media in any way or if there is any publicity at all about this. We are most serious, and if you betray us in any way, your daughter will be executed promptly.

There was a pause on the tape and then some muffled and unintelligible sounds, and I noticed Rankin's body stiffen rigidly at this part of the tape. A girl's voice spoke:

Daddy, they're holding me here. I'm all right, and they haven't harmed me. But they—

And the voice broke off abruptly, and the man's voice returned:

That was your daughter, Rankin. She's unharmed and she will continue to be so, as long as you follow our instructions exactly. I will contact you seven days from today, and I will tell you where to deliver the money so that your daughter can be released. The next contact from the NFA will be either by tape like this, or by phone. So stay close to your phone at home. This is General Camillo.

That was the end of the tape, and Rankin walked over and snapped off the machine. "It came in this," he said, handing me a plain manila envelope with his name and address printed on it in crude block letters. "And inside was the half of her driver's license. And also this." He reached in his pocket and handed me a small slip of paper with a clumsy drawing on it. The drawing showed a man's clenched fist holding some streaks of lightning, and beneath the drawing were the letters NFA. The symbol of the National Federation Army, I supposed.

"Was that your daughter's voice on the tape, Senator?" I asked.

"Oh, yes, indeed," he answered.

"Are you sure? It was only a scrap of conversation."

"I'm quite sure. I'd know my daughter's voice anywhere."

Perhaps, I thought. In Rankin's present state of mind he might be led to believe anything that was programmed for him to believe. And some girl who was familiar with Ellen Rankin's voice could have given even a poor imitation of it in that scrap of dialogue, and Rankin might have accepted it. If that were the case, then Ellen Rankin might be dead at this time. However, I tended to doubt that. It was the other side of the coin which bothered me. Suppose it was really Ellen Rankin's voice, but suppose she was faking it, pretending to be kidnapped. There was a definite note of terror in her voice on the tape, but that could be easily faked.

Another reason why my mind was running in those channels was because of something peculiar this General Camillo had said on the tape. (His real name was probably something quite undramatic, like Harry Smith.) He had specifically instructed Rankin under threat of killing his daughter not to inform the media or the press about the abduction. And that was most unusual. The radical activist groups of the past have always wanted as much publicity as they could get to advertise their cause. They went out of their way to get publicity, manufacturing it if necessary, contacting newspapers and TV stations directly. But this crowd was taking the exact opposite route. They wanted to make it a strictly confidential transaction between Rankin and themselves. If this Camillo believed so passionately in his cause about freeing the people, then why in hell didn't he want the people to know about it? It sure had the peculiar feel of a rip-off.

"About the money, you'll be able to take care of that, won't you?" Rankin was saying to me.

"Yeah, I think so."

"That's our only problem, as I see it now. I told you, we don't want to take the money out of one source in a large amount of unmarked bills because the police would be alerted, and that would jeopardize Ellen. And I suppose I could go around to a number of sources to—as you say—launder it. But I've never done anything like that, Petersen. And I might botch it up."

"Okay, leave the laundering to me, Senator."

"What I'll have to do is get the money from a number of different accounts and investments I have around the country. Perhaps I might sell some securities, and perhaps I might take a quick loan on some properties. I want to get the cash in a hurry. I imagine it will take me a day—two days at the most—to assemble the three hundred thousand in cash. Does that give you enough time to comply with the seven-day limit this lunatic proposes?"

"It will have to be enough time. A good laundering operation usually takes a month or six weeks. You have to move the money all over the lot, even using banks outside the country, in Mexico or the Bahamas or even Switzerland. There are real pros at doing that, and when they've finished there's no way you can trace the money back to its original source. But that's not our problem, Senator. We're not so much concerned about whether the money is eventually traced back to you after this is all over. What we simply want is a large pile of unmarked bills without alerting anybody official that we're doing it."

"Precisely."

"And I think I can get that done for you in the seven-day limit. Why don't we do it this way: you have those monies deposited right into my account at the Riggs Bank, and I can draw on it from there and get it laundered elsewhere. Then when I'm finished I'll bring the whole three hundred thousand out here to you in the small unmarked bills. That's the fastest way."

Rankin agreed to that, and I gave him my account number at the bank. I also gave him phone numbers where I could be reached at any hour of the day or night—my home phone, my office phone, and my answering service—and I asked him to call me immediately in the case of any developments of any kind. Then I said to him: "Senator, I'd like to ask you some questions about your daughter. Just to help me get this in perspective. When was the last time any one you know was in contact with her?"

"Well, as I said, I talked to her a week ago. And this morning after I got the tape I called her office, but they said she hadn't been to work in two days. So I guess that's the last that anybody I knew talked to her. I tried to get in touch with her roommate, but I couldn't locate her."

"Her roommate?"

"A girl named Cathy Morrison. Ellen had decided that she didn't want to live alone, and she had met this girl someplace in town. She's a rather nondescript person, from someplace in the Midwest, if I remember. When I was trying to locate her this morning, I had my AA make some inquiries, and he located her place of business, but she hasn't shown up there for two days, either. And, of course, there's no answer to the phone in Ellen's apartment."

"Didn't the disappearance of Ellen's roommate seem strange to you, Senator?"

"Well, I don't know if it's a disappearance; she might be on vacation, or a trip or something. Maybe it *is* strange, I don't know, I haven't really considered it. There have been so many strange things happening to me since I opened that envelope this morning."

It may not have appeared strange to Rankin, but it certainly appeared strange and suspicious to me. Ellen Rankin disappears two days ago, and at the same time her roommate disappears. Could they have engineered this together? Or could the room-mate—Cathy Morrison—be part of the NFA and participated in the kidnapping of her own roommate?

"Where did Ellen work?" I asked Rankin.

"At some consumer protection advocacy group on K Street. They fight for better consumer prices, or something like that. It wasn't really a job, because they only paid Ellen peanuts, and I was really supporting her."

I raised my eyebrows at that, because it didn't sound like the kind of public activity which would please the elder Rankin. "Is she an activist?" I asked him.

"Certainly not," he said indignantly. "Ellen and I don't exactly see eye-to-eye on politics, and I suppose you'd say she was something like a liberal." He said the word "liberal" with discomfort, as if it left an unpleasant taste in his mouth.

"Let me ask you, Senator, do you think there is any chance that Ellen herself is a member of this National Federation Army, and that maybe this whole kidnapping thing is a charade?"

Rankin really got upset by that remark. "That's absolutely preposterous," he almost shouted at me. "Ellen would never get mixed up with a bunch of idiots like that. I know my daughter, and she's a sound, level-headed girl. She's been kidnapped, I tell you, and all you have to worry about, Petersen, is helping me get her back."

"All right, Senator, calm down. I'll help you get her back." There was no use discussing this any further with Rankin in his emotional state. He might think that Ellen Rankin's membership in something like an NFA was preposterous, but I didn't think it was beyond the realm of reason at all. I've heard lots of guys like Rankin say that they knew their children quite well, when in actuality they didn't know them at all. But Rankin was right about one thing: the immediate task was to get Ellen away from the NFA, whether she was there willingly or unwillingly. And although I wasn't at all convinced about the genuineness of the kidnapping, I nevertheless felt the safest way to proceed for the time being was to work on the assumption that Ellen Rankin had actually been abducted. And then, when we finally located the NFA, we could decide just how real the whole thing had been.

I said to Rankin: "There's one other thing I think we should do right away, Senator: put a tape-recording machine on your phone."

"Why do you want to do that?"

"I feel quite sure that when this General Camillo contacts you in seven days, or before, he'll use the phone as he intimated. If he wants to arrange a drop for the money, the tape cassette device is too clumsy—it would give you time to set up something. No, I think you'll get a phone call, telling you where to report with the money in a short time. And I'd like to get that phone call on tape. We can use it later after Ellen is returned, to prove the extortion attempt." Actually, I had other reasons for wanting to put a taping device on the phone, but I wasn't telling them to Rankin.

The Senator agreed to the tape, and I told him I would return later in the day with an expert to install it for him. Both Rankin and Hank Phillips looked drained, and I asked them if they had eaten anything. They said no, and I suggested they go out to the kitchen and have the maid fix them something. I wanted to listen to that tape one more time before I left, and I didn't think they would want to hear it again.

Sitting alone in Rankin's study, I rewound the tape to the start, and listened again to General Camillo's message. I didn't really learn anything new from the second playing, but I found myself becoming increasingly concerned about Camillo himself. The voice was flat and uninflected, and it was, in fact, rigid and overcontrolled. Like the calculated voice of a ruthless fanatic; or perhaps the voice of someone who was severely mentally disturbed.

And whether Ellen Rankin was with the NFA willingly or unwillingly, I certainly felt she wasn't in very good hands at all.

CHAPTER THREE

Senator Harold Phillips drove me back into town in his Cadillac El Dorado. It was an unusually warm day for early April, and Hank had rolled up the windows and flipped on the air conditioning, which was gently whirring away. Shortly after we had pulled away from Rankin's house, he thanked me for agreeing to help in returning Rankin's daughter from the kidnappers.

"If it *is* a kidnapping," I said to him.

"What makes you think it may not be a genuine kidnapping, Brian?"

"A lot of little things. Oh, it may be a real kidnapping, all right, but I'm still going to keep my options open about it. But if it *is* a real kidnapping, Hank, I'm still not happy about not getting assistance from the FBI. Rankin's taking a big risk."

"I know," Phillips said, a troubled expression on his face. "But I think all things considered it's a risk he has to take to get his daughter back. If he doesn't do what those people ask they could very well kill Ellen on the spot. After all, Brian, if it were your daughter—" He stopped suddenly, aware of what he had said.

"Yeah," I said, slumping down in my seat.

"I'm sorry, Brian. You know I didn't mean …"

"Yeah, I know, Hank."

Hank was obviously embarrassed by his unintentional reference to my daughter, as if he had clumsily reminded me of something I was trying to forget. Don't worry, Hank old boy, I can't ever forget it. That last day is etched indelibly on my mind, and

I can still recall the sequence of events with terrifying clarity. Indeed, I often wake up abruptly in the middle of the night, my chest and forehead streaked with perspiration, and go through it all over again.

That afternoon I had been in my father-in-law's, old Zachery Edwards', office, helping him pack his books and memorabilia. And that in itself should have been an omen that things were about to fall apart. Zach, a three-time senator from the Midwest, had been surprisingly—some newspapers said, unbelievably—beaten in what appeared to be a routine re-election bid by a young and fairly unknown crusader, who campaigned on the issue that Zach was too old and that new blood was indeed needed in the Senate. Sure, new blood was needed, but it didn't make any difference if that new blood was old or young; it only had to be honest, competent, intelligent, and diligent. And Zach had all of those qualities, somewhat of a rarity, unfortunately, in this capital city. I know his retirement is still being mourned in many of the corridors of power where they realized what an outstanding senator he was. And the young crusader who defeated him still has to show me that he can do half the job Zach did.

The phone call came to Zach's office where they had finally tracked me down. They first tried my own office—not the little one I have now, but that big one on Pennsylvania Avenue, which I had when I was really going great guns as a lobbyist and assembling a large staff—and they referred the call to Zach's. It was some Virginia policeman telling me that Marge and our six-month-old daughter Debbie had been in a car accident on Columbia Pike, and they were both at Faquier Hospital. Later I learned that when Marge was taking Debbie to the pediatrician, some kids in a souped-up car had lost control of their high-speeding vehicle, crossed over the center lane, and smashed into our car almost head-on.

22

Zach drove out to the hospital with me, and I must have broken every speed record for getting out of the District and across the Potomac into the Virginia suburbs. We dashed into the emergency room entrance, and some young doctor in a white jacket was waiting to intercept me. He tried to do it gently, apparently reaching back into some old psychology course, but I knew what he was going to tell me. They were both dead. The baby was killed instantly, and Marge died later in the hospital emergency room. I guess I must have gone berserk, and when I saw the cops leading out one of the kids in the other car, a fellow about nineteen or twenty with only a large strip of plaster over one eyebrow, I went for him. I got him to the floor, and I had my hands around his throat and my fingers were squeezing those pressure points behind his ear in that fast-kill technique I had learned in Army Intelligence. I was later told that the cops tried to pull me off, but when they couldn't, and the kid's face was starting to turn purple, they finally had to knock me out from behind with their clubs.

That was the beginning of the end for me, as far as I was concerned. Somehow I got through the funeral, looking at those two coffins, the large one and the tiny white one, with dazed and stony eyes. Then I broke apart completely. I wasn't interested in the damned lobbying business anymore; I wasn't interested in going into Washington every day; I wasn't interested in anything. Suddenly, I threw a few things in a bag, and took a plane. I didn't really care where I was headed, but eventually I ended up in the Florida Keys.

That's where Zach found me some six months later, when I was well on the way to becoming the champion beach bum of the Keys. I had settled into a fairly regular mind-numbing routine of indistinguishable days: roll myself out of bed late in the morning, try to come around with as many Bloody Mary's as it took, bake out on the beach in the afternoon, start gulping Gibsons as the shadows lengthened, and then the endless scotches into the long dark night. I even picked up a string of faceless girls and got laid a few times, but they only made me feel even more lousy. By the time Zach found me I had ballooned up to 240 pounds, and my only concern was forgetting about yesterday and trying to get through tomorrow.

I woke up one morning in a beach shack I was renting on the far end of the Keys, and there was Zach sitting beside the bed, a troubled and tender expression on his face. He said he had come to take me back to Washington. I didn't want to go, of course, but we talked about it the whole day. I don't know how he finally convinced me to get on a plane with him and come back. Maybe my mind was so sodden with the booze that I couldn't think properly. Maybe that hurt expression on Zach's face got to me, and I didn't want to inflict any more injury on him. Maybe it was because I just didn't give a damn about anything, and at that moment one place was as good—or as bad—as another.

My old lobbyist office had been closed after I blew the Washington scene, but Zach helped me find the small place I have now and he stayed around for a while trying to get me started again. Oh, I guess Zach's therapy worked for a while. With all his contacts around town and with my former lobbying record, I picked up some nice accounts fairly quickly. And I got myself back into physical shape, bringing my weight down to 220. That's a little hefty, I know, but it hangs well on my stocky six-foot-two frame, and it is indeed the same weight I carried when I played football at UCLA some years ago.

But I knew it wouldn't really take. I just couldn't seem to keep my mind on it, and I quickly lost interest in my accounts. Nothing seemed to matter much anymore. And I found myself thinking wistfully again of those lonely beaches in the Keys. And perhaps after not too much longer I would have indeed ended up in the Keys again. I know that I was giving most serious thought to packing it, to closing the small office in Washington and taking off. There was nothing to keep me here any longer.

Then one of my clients asked me if I could help him out somehow on a distressingly personal matter. He was being forced to pay hush money for some indiscretion in his distant past, and he was being bled dry with constant threats of exposure. Reluctantly I agreed to do what I could for him, and it led to a fierce chase which ended up in a motel room in Baltimore. The guy—or the guys, rather, for there were two of them—tried to muscle me at the end, and I had to thrash the hell out of them to protect myself. I'm not too proud of this, but I do remember the curious and almost savage satisfaction I got when I pummeled those two louses. It was almost like a catharsis, a way of venting my fury at the evil forces of life.

Word of that little episode quickly shot around the Washington cocktail circuit, as stories tend to do in this town, and soon I found other people coming to me for similar services. Petersen's discreet services, as someone on the circuit called it. And in a snake pit of a town like D.C., there's a world of need for lots of discreet services. And for some reason, which was not quite explicable to myself, I found myself agreeing to accept some of these assignments. And so I stayed in Washington. I continued my lobbying business on a minor key, doing a few little tasks for a selected number of clients, but I found myself doing more and more of this other activity. There was a government contract fraud affair I broke up; a leak from a high Senate committee I uncovered; a mysterious killing I unraveled. Those sorts of things go on in Washington, and there are lots of people who want them cleaned up quickly, incisively, and with no public notice.

And I guess Brian Petersen seemed an apt man for that role. I certainly knew my way around this city, and I had a lot of contacts. And even though Zach had retired to Indiana to read and fish, he was still able to plug me into good contacts whenever necessary. Furthermore, my short stint in Army Intelligence had given me some good investigative background, as well as some excellent training in the martial arts—whether hand-to-hand combat, or the use of weapons.

But from the rumors which circled back to me on the gossip circuit, the aspect about me which seemed to appeal to people was that I just didn't seem to give a damn anymore about myself after the death of my wife and child. I'd take that dangerous risk, I'd stick my head in the lion's mouth, I'd get the damn job done somehow. And above all, I'd be discreet about protecting the reputations of my employers. Oh, they knew I wouldn't do anything corrupt for anybody, because I felt there'd already been too damn much corruption in this town. But if you had an honest beef, I just might try to help you out of it if there was no other way to get it done.

I don't know what strange satisfaction I got out of doing this, and I knew it wasn't doing anything to increase my popularity. Sure, people came to me when they were in trouble, but a lot of people were beginning to feel quite uncomfortable about my presence around town. You never feel quite sure about a person like me who doesn't seem to give a damn about himself; you never know when someone may start him on your trail.

That didn't bother me too much, and I suppose I got a perverse satisfaction from seeing some of the big boys around town come tip-toeing into my office, looking anxiously over their shoulders, asking for help with their ever-so-delicate problem. However, I made it clear to them I was no knight in shining white armour: I made them pay for my services, and I made them pay well. That way, I thought sardonically, they would appreciate the services more. Even at that, I didn't accept everybody who asked me. At this stage of my life I felt I could be quite selective about what I chose to do. And I was.

Sitting in Hank Phillips' car now, as he drove us down Massachusetts Avenue toward the city, I was somewhat amazed at my sudden involvement in Lester Rankin's problem. Ordinarily, I would not have even bothered to return Rankin's original calls, but under Hank's prodding I was now tied up in this, wherever it took us. Even more amazing, I suppose, is what had happened to me in these past two and a half years. Just that short a time ago Lester Rankin would never have dreamed of calling upon me for help in a problem of this magnitude, because at that time Brian Petersen was just a bright, pleasant young lobbyist, making a name for himself in Washington. And now? What the hell was I now?

Hank Phillips dropped me in front of my office building on Connecticut Avenue, and as I started to get out of the car he asked me: "Brian, is there anything I can do to help in this dreadful business?"

"Just stay close to Lester Rankin, and bolster him up. We don't want him falling apart on us."

"Of course."

I paused as I was alighting from the Cadillac. "One more thing, Hank. They say that you're a good man with the prayers. If you know any appropriate ones, I'd start saying them now for Ellen Rankin."

I didn't go up to my office because I knew that now in the late afternoon Annie would be gone. We don't have that much lobbying business anymore, and I tell her to scoot out of there by two-thirty or so every day, so that she can be at home before her kids arrive from school. Furthermore, I wanted to get my car out of the garage in the basement right away and get cracking on this Rankin thing.

My big Olds was brought up quickly from the garage, and I drove over to Rhode Island Avenue, parking in front of Eddie Perkins' radio shop. There were a few customers in the front of the store looking at some stereo equipment, and I immediately spotted Eddie in the rear of the store, leaning over a glass display counter, a toothpick in his mouth, staring vacantly into the air. His eyes snapped to attention when I pushed open the door, and I saw them narrow appraisingly. Then he recognized me. Without saying a word, he gave a short, almost imperceptible nod of his head toward the private area in the back of the store. I followed him, and we entered a large cluttered room, which was completely lined from floor to ceiling with shelving. There was a myriad of electronic devices on those shelves, a vast collection of gadgetry which never failed to amaze and mystify me. Eddie closed the door firmly behind me, and then he turned, his features breaking into a crooked little grin for the first time.

"Good to see you, Mr. Petersen," he said.

"I need your services again, Eddie."

"Always glad to work with you, Mr. Petersen."

I knew that Eddie meant that, because he is quite selective about his clients, as he can afford to be. You see, Eddie Perkins is one of the best—if not *the* best—electronics surveillance experts in the city. Indeed, there are some people who say he's the best in the country. Eddie got his early training at the CIA, but like so many of those fine specialists, he got fed up over the years with the regime out at Langley and went into business for himself. He not only learned all the CIA had to offer, but his creative mind has invented an astonishing amount of highly sophisticated devices, which he keeps closely guarded. I don't know anybody around who is any better at installing a bug, whether close up or from a long distance, and there's nobody more capable of sweeping an area and picking up even the most sophisticated of listening devices. Electronics surveillance is a growth industry in a city like Washington, and Eddie has all the clients he can handle. Ironically, even the CIA hires him occasionally for a particularly difficult job.

We sat down at a long wooden table, and Eddie cleared away a pile of wires and circuits. He was a small man with a thin, bird-like face, and now he looked inquiringly at me.

"I've got a whole laundry list of things I need," I said. "One device, the easiest one, I need right away. The others I need in six days."

"What's the easy one, Mr. Petersen?"

"I want to put a taping device on a person's phone to record all conversations. It's Senator Lester Rankin's phone, and we're doing it with his permission." I realized that this was an unbelievably simple job, something which wouldn't demand the talents of an Eddie Perkins, and I quickly added: "I'd also like you to sweep the Senator's phones to see if there is a tap on them now. And ..." I paused.

"And?" Eddie asked.

"I was just thinking, Eddie, that there might be a time in the future when I might want to listen to Rankin's phone conversations from someplace outside his house and ..."

"Gotcha," he said.

"I don't know if I'll ever have to do it, but I'd like to be prepared if it becomes necessary."

"Can do. It's a piece of cake."

"Now, for the other stuff."

Eddie took out a long yellow pad, and made some notes while I talked, and then he sketched a few fast diagrams with a stubby pencil. We talked for about a half-hour in the back room of his shop, and he continued to make notes and diagrams while I explained about the other devices I needed. He said he could have them all ready for me within the six days, earlier if necessary.

"And, Eddie, don't worry about the expense. Get the best equipment you can."

"The best you'll get, Mr. Petersen."

"My client doesn't realize it yet, but he's going to be paying for all this."

Eddie told me he could come out to Senator Rankin's house with me right now, and he spent a few minutes selecting some equipment from his shelves and packing it in a large metal carrying case with a handle. We went out through the store together, and Eddie glanced casually at a young man and a woman who were inspecting a stereo set. I'm sure Eddie made a few dollars each year on this conventional electronic equipment he sold, but his real business was that in the shelf-lined room in the back of the store.

We drove out Massachusetts Avenue in my car, and during the ride to Kenwood Eddie told me about the new minute telescopic listening device he was developing which could pick up voices almost a mile away. When we turned into Rankin's driveway I saw his eyes widen with appreciation at the large Tudor house. Eddie, of course, did not ask me the reason why I wanted the electronic equipment I had ordered from him, and that was his usual business practice. He felt he was just a surveillance expert, and the less he knew about the reason for the surveillance the better for him.

A maid answered the door and ushered us into the study where Rankin was seated on the leather chair, talking to someone on the phone. He waved toward me, and then looked suspiciously at Eddie Perkins. He indicated he would be through in a minute, and I could tell from the end of the conversation that he was talking to a banker somewhere, instructing him to deposit money into an account at Riggs Bank. The ransom money for Ellen Rankin.

I introduced Eddie to the Senator and Rankin greeted him somewhat curtly and coolly. The conservative Senator usually didn't deal with people like Eddie Perkins. I could also see that Rankin looked more composed now, and I thought that perhaps the effort to gather the ransom money had steadied him down by giving him something positive to do in obtaining the release of his daughter.

Rankin explained the phone system in the house to Perkins, and then the Senator and I went out to the spacious living room where the maid brought us some drinks while Eddie went to work. Forty-five minutes later Eddie came back, still carrying the metal case. "It's done," he said.

"You covered all the phones?" I asked.

"There's three phones downstairs and one phone upstairs, all on the same number. I've got them all hooked up so that whenever you pick up any one of them a recording machine in the study is activated. It deactivates when you replace the receiver."

"Do we have to change tapes, or anything like that?"

A thin smile of pride came over Eddie's lips. "The recording machine is one I built myself, and it has a monster of a tape deck. The tape looks something like a big pizza, and it can take thirteen hours of phone conversations on one side. And if you flip it over, you can get thirteen hours on the other side. That's twenty-six hours of phone conversations. I also left another big tape reel there if you need it."

"I doubt if I will," Rankin said dryly. "I'm no magpie on the phone. Now, if you gentlemen will excuse me, I do have to make another brief phone call about a financial matter." He glanced significantly at me.

Rankin walked us to the door, and when Eddie went on ahead to put his case in my car I said to Rankin: "Senator, how much do you know about Ellen's roommate, Cathy Morrison?"

"Not much, really. Ellen had her out to the house here once or twice, but I only talked to her for a few minutes. I believe she's fairly new to the city, and she came here from someplace outside Chicago. Winnetka, or Wilmette, or someplace like that. Why do you ask, Petersen? Do you really think she may be implicated in this?"

"If she's suddenly disappeared, there's a very good possibility, Senator."

Rankin pondered that for a few seconds, and then asked: "Well, is there something we should do about it?"

"There's a lot we could do about it if the FBI or some law enforcement agency were brought into it. We could research her background, her friends, her contacts, and try to get a lead on her and where she might be now. But since we're playing this your way, Senator, we can't afford a full-scale investigation because it might get back to the NFA that we're trying to track them down."

"Of course," Rankin said stiffly. "That's what we'll do then. Nothing. Our only concern is getting Ellen back. After we get her back we can do whatever investigation of her roommate is necessary."

"Okay," I said, and I walked off, leaving him there with a troubled expression on his face.

Eddie was waiting for me in the front seat of the car, and when I started the engine and pulled out of Rankin's gravel drive I asked him: "Were the phones clean?"

"I think so. I checked all the phones carefully, and I even followed the wires into the basement, and I couldn't find no taps."

"They're clean then, Eddie. If you couldn't find a tap."

"Yeah, Mr. Petersen, I don't think there's no tap I couldn't find."

"And about the other thing?"

A thin smile spread over Eddie's lips. "I put a microscopic bug in each phone, and I really concealed it up in the wires. It's sending off now, and it should last for about a month. I ain't set up no receiver yet, but anytime you want to listen to those phones, you just let me know. I could pick them up from a distance of a half a mile away from the house. We could set up a stationary receiving spot, and we could cruise around the area in a car and pick up the signal."

"Thanks, Eddie. We may never have to do it, but then again we might."

Who the hell knows, I thought, what I may have to do before this weird thing is over?

CHAPTER FOUR

After I had deposited Eddie Perkins back at his shop, I grabbed a quick sandwich at a lunch counter, and then I headed out to the Dupont Circle area. I had obtained the address of Ellen Rankin's apartment from the Senator before I left, and now I was going to do a little bit of extremely cautious sniffing around to see what odors I could perceive. As I told the Senator, we couldn't risk a regular investigation. But nevertheless that wasn't going to prevent me from doing a little casual snooping of my own to see if I couldn't get a better angle on the alleged kidnapping of Ellen Rankin.

Dupont Circle was fairly crowded on this balmy spring evening, and some young people were wading in the large fountain in the middle of the park area. On the far side of the circle, near where Connecticut Avenue continues north, a group of people were gathered around two young fellows who were noisily strumming away at guitars while moaning lyrics to something that sounded like a cross between hard rock and old spirituals. Everybody was casually dressed in old clothes, with a heavy sprinkling of jeans and denims, but I knew that these were the costumes they had donned after they had arrived home from work. A few years back the Dupont Circle area was the hippie hangout in Washington, the logical place where runaway kids from all over the East Coast eventually drifted. But that's pretty much changed now. This slightly later generation hasn't dropped out on the drugs, hard or soft, but rather they usually go out to jobs every day. Oh, they share the same disillusionments about establishment values as their almost immediate predecessors, but they feel that the way to change things is to work within the system somehow. And that's why many of them, like Ellen Rankin apparently, want to work for consumer groups or advocacy organizations or Naderlike groups.

Ellen Rankin lived in an older apartment building on a small side street just north of the Circle, and when I entered the lobby I was relieved to see that there was no doorman or desk clerk. It was a walkup, and I started up the stairs to the third floor. Her apartment number was 304. On the second landing I encountered a young man who was bounding down the stairs. He was dressed in the traditional levis, and he had a huge mane of hair and a sizeable beard. He paused, regarded me curiously for a moment, and I said: "Nice evening, isn't it?"

His face broke into an unaccountable grin. "Beautiful, man, beautiful," he said, and he passed on. I could hear him humming all the way down.

I knocked softly on the door of apartment 304, but of course no one responded. There was only one, rather ancient, lock on the door, and any amateur could snap it open easily. I sure as hell wanted to get inside to take a look around, and I regretted that I hadn't asked Rankin for a key. But then I suddenly realized that Ellen Rankin undoubtedly wouldn't have given her father a key to her apartment. I glanced up and down the corridor. There was no one around. From my wallet I extracted one of my plastic credit cards, and began to work it through the door jamb and up against the lock. One twist did it, and I was able to open the door and step in.

Despite the age of the building, the apartment itself was a nice one, large, light, and airy. Walking softly on the balls of my feet, I made a fast inspection of the apartment to see if anyone was home. No one in the living room or kitchen. I pushed open the door to what was apparently one bedroom, and found no one there. The other bedroom was also empty. And so was the bathroom. I hadn't made a careful inspection of anything yet, but I had learned one important fact. The apartment was quite neat and tidy, and there wasn't the slightest sign of any struggle having taken place here recently. If Ellen Rankin had been abducted, she sure as hell hadn't been forcefully taken from these premises.

And so, if Ellen Rankin had been kidnapped, where did the snatch take place?

I went to work on the living room, but I didn't find anything interesting there, and then I turned my attention to the two bedrooms. There were some letters, bills, and papers in each room which told me which of the rooms was occupied by Ellen Rankin and which was occupied by her roommate, Cathy Morrison. But I could have made the identification without those papers. The closet of one bedroom was filled with a lot of expensive clothing, such as Pucci dresses, Italian shoes, and designer slacks. Obviously, Ellen Rankin's room. The clothes in the other room were neat and serviceable, but much more modest off-the-rack stuff from average department stores. Cathy Morrison's room.

Thus a rather wealthy girl had shared a place with a girl of much more modest means. Rich girl, poor girl. Had the poor girl become obsessed by the wealth of her roommate? Had she come under the influence of this General Camillo and under his direction planned Ellen's abduction as an act of retaliation for capitalistic sins? Hell, I didn't know. There were some letters on a small table by Cathy Morrison's bed, and I read them carefully. A few bills, some advertisements, and two letters from a woman in Winnetka, Illinois, who was obviously the girl's aunt and was writing to complain that she hadn't heard from her niece lately and she wondered how she was.

Auntie, I'd like to know how she is, too.

I took some of the papers and put them in my jacket pocket. Maybe I could do a little more checking on Cathy Morrison, starting with her Winnetka background. I stood there for a few more seconds, my lips pursed, wondering if there was anything else I could learn here. Then I tensed, and let my hands drop casually to my sides. My back was to the door of Cathy Morrison's bedroom, and I didn't know what was behind me. But I sure as hell knew someone was standing there.

There might have been a slight sound, and again there might not have been. But I knew, by perhaps some kind of deep feral instinct, that someone was standing behind me. Over near the door. I turned slowly, and I saw her. A girl, early twenties, with short, almost bobbed dark hair.

She was holding a pistol, and it was trained directly on me.

"Don't move, mister," she said.

The pistol looked like a .22, probably a hunting weapon, and she was holding it tightly, as if she were not too familiar with it. We were about five or six feet apart, but even an inexperienced marksman with a small weapon like that can put a lethal hole in you from that distance.

I tried to make my voice casual. "Oh, you must be Cathy," I said. "I was looking for Ellen Rankin." I started to take a step toward her.

"I told you not to move," she said. "I'm not Cathy, and you weren't looking for Ellen. I saw you break in here."

Damnit, I thought to myself: I must have failed to snap the outside door of the apartment firmly closed behind me when I broke in a few minutes ago, and now this girl had been able to slip in behind me and then sneak up on me with a pistol. The very last thing I wanted to have happen was to get caught breaking into Ellen Rankin's apartment. I wasn't too concerned about the criminal aspects of it, because I was sure I could talk my way out of it to the police. But the notoriety might be something else, and the police might start asking questions about the missing Ellen Rankin. And that could blow the whole thing, and bring the police and the FBI charging in. I felt, in fairness to Senator Rankin, that I couldn't let that happen.

So I tried to con this girl who was holding the pistol on me. Feigning a little smile of embarrassment, I said: "Oh, no, I wasn't breaking in to steal anything. You see, I'm a friend of Ellen Rankin—well, really, not Ellen herself, but her father, Senator Rankin. I was with the Senator a little while ago, and he asked me to stop by and see if Ellen's all right. He hasn't heard from her for a couple of days."

She didn't seem to be buying it, but I continued doggedly on. "When I didn't get any answer to my knock, I thought I'd just take a look in here to see if everything was okay. That's not much of a lock on the door. Oh, I guess it was a foolish thing to do, but I didn't think it would cause any harm just to take a peek in here. Then I could tell the Senator—"

"Bullshit," she interrupted.

"Really," I said lamely.

Her eyes narrowed, and she said: "You wouldn't be fuzz, would you? A narc, or something like that?"

"Not at all."

"Do you have any ID?"

I didn't like the way this was going, but I thought I'd better take it easy and play along with her for a while. And, of course, she had that damned gun trained on me. You can't argue very well with a person who's got you covered with a pistol.

"My wallet," I said, and reached around to my hip pocket to fish it out. She was an amateur, all right, because she shouldn't have let me do that. In tacky situations over the years, I have carried a small .32 in a belt holster which is snapped on my belt right at my spine, and if I were wearing it now I could have whipped it out. This Rankin affair had developed so quickly that I hadn't a chance yet to get armed. But I sure as hell was going to get armed as soon as I could.

I pulled out the wallet, and again started to step toward her to hand it to her. But she waved the gun. "Stand still. And throw it to me."

I gently lobbed it in the air, and with a surprising amount of deftness she caught it with her left hand. With that same left hand she flipped it open and riffled through it, as she kept darting glances from me to my wallet. I didn't give a damn about that wallet because there was nothing in there to contradict my story—just my name, a driver's license, and some credit cards. But I was getting increasingly disturbed about the way this was developing. She could very well march me down to a police station, or she could call the cops, and then I'd have to do a lot of explaining.

Furthermore, I don't like being held with a gun like this, especially when it drags on. You never know what the pistol-wielder is going to do next. Some chance remark could set them off and they start blazing away. I measured the girl carefully. Five one, perhaps five two, intelligent but rather plain features, small frame. She was wearing faded jeans and a pullover sweater. I wondered how physically adroit she was. We'd soon find out.

She seemed satisfied that there was no police ID in my wallet, and I saw a troubled frown come over her face, as if she were thinking about what to do next.

"Could I have my wallet back?" I asked gently.

She had the wallet in her left hand, and I held my two hands up high near my face, like a baseball catcher signalling for a high pitch. And she tossed the wallet to me, high, toward my hands.

I took a half-step forward, balancing the majority of my weight on one foot, getting set for the lunge. But she didn't notice that; she was watching the wallet sail through the air toward my outstretched hands. I let the wallet go right by me. And at the same moment I lunged right at her, my hand slapping down and grabbing that right wrist, which was holding the pistol.

I jerked her hand down violently, and held her wrist tightly so that the barrel of the pistol was pointed at the floor. She gave out an anguished gasp, but she managed to keep her fingers around the pistol. I was afraid the damn gun would go off in a few seconds. I had her wrist in my right hand, but my left hand was free. I slapped her across the side of the face with my open palm, not too hard, but hard enough to stun her. Her knees sagged, and I twisted her wrist once more and the gun clattered to the floor. I caught her as she started to slump to the floor, but at the same time I kicked the gun away with my foot.

My hands were under her armpits, supporting her, and I gently turned her and sat her down on the edge of the bed. She leaned forward, putting her hands over her face, and quiet sobs began to rack her body. I picked up the pistol from the floor, put it in my jacket pocket, and then walked into the bathroom where I prepared a damp face cloth and a towel. The sobs were subsiding and I poked her softly and handed her the face cloth and the towel. She accepted them, but I could see the terror in her eyes as she looked at me.

I was stuck with the story I had spun off the top of my head a few minutes ago, and I felt I had to continue it if I were going to get out of here without raising a lot of questions in people's minds about Ellen Rankin. "I'm sorry I did that," I said softly. "I get nervous when people hold a gun on me. It's a conditioned reflex I learned when I was in the Army a long time ago. I really was just looking for Ellen Rankin."

She looked at me skeptically now, but all she said was: "I don't like armies."

"Neither do I. But again, I apologize. Suppose you tell me who you are, and why you barged in here with a gun."

"My name is Judy Powell," she said. "I live down the corridor, and I was just about to go out when I heard somebody fiddling with the door here. I opened my door on a slight crack, and I saw you breaking in. There have been a lot of robberies in the building the last few months, and I thought this was another one. And so I got that pistol, and tried to catch the thief."

"Where'd you get the pistol?"

"My brother gave it to me some time ago. It's an old hunting pistol of his, and he said a girl living in the city needs some protection today. I keep it in a box under my bed, but I've never even fired the damn thing. In fact, I've never fired a gun in my life."

"That was quite evident. But, Judy, that wasn't a very smart thing to do. You should have called the police."

She studied my face, and I think I was beginning to convince her now. "Yeah, I guess I should have," she said. "But the cops take so long to get here, and I thought you would have looted half the place and be gone before they arrived."

"When you pull a gun on a person all sorts of things can happen. Okay, you made a mistake. But so did I by entering the apartment. It was a stupid thing for me to do. Let's say that one mistake cancels out another. Can I make amends by buying you a drink someplace near here? There are some nice little places down on Connecticut Avenue." I didn't particularly want to have a drink with this girl, but I thought it was a logical part of my little act—the embarrassed guy trying to make amends.

"No, I don't think so," she said.

"I'm awfully sorry about that slap across the face."

She rubbed the side of her face. There was a red mark there, but I didn't think a welt would form. "I'm sorry about it, too. All right, one drink, that's all. Then, as you say, we've cancelled out each other's mistakes."

We went to a little bar on Connecticut Avenue on the south side of Dupont Circle, a noisy place that was filled with a lot of young people. She had a glass of white wine, and I had a scotch, while I continued my little charade, hoping to allay any suspicions she might have in her mind about something sinister being involved in my breaking into the Rankin apartment. We were at a little table in the rear, and I had to lean over to hear her against the din emanating from a loud record player behind the bar.

"So, Senator Rankin has lost contact with his daughter," she said.

"Not really. He just hasn't heard from her in a few days." I let my voice drop to a conspiratorial tone. "You see, Ellen and her father don't get along too well. Different political views."

"That's a gas. The great Rankin doesn't understand his daughter. That's what's going on all over the country today. The older generation doesn't understand us."

"What's Ellen Rankin like? I don't really know her."

"I don't know her well, either. She's just a neighbor I know casually. She and her roommate, Cathy. We bump into each other in the corridor now and then, and we were at a big Christmas party together in the building last December. But I'd say she seems to be a nice kid. Quiet, pleasant. I know she's a senator's daughter, and she's supposed to have a lot of money, but she doesn't flaunt it around. I guess I'd like to know her better."

"Do you know her roommate, Cathy?" I was pumping now, trying to get any little scrap of information I could.

"No, not really. I did have a rather long conversation with her at that Christmas party. She seems to be quite different from Ellen."

"Oh, in what way?"

"More outgoing, I guess. An extroverted type. Perhaps you'd have to call her an activist."

"You would? Why?"

"Just some things she said at that party. And I understand she works for some activist group. Listen, I don't know either of those girls very well."

I thought I'd better let it go at that, because if I kept pumping her anymore I was just going to arouse some more suspicions. And I thought I had her calmed down pretty well by now. She'd probably tell her story to her friends about trying to apprehend a person she thought was a thief in the Rankin apartment. But I didn't think she'd go to the police now. And that's all I wanted.

True to her word, Judy Powell had only one drink, and I walked her back to her apartment in the balmy night. I left her at the street entrance to the building, and as we parted I said: "Am I forgiven now for that slap across the face?"

"All forgiven." She turned to go, and then she stopped. "One more thing, that pistol."

I still had it in my jacket pocket, and I extracted it now. "What do you plan to do with it?"

"I'm going to give it back to my brother."

"That's a good decision. You see how easily I took that away from you? And when that happens a person can very easily find herself getting shot with her own gun."

"Yeah," she said. "Lesson learned."

I drove leisurely back through town, and then took the Fourteenth Street bridge over the Potomac toward Virginia. I could see to my right that there were a lot of people milling around the Tidal Basin where the Japanese Cherry Blossom trees had been planted way back in the Taft Administration. The blossoms were just starting to come out now, and for the next week or so both tourists and locals would be coming out here far into the night to look at those graceful pink and white blossoms.

I drove down Route 1 on the Virginia side, then took a sharp turn up a rather steep hill in Arlington toward my house. My house was a brick building with wood trim, and it was situated on the side of a hill which afforded me a rather breathtaking view of the nation's capital across the river. Marge actually located this gem of a house for us a few years back, right after our marriage. She was born in Washington while her father was here in the Senate, and for all practical purposes she was a native Washingtonian. I, of course, was a Californian, but I had landed here during the last few months of my Army hitch when I was stationed at Fort Myer and working in the Intelligence office at the Pentagon. Marge and I met at one of those garden parties to which they are always inviting eligible young officers, and six months later we were married. I never had any intention before of settling down in Washington, and as a matter of fact I had no idea of what the hell I wanted to do with my life. But Marge changed all that, and then Zach, her father, got me set up in the lobbying business. Then Marge found the house. Then our child arrived. And I liked every bit of it. God, did I like it.

And now I was coming home to the empty house again, and that feeling of almost unbearable emptiness came over me. I left my Olds in the carport, and immediately went down to the game room in the basement where I poured myself a tall scotch. From the small fridge under the bar I took out a piece of cut lime and plopped it in my drink. A little idiosyncrasy of mine. And an expensive one, too, because limes were out of season and I had to buy them at a gourmet store which really made you pay for having them flown in.

My pool was situated on the ground level, and through the sliding glass doors I could see the water shimmering on that moon-filled night. Since we were having such a warm spring, I had removed the tarp and filled the pool with fresh water in hopes of getting in some early swimming. Carrying my scotch, I walked out to the pool area and sat in an aluminum chair near the edge of the pool. It was still fairly early in the evening, but nevertheless I felt unusually tired after the perplexities of this strange day.

Sitting there alone, sipping my scotch, I went over it all again in my mind, but no matter how I looked at it I kept coming back to the peculiarity of the disappearance of the roommate, Cathy Morrison. It just didn't seem to fit in with the whole kidnapping scenario. And just a short while ago I had learned another interesting thing about Cathy Morrison. The girl down the hall, who admitted that she only knew Cathy casually, nevertheless felt that she was an activist. Cathy Morrison must have telegraphed that pretty loudly. But I wondered how much of an activist she was. Enough to join a group called the National Federation Army?

That reminded me of something else, and I put my drink down on the flagstones and went into the furnace room in the basement. In the far corner was a metal foot locker which I had bolted to the floor. I found the key, and opened the lid. Inside I kept some weapons, and I inspected them now—a small .32; a hefty .38 Police Special; and a .357 Magnum. I extracted the .32, and also a small belt holster and a box of .32 shells, and I took them back out to the pool area with me.

I sat down again, placed the box of shells in my lap, and looked closely at the .32. It was a small Smith & Wesson weapon, only eighteen ounces in weight, and it didn't have the blast or the longer range of some of the other weapons. But it was light and could be carried easily and inconspicuously, and I knew it could still do a hell of a job for you when you needed it.

I balanced it in my hand, and then aimed it across the other side of the pool. Gently I squeezed the trigger, but there was no report, of course, because the chambers were empty. I swung out the cylinder and inspected it carefully. It looked fine, because I kept the weapon well oiled.

Then, slowly and thoughtfully, I began to slide in the six shells.

CHAPTER FIVE

The first order of business the next day was the money-laundering operation for the ransom demand, and so shortly after nine I was in the reception area of Daniel McFarland's office on Pennsylvania Avenue just down from the White House.

It's hard to get in to see Dan without an appointment, but he had been an old friend of Zach and I had gotten to know him fairly well over the years. I had to wait for about a half-hour, but then the receptionist told me that Mr. McFarland could see me now. Big Dan—as he is known around town—was seated behind that enormous mahogany desk at the far end of his huge office, and he laboriously pulled himself up from his chair to greet me as I entered.

Dan is a big man in Washington in more ways than one: he is well over 250 pounds in weight, and he has large jangling jowls. He has remarkably blue eyes, and gives the impression of a jolly fat man, an impression he deliberately cultivates. Dan is as shrewd as a fox, and he can be as dangerous as an angry rattlesnake in this jungle of a town when the situation warrants it. Technically, Dan runs a law practice just a stone's throw from the White House, but actually he is a political can-do man in town. A former national treasurer of his party, he has been on close terms with a number of presidents, and today he is on a first-name basis with practically every important figure in town. He can put you in touch immediately with the right person about your government problem; he can work with you on getting that government contract; he can do some political fund raising for you. You name it, Big Dan can do it. And his contacts, and his clout, extend throughout the country. He was the man to see about my money problem.

"Long time, Brian," he said, extending his pudgy hand, a broad smile breaking out over his fleshy face. That overpowering heartiness, which had become his trademark.

"Sorry to break in on you like this, Dan. I only want a few minutes of your time." I glanced at the intercom system on his desk. "I hope the President won't interrupt us."

Dan laughed easily. It was an old story around town. According to the story, when Dan wants to impress new out-of-town clients who come to him for the first time, he arranges for his secretary to buzz him on the intercom a few minutes after the new client enters Dan's office. The secretary says loudly on the intercom that the President is on the phone and would like to speak to him. Dan politely excuses himself from the client for a few minutes to take the call in a private office down the corridor, and the client is really impressed. Dan's critics say that it is all a put-on: that Dan merely goes down to the bathroom where he smokes a cigarette for a few minutes before returning to the office, a pensive frown on his forehead. Dan merely smiles whenever he hears the story, and he won't either confirm or deny it. Why should he? Presidents really do call him on the phone.

"I'll get right to the point, Dan," I said. "I need a favor."

"So does everybody who comes through that door. What's your problem, Brian?"

"Let me put it this way. I have—or I will have in a few days—three hundred thousand dollars—"

"Good for you," he interrupted. "See, hard work and honesty pay off, don't they, Brian?"

I ignored that. "The money is in new bills, perhaps large denominations. Hundreds, maybe."

"I'm beginning to see where this is leading."

"And I'd like them converted into smaller bills, and older bills. Nothing larger than a twenty."

"The banks can do a fairly good job of that. And we have a number of good ones. Do you want me to put you in touch with the executives of a few of them?"

"Come on, Dan. You know what I want. I want the bills converted, and I don't want any notice or publicity about the conversion."

"Christ, sure I know what you want. You want me to launder some money for you. No thanks. This town is still trying to get over the stink of that stupid laundering operation during the Watergate days."

"This has nothing to do with a Watergate operation."

He held up his hand. "Please don't tell me what it is. I don't want to know any more about it."

"Dan, I can't tell you what it's all about. But I can guarantee you that it's a perfectly honest operation."

He eyed me shrewdly. "Would you be willing to sign an affidavit to that effect?"

"I certainly would. In fact, I'd insist that I'd sign it, so you could keep it in your safe to protect yourself."

Daniel McFarland closed his eyes and placed his two forefingers on his lips, as if he were in prayer. After a few seconds, he said: "Let me see. Brian Petersen comes in here and wants three hundred big ones laundered. He assures me it's all honest. And I know his reputation. He wouldn't screw you. But why then does he have to convert new bills into old bills? Who does he have to pay in old, unmarked bills? You know what it sounds like to me? It sounds like—"

"Don't say it," I interrupted.

"Okay, I won't say it. But I want to ask one other question. Are the police or the FBI involved in this?"

"No."

"I see."

"Dan, I can't tell you much about this. But when this is all over there are going to be some mighty important people in town who will be very appreciative that you've helped."

That was language which Dan understood, and he mulled it over now.

Finally, he asked: "And you'll be willing to sign that affidavit?"

I nodded agreement, and I added: "And perhaps I might be able to get a commission for you, if that's necessary."

"Fuck the commission. I just don't want to get my fingers burned."

"You won't."

"I'd better not. Or else I'll cut your balls off, Brian." He leaned over, flipped the intercom, and had his secretary come in. While I sat there he dictated a short statement describing the secret money conversion he was going to do for me and my assurance that it was an honest transaction, not in defiance of any law.

When the secretary left to type up the statement, Dan said to me: "When are you going to deliver the money to me?"

"Tomorrow at the latest. There's one other thing I forgot to tell you, Dan. I have to have it done in six days."

"Christ, I'll bet you forgot to tell me. Six days! This takes time, Brian."

"Time is what I haven't got. And I know you can do it, Dan."

He scowled at me. "Let's see, you'll bring me the money tomorrow, and then I've got five days. What I can do is break that three hundred thou up in ten lots of thirty each. I think I can find ten respectable guys up and down the eastern seaboard in different cities who can convert thirty thou into old bills without causing suspicion. But it'll mean flying the money around and special messengers and all that. Expensive. I'm not charging you any commission, Brian, but I'm going to charge you expenses."

"A deal."

The secretary came back into the office, and she laid the typed statement on the desk in front of Big Dan. He read it over carefully, nodded his head, and then he passed it over to me. I picked up a pen from the desk, and without even reading it, I signed it.

The laundering operation was underway.

Annie looked up from her desk as I entered, surprised to see me in the office so early, and then she noticed the frown on my forehead. "Trouble, Brian?" she asked.

"Trouble isn't the word. Get your notebook and we'll go over it."

She picked up her stenographer's pad and followed me into my office. I sat back in my chair, loosened my tie, and for the next half-hour proceeded to dictate all my recollections of the Rankin kidnapping, beginning with my first interview with Senator Rankin. While I promise my clients complete confidentiality, I nevertheless reserve the right to share the details of these cases with Annie Campbell. It's not only that I find it useful to have someone with whom I can talk it over and perhaps find a new perspective—that's part of it. But I also wanted a written record of some of these secret and lone assignments I was beginning to accept—in case the thing should blow up in my face and I needed a written record to prove what happened; and also in case I should get killed on one of these assignments, because then there would be some notes and observations available which someone else might pick up and follow to their conclusion. Annie, of course, observes the same confidentiality as I do, and after she types up my notes and I place them in my wall safe, I'm quite sure she never discusses the matter with anybody else.

Finding Annie was undoubtedly the best bit of pure luck I've had since Zach brought me back to Washington from the Keys. When I was trying to get my lobbying business started again I placed an ad in the paper, looking for someone who could give me a few hours' parttime help at the beginning. Annie was the first one to answer the ad, and that was it: she had the job. She's in her early thirties, a suburban housewife, and her two kids are now in school. Her husband has a middle-level government job in one of the agencies, and Annie was looking for a few hours' work to supplement their income. She was just what I needed: she came in mornings, got the office in shape, and she was able to wrap up my business by two o'clock in the afternoon and arrive home before her children. And, indeed, as I found myself doing less and less actual lobbying and more of this other stuff, that was all the office help I required.

I looked at her now as her pencil raced across her steno pad: a pert brunette with light freckles across her forehead. She had become more than a secretary to me. A friend? Yes, of course, but something more than that. A confidante, perhaps. Someone with whom I could share the details of these murky and often depressing affairs I was encountering here in Washington.

When I had finished dictating, I reached in a desk drawer, extracted a cigarette, and slowly lighted it. "The damnedest thing about this," I said to Annie, "is that I feel completely handcuffed. Since Rankin wants to play it exactly as this General Camillo directed, we can't enlist the help of investigative organizations and conduct the kind of inquiry I'd like."

"But, Brian," she said gently, "Senator Rankin isn't asking you to catch the kidnappers, he only wants help in the mechanics of getting his daughter back."

"I know," I said sourly. "But maybe Rankin is never going to get his daughter back, maybe he's the victim of a giant fraud. And in that case, Rankin needs more help than he realizes. I'm not going to tell Rankin anything about it, but I'll be damned if I'm going to let this General Camillo have it all his way. I want to know a little more about what's going on, but we'll have to do it extremely carefully."

I reached in my pocket and pulled out the sheaf of papers I had taken last evening from the table next to Cathy Morrison's bed. I handed one to Annie. "Here's a pay voucher from some group called Action for Environment, on Twenty-fourth Street, apparently the place where Cathy Morrison works. I'd like you to call there and see if anybody knows where she is. But do it very deftly. You're an old friend of hers who just arrived in town, or something like that. And also, see if you can find out what the hell that group does."

Annie took the voucher, and went out to her own office to make the call. I pulled the phone on my desk toward me, and then I flipped open my address book and looked up Tom Breyer's number in Chicago. While waiting for the call to go through, I picked up the letter from Cathy Morrison's aunt and studied the Winnetka address.

Tom Breyer's secretary put me through to him immediately. He is a partner in a rather prosperous real estate business in Chicago, but I first met Tom a number of years ago when we were both stationed in Europe in Army Intelligence. He was a good operator, but more than that we became buddies and spent a lot of our leave time together in Europe. And we both vowed that when we finished our hitches we were going to get out of that damned business.

I hadn't talked to Tom for over a year, and after we had chatted for a few minutes, I asked him my favor.

"I'm trying to locate a girl, Tom, who comes from Winnetka, I think. She's been here in Washington for a while, but she seems to have dropped out of sight. Maybe she's returned home, I don't know. But I'd like to find out. Her name is Cathy Morrison."

"Sure, Brian, I can check it out for you. Do you have some place I can start?"

"I do," I said, and I gave him the aunt's name and address in Winnetka. "That's all I've got to go on so far, Tom. But there's one extremely important thing about this one. It's got to be an absolutely covert inquiry, like the kind we used to do in Intelligence. I don't want anyone to know that anyone is trying to locate this girl. If anyone gets suspicious, drop it immediately. Walk away from it."

"Cripes, are you working for the Company now, Brian?"

"Not a chance, Tom. This is my own deal."

"Sure, Brian, I'll nose around. I'll do it this afternoon, in fact. I've got some business north of Chicago. I'll make a stop at that address, and use some of our old tricks. I'll get back to you."

After I had finished the call, Annie came back into the office and told me she tried to get in contact with Cathy Morrison at Action for Environment.

"And I suppose, Annie, that she hasn't shown up in three days."

"That's right," she said. "I talked to some type of office manager or something, and he said they were beginning to wonder if Cathy Morrison just hadn't quit for some reason. She hasn't called in sick, and she apparently can't be reached by phone."

"Yeah," I said thoughtfully. "Did you get any kind of an angle on the organization?"

"It doesn't sound very activistic to me. They're mainly interested in protecting endangered species of wild fowl."

I shook my head in puzzlement. "For God's sake—birds!"

I had a luncheon engagement with Steve Harrison at Paul Young's Restaurant on Connecticut Avenue; I owed him a luncheon in return for some favors he had done for me. Steve is a reporter on the congressional desk of the *Washington Post*; one of the newer breed of investigative reporters who have become so important in this town in the last few years. He is an intense, thin, young man in his early thirties with prematurely thinning hair and thick eyeglasses, and today he spared no effort in tagging me for the lunch I promised him. Oysters on the half-shell, steak diane, Caesar salad, cheese cake. And a fine bottle of red burgundy to accompany it.

I ordered a chef's salad and a glass of iced tea, and I watched him stuff away the victuals. "Don't they pay you guys enough to get a good meal at the *Post*?" I asked.

"We artists are always underpaid." he said, and motioned to the waiter for more coffee.

"Be my guest. Does this bacchanalian luncheon entitle me to pick your brain again?"

"Try me."

"An organization called the National Federation Army. Ever hear of it?"

He shook his head. "Never. Should I?"

"I don't know," I said, lighting a cigarette. "Maybe you could do a little research on it for me. It's probably a young radical group. Located here in Washington, I think. But I have a suspicion it may have started in Chicago. Maybe the University of

Chicago. But, Steve, this has to be an absolutely deep background inquiry."

He nodded his head slowly. In the jargon of the journalistic trade, a deep background inquiry is one in which Steve would keep my name out of it and refuse to reveal the name of the person who was seeking the information. Of course, I was also obligating myself to Steve, because if he did discover anything, he could then come back and request deep background information from me.

"Okay," he said. "But it's going to cost you another meal." He signalled for the waiter to bring him some brandy.

I groaned. "I don't know if I can afford you, Steve."

Later that afternoon I made a stop at the National Press Building on Fourteenth Street to see Tom Walsh. He was in his small office, banging away on an old manual typewriter when I entered, and he gave me a big wave of greeting. Tom is also a Washington journalist, but he is a veteran from an older school. And, unfortunately, Tom has been on the skids for the past few years. A former chief of the Washington bureau for a chain of midwestern newspapers, and a top writer for both wire services, he started to get drowned in the bottle. As the sauce took over his life, he began to lose one good job after another until now he was reduced to doing a few freelance pieces now and then for out-of-town papers. In the past year or so Tom has straightened himself out a little bit so that he is able to function at least marginally, but you never know when the poor guy is going to come crashing off the wagon again. Despite Tom's personal problems, he's an extremely well-liked person, and I doubt if there is anybody around who knows Washington better than he does. If you really want to find the scoop on somebody, Tom Walsh is the man to see. That is, if you can get him at those periods of his life when he's not all juiced-up.

He looked fine now, and I got right into it with him. "What do you know about Senator Rankin's daughter Ellen?" I asked him.

"That's his youngest kid, isn't it? Not much. She seems to stay out of the limelight. I think she's some sort of do-gooder, Brian."

"I'd like to see if I could get any more information about her."

"Sure. I can ask around."

"Well, Tom, this is a tacky one. I don't want anyone to know that there's any present interest in Ellen Rankin."

He frowned. "Well ... maybe I can engage in some casual bar talk, or something like that, with some of the press boys. It wouldn't be as good as pulling out the stops and asking some hard-hitting questions around town."

"No, let's not have any hard-hitting, Tom. For the time being. One more thing: have you ever heard of a radical group called the National Federation Army?"

He smiled, and shook his head no. "That wouldn't be a temperance group, would it?"

On the cab ride back to the Connecticut Avenue business area I sat huddled in the corner of the rear seat, smoking a cigarette, and wondering about the NFA. Two very knowledgeable guys—Harrison and Walsh—had never even heard of it. And it seemed from the tape cassette Rankin had received that the NFA was very much interested in preserving that anonymity. All they wanted was the three hundred grand from Rankin. And no publicity. It didn't fit the pattern of recent radical and terrorist kidnappings.

I had the taxi drop me at the health club I frequent near my office, and for the next three-quarters of an hour I did my usual workout of calisthenics: the low bars, the rings, the weights, and the fast session on the hanging boxing bag. When I was finished I stripped off my shorts and sweat shirt and showered down, starting with the warm water and gradually turning the faucet until it was spraying cold water over my body. I glanced at myself briefly in a full-length mirror as I was toweling myself dry—despite the wounds and bruises I had taken over the years, the old body was still in reasonably good shape.

Annie had, of course, departed the office for the day, but I went up there to see if she had left any messages for me. There were no messages, but she had neatly typed up the notes I dictated this morning and left them on my desk in a manila folder. Propping my feet up on the desk, I read through them very slowly, hoping to see something I hadn't noticed before. But nothing hit. I closed the folder, and took it over to my wall safe. There's nothing particularly clever about the location of that safe, because it is covered only by a Gauguin print. But the fellow who sold it to me, an old Army ordinance man, told me that he worked it into the basic structure of the building and it was a durable job which would baffle even an experienced safe man. I didn't know about that, but at least I knew it wasn't a tin can.

The phone rang and I answered it. "Hello."

"Petersen?"

"Yes."

"This is Lester Rankin. I think we'd better have a conference immediately."

"What's happened?"

"I've just had another communication from those people."

"The General?" I asked.

"Yes."

"By mail?"

"No, by phone. He called about a half-hour ago. There's been a most disturbing development. I've called Senator Phillips, and he's coming right over. I think you'd better meet with us."

"I'm on my way."

CHAPTER SIX

ester Rankin was in his study when I arrived, talking seriously with Senator Harold Phillips. They stopped talking abruptly when the maid showed me into the room, and Hank Phillips caught my eye and lifted his shoulders in a slight shrug, as if to say that he didn't know what this was all about.

Rankin wheeled to face me and there was a thunderous expression on his face. "Petersen, have you violated my confidence?" he asked sternly.

"Of course not, Senator."

"Have you told anybody of Ellen's kidnapping?"

"Definitely not." I had told Annie about it, of course, but that didn't count.

"Then how do you explain that phone call from General Camillo?"

"You're getting ahead of me, Senator. Perhaps you'd better start at the top."

Rankin waved at the telephone sitting on a small table next to a large leather chair. "About forty-five minutes ago that maniac phoned me directly, and I had to do some pretty smooth talking to calm him down. It seems that he has somehow learned that you are associated with us in this, and he was most disturbed. He thought I was double-crossing him by calling in the authorities."

"Have you made any phone calls since then?" I asked, and when he shook his head no, I went over to Eddie Perkins' recording machine which was on the floor and began to work the tape backwards. "Let's listen to the conversation, and then maybe I can tell you more about it."

I had to fiddle with the machine for a while, stopping it and listening to snatches of conversation, until I finally got it set at the start of the phone call when I heard Rankin answer the phone. The three of us stood there, like three wooden Indians, looking stonily at the machine while it replayed the call.

Rankin: Hello.

Camillo: Is this Lester Rankin?

Rankin: Yes.

Camillo: This is General Camillo speaking for the National Federation Army. Rankin, you're double-crossing us, and your daughter is going to die.

Rankin: What do you mean, I'm not double-crossing you. I'm following your directions implicitly. I'm in the process of gathering the money, and I'll be waiting for your instructions on where to deliver it.

Camillo: Maybe you are. But I'm not talking about that. I told you not to contact the authorities or the media.

Rankin: I haven't.

Camillo: Then why have you brought that Brian Petersen into this?

Rankin: Brian Petersen. Why he's an old family friend.

Camillo: He's some sort of undercover agent, isn't he?

Rankin: Nonsense. He's a lobbyist. And he's had a lot of personal tragedy in his life. But that's beside the point. He's an old family friend, and I've asked him to help gather the money you requested. You said you wanted it in unmarked bills, and he's the man who is doing it for me. I believe they call it laundering the money. It's something I know very little about, and it's something I just couldn't manage myself, and I had to get Mr. Petersen to assist me. After all, you wanted the unmarked bills.

Camillo: You'd better not be double-crossing us. The NFA will not be fooled.

Rankin: I assure you I'm not. I'm following your directions to the letter.

Camillo: That Petersen guy better not be cops.

Rankin: He has no connection of any kind with the authorities. As I told you, he's an old family friend.

(Listening to the tape of the phone conversation, I was already beginning to churn it around in my mind—how the hell had they learned that I was working on this thing for Rankin? I must say, however, that Rankin was handling it extremely well, and he was adopting exactly the right tone for dealing with Camillo. He didn't act intimidated, and yet he wasn't aggressive. Rather, he adopted a soothing tone which wasn't at all patronizing. And I liked his pitch about my being an old family friend, which wasn't true at all, of course. I guess Rankin's years of debating on the Senate floor must have schooled him well in the techniques of dialogue with a difficult opponent. The conversation ran on for almost five minutes, as Rankin continued to assure Camillo that I had no police connections of any kind. Finally, Camillo appeared to be mollified, if not completely convinced.)

Camillo: We're playing square with you, Rankin. That's the way the NFA operates. And you fascists are going to have to learn to play square with the people.

Rankin: I'm playing square with you.

Camillo: Otherwise, the high tribunal of the National Federation Army will be forced to execute your daughter.

Rankin: I want to speak to my daughter.

Camillo: She's not here. I'm not speaking from NFA headquarters. I don't want the fascist pigs tracing phone calls.

Rankin: Is my daughter all right?

Camillo: She is unharmed.

Rankin: What assurances do I have?

Camillo: You have the assurances of the National Federation Army, and that should be enough.

Rankin: I don't know anything about the National Federation Army. I've never even heard of it.

Camillo: Someday the whole world will hear about the National Federation Army. But for the time being you'll have to trust us. You have no choice. The only thing you have to do is get the money.

Rankin: I'm in the process of gathering it now and having it laundered.

Camillo: You only have five more days.

Rankin: I'll have it by then.

Camillo: You'd better. Or else—

I heard the click of the phone being hung up on the tape, and then the tape rolled soundlessly on. I reached over and shut off the machine.

"Well?" Rankin asked me, asperity in his voice.

"First of all, Senator, I have not violated your confidence. I have not told anyone about your daughter's kidnapping."

"But then how do you explain that strange conversation?"

"There are a number of curious things about that conversation, Senator. The first, obviously, is their knowledge that I'm somehow involved in this now. And that's certainly disturbing them because they think that I might be the police. And I have to say, Senator, you handled Camillo extremely well on the phone, assuring him that I wasn't. But how the hell did they even know I was involved in it? Let's start at the beginning. After you received that tape yesterday, Senator, what was the first thing you did?"

"Well, after I recovered from my initial shock, I guess the first thing I did was call Senator Phillips. I got him at home before he left for the Hill, and he came right over. It was then he suggested we employ your services to advise us on how to handle this tricky business. Senator Phillips then left because he said he had some extremely important business at the office, authoring that new bill on nuclear reactors which has to go before committee today. But he said he'd return as soon as he could, in a few hours."

"And then you phoned me. Twice, I believe."

"Yes. And I couldn't seem to get you, and your secretary didn't know where you were."

"So, then you phoned Hank at his office and told him about it?"

"That's correct. And he said he thought he could find you."

I pointed to the phone. "Therefore, three times yesterday, right after you received the kidnapper's message, you used that phone to try and get in contact with me. Did you ever think your phone might be bugged, and the NFA listening in? They're paranoid about police involvement, and they thought you might be calling in some undercover man or something."

Rankin stared at the phone. "Yes," he said slowly. "That might be the answer."

I knew it wasn't the answer at all, of course, because Eddie Perkins had told me he swept the place yesterday and discovered that there was no tap on the phones. But I was just trying to calm Rankin down, and give him something to think about while I tried to sort it out in my own mind. I turned toward Harold Phillips. "And I don't think you'd make the mistake, Hank, of telling anybody about it."

"Of course not, Brian. After I left Lester yesterday I drove right to the office, and I was just trying to put the finishing touches on that bill for committee when he called and said he couldn't find you. You're notorious, Brian, for not returning phone calls, but I thought I could get you. Even though I was getting ready to come back here to Lester's, I decided to wait in my office for you to return the call. But, no, I didn't mention your name to anyone."

"Then, again," I said, "there's the possibility that they may have people staked out around the house to make sure that the police don't come charging in. And then they saw me arrive here yesterday a few hours after you should have received the kidnapping message, and then I returned later in the day with Eddie Perkins. Maybe they got suspicious that you were calling in the police. And they didn't know who I was, but they somehow found out. Maybe they got my license plate and somehow were able to check it out. Maybe they followed me and found out my name."

Rankin slumped in a chair. "My God, bugged telephones. People putting my own house under surveillance. Those people are monsters."

"Yes, Senator, but I think you brought that off very well on the phone. You don't have anything to worry about, even if they do tap your phone and keep your house under surveillance. You're following their instructions. They can't fault you on that."

"I guess not," Rankin said glumly. "I've already had deposited in your account about a hundred and fifty thousand dollars. The remainder of it should be there shortly after the bank opens tomorrow. Say, about ten o'clock. You'll be able to do your part of it, Petersen?"

"I will."

"I guess I should apologize for accusing you. But it's been an unsettling time. And when I got that phone call from that maniac I didn't know what to think."

"I understand, Senator."

He rubbed his hand over his eyes. "Is there anything else you think we should be doing?"

"No, the only thing we can do now is wait. The next move is theirs. We just have to wait for the phone call telling us where to deliver the money."

I was making motions to leave now because I was getting itchy to try out a little theory which was jumping through my mind. Hank Phillips said that he would stay with Rankin for a while and talk to him.

But Rankin shook his head no. "I appreciate that, Hank. You're very kind. But I think I'd just rather be alone for a while, if you don't mind."

Phillips and I therefore left the study together, and when I looked back Rankin was still slumped in his chair. I followed his gaze and I saw he was looking at a large photograph on the wall. It was a studio portrait of Ellen Rankin, obviously taken a few years ago, because she wasn't wearing the long hair I had seen in the photograph on her recent driver's license. I wondered where Ellen Rankin was right now.

It was dark when we left Rankin's house, and I walked Hank Phillips over to his Cadillac. "I'm worried, Brian," he said.

"So am I, Hank."

"Isn't there anything else we can do?"

"Not unless you want to call in the police."

"No, we've made our decision on that, and we're going to have to live with it now. But after we get Ellen back we'll certainly call in the police, and then I'd like to see that Camillo and his whole NFA rot in jail for the rest of their lives. Brian, what in God's name do you think this NFA is?"

"I'm not quite sure, but we're beginning to learn a little more about it."

"We are?"

"That phone call. Camillo was obviously terrified that I might be police, and he wanted to put it right to Rankin. And Rankin handled it well. I can understand Camillo doing that, but he made a colossal mistake. He talked on that phone for almost five minutes. If he had any suspicion that the police might have been called in—and he obviously did—then he should have made the call as brief as he could. Certainly no more than a minute. Any professional criminal knows that the longer you hang on the phone the easier it is to put a trace on it. But Camillo allowed himself to get involved in a relatively long, five-minute conversation. That can only mean one thing. He's no professional criminal, he's an amateur."

"Well, I suppose that's reassuring."

"Not at all, Hank. I don't like amateurs because they panic too easily. They can be much more dangerous than professionals."

I watched Hank Phillips drive away, and then with extreme deliberation I extracted a package of cigarettes from my pocket. I was trying to make it look as casual as possible, but my eyes were darting around, trying to see if I could spot a stakeout of any kind around Rankin's house. However, everything looked quite normal. No suspicious cars parked near the house. Nobody standing idly around. That nevertheless didn't mean that there wasn't someone out there whom I couldn't spot at the moment. And the stakeout of some sort was still my favorite theory of how the NFA had gotten suspicious of me.

No other theory seemed plausible. I certainly hadn't told anyone directly about the alleged Rankin kidnapping, except Annie, and I would bet my very life that she would preserve my confidentiality. During the past twenty-four hours I assuredly had mentioned either Ellen Rankin or the NFA to a number of people, but each one only was given a piece of the puzzle. I couldn't imagine them running to the NFA with it. I thought of all the people I had talked to since this wretched affair started. Eddie Perkins. No, I couldn't imagine him with NFA connections. The girl who thought I was breaking into Ellen Rankin's apartment. No, she appeared pretty genuine, and I think she bought my story fairly well. Furthermore, even if she had some connection with the NFA, she had seen my ID and she knew that I wasn't police. Dan McFarland—I hadn't mentioned either Rankin or NFA to him. Steve Harrison or Tom Walsh. No, that was preposterous. It simply had to be a stakeout of some kind.

And so I casually lit a cigarette, allowing the match to burn brightly before my face, and then I slowly walked over to my car. As I pulled open the door I took one last look around. I still couldn't see anybody, but if there was someone out there in the darkness, I had deliberately given them enough time to see me. Maybe I could draw them out.

I turned the key in the ignition, and allowed the engine to run for almost a minute before I slowly started to pull out of the gravel driveway. Driving at an extremely low speed, I left the Rankin property and turned into the narrow, tree-lined street in front of the house. I was probably only about ten or fifteen yards from the driveway, carefully looking in all directions, when I spotted it. Way down the street behind me, about a hundred yards back, I saw the lights of an automobile flick on. As I continued my slow drive, I watched it through my rear-view mirror and I saw it pick up a little speed and then slow down so that it was trailing me by about fifty yards. It could be just a coincidence of course, someone who happened to be leaving another house at the same time I was leaving Rankin's. But I knew it wasn't.

Nevertheless, I'd give it a fair test. The streets in residential Kenwood are narrow and circuitous, and I drove along at about twenty miles an hour, allowing the car behind me either to pick up speed or to pass me. But it didn't—it just hung back there, following me. It was still behind me when I reached River Road, and instead of turning right as I usually would to head back toward the District, I turned left toward Potomac, Maryland. And the car behind me came right along.

There was a considerable bit of traffic along River Road, and I hit the accelerator, increasing speed. I could see the car behind me more clearly now under the bright streetlights: a four-door Chevrolet, rather old and battered looking. It picked up speed to keep close to me. And then when I slowed down, it slowed down too, remaining that same distance behind me.

No doubt about it. I was being tailed.

And I was sure that was how General Camillo had learned of my involvement in the Rankin affair. The NFA, terrified that Rankin might go to the police, had been watching his house for any suspicious activity. And then they saw me drive up there a few times yesterday, and that aroused their suspicions. Somehow they had been able to find out who I was, perhaps from a license plate, or perhaps they had been trailing me around for the last twenty-four hours and I didn't notice it. That was quite possible, because it hadn't even crossed my mind that anyone would want to follow me, and I hadn't even bothered to check for a tail.

But they were tailing me now. Undoubtedly, Rankin hadn't completely stifled General Camillo's suspicions about me, and they still wanted to make sure I wasn't some type of undercover agent working for the police or the FBI. They would trail me, therefore, to see where I went, and to find out if I were reporting back to the police or any other law enforcement agency.

That was fine with me, because I really wanted this tail, and I was going to make sure as hell the Chevrolet didn't lose me. It was the closest I had gotten yet to the mysterious National Federation Army. But even at that, the Chevrolet almost lost me a few times, and I had to slow down to make sure it could catch up through the heavy traffic. They were amateurs, all right, and this was one of the worst tails I had ever seen. The way the Chevrolet had flicked on its lights right behind me when it was starting out was lousy technique. And then it had followed me too closely in the Kenwood area when there were no other cars around. Now, it was having great difficulty in tailing me in heavy traffic. Amateurs. But, as I told Hank Phillips, amateurs can be extremely dangerous.

We came to a red light, and the Chevrolet stopped a few cars behind me. I could see now through my rear-view mirror that there was only one person in the Chevrolet: a young man, perhaps somewhere in his early twenties, and he appeared to be wearing a khaki bush jacket.

The light flicked to green and the traffic started up again. Come on, baby, I thought to myself, stay with me. You think you're trailing me. But I'm really dragging you along. And when I find the right spot, I'm going to double back on you. Then I'll meet one member of the National Federation Army face to face for the first time.

With my right hand I reached around my back to the belt holster, and withdrew the .32. I held it in my hand for a moment, and then I clicked off the safety, laying it on the seat beside me.

CHAPTER SEVEN

We drove out River Road, through the village of Potomac and then into the countryside, the old Chevrolet following right behind me.

The traffic had dwindled to practically nothing, but it still wasn't the right place to work a turnabout. That occasional car passing by could very well interrupt the little project I had in mind. At that moment I was thinking that I could blow the whole Rankin kidnapping wide open and find where Ellen was without the risky business of having to pay ransom. All I needed was one member of the NFA, and I had him right behind me now. There was no doubt that if I could get my hands on him I could make him talk, and then have him give me the trail right to Ellen Rankin. I learned some rather effective methods in Intelligence for getting people to talk in a hurry without the necessity of using the slow process of drugs. The methods aren't very pretty and you don't find them printed in any government manuals, but they work. For instance, you won't find many people who won't start blabbering like idiots when you tie them down and shoot off one of their testicles. When you hold that pistol over the one remaining testicle they start talking all right, telling you whatever you want to know. Those aren't Marquis of Queensbury rules, of course, but when you start playing the kidnapping game, real or bogus, you forfeit your right to any rules as far as I'm concerned.

I didn't know this section of Maryland very well, but I thought I could eventually find the spot I wanted. There were large, estatelike homes out here with plenty of open fields and wooded areas, and if I turned off River Road someplace I was sure I could find a deserted lane. I made my decision at the next intersecting road, and took a sharp turn to the right. The Chevrolet came right behind me, maybe about a hundred yards back, and again I marvelled at what an incredibly bad tail it was.

I drove along the lonely road, looking for some kind of even smaller road I could turn into. I had my high beams on, and I finally thought I spotted something attractive up ahead. Pushing the accelerator to the floor, I shot way ahead of the Chevrolet and I must have been almost a quarter of a mile in front of it when I made a sharp, screeching turn into what appeared to be a narrow country lane. It was a dirt road and I bounced along at the highest speed I could manage until I felt I was far enough in. Then I flicked off the lights, slammed on the brakes, and did a roll out of the car, sliding across the front seat and out the passenger door. I had my pistol in my hand when I hit the ground.

The Chevrolet was just starting a slow, tentative turn into the lane, and I kept my eyes trained on it as I crawled away from my car. There was a low stone wall, maybe three feet high, along the edge of the lane, and I kept close to it, crawling on my hands and knees back toward the entrance of the lane where the Chevrolet had appeared. Some high grass along the ground next to the wall also helped to shield me from view. I had managed to crawl about ten yards in the grass when the Chevrolet drew up. The driver saw my parked car, and stopped immediately, shutting off his lights.

I lay perfectly still in the tall grass at the base of the stone fence, and waited. It was his move now. His car was parked about thirty-five or forty yards behind mine, but I was hidden in the grass at the side of the road between the two cars. It took him almost five minutes to make up his mind about what to do next.

He couldn't see any movement in my car, and he was apparently thinking that I had parked and hiked off someplace, perhaps to meet somebody. I could almost feel his brain working; he had to find out where I had gone, and he had to find out whom I was meeting out here in the middle of the woods.

The door of the Chevrolet opened and the driver stepped out cautiously, and moved toward my car in a low crouch. He was checking to make sure that I wasn't still in the car, and on that moonlit night I could get a good look at him. My original appraisal was correct: the young man in the bush jacket appeared to be in his early twenties, white, moustachioed, and was holding a pistol which looked like a snub-nosed .38, a Colt Special. It was a bigger, more powerful weapon than my .32.

He was trying to stay close to the edge of the road, and he was only a foot or so away when he passed right by me, his eyes trained on my car. I let him get another five yards along when I jumped up. His back was to me now, but he heard the movement and started to wheel around.

"Hold it!" I shouted. "You're covered."

He was almost completely turned toward me, but he froze, the pistol still in his hand. However, as I was to learn, he had exceptionally quick reflexes. He took one quick step in the direction of the low stone wall and flung himself into the air, hurtling over it headfirst. I had my .32 trained on him all the way, and he was an easy target as he went sailing through the air. I could have riddled him right up the middle, but I didn't want that; I wanted him alive. And that caused me to miss. I fired, trying to aim for the lower part of his outflung body, somewhere around the hips or legs, but I didn't hit him.

He landed in some grass and foliage on the other side of the wall, and I went right after him, my pistol in front of me. But he was quick. He had managed to either do a somersault landing or he had scrambled quickly to his feet, because he was dashing into the woods ahead of me. I could hear him thrashing through the foliage, and I followed after him. He wasn't making any effort to be quiet or conceal his movements and I had no trouble following the sounds. We went on for forty or fifty yards, and then suddenly it was quiet. I couldn't hear him.

I went down on one knee, listening, waiting for him to make his next move. But there was no sound. All right, it was going to be a waiting game. He couldn't be any more than ten yards ahead of me, but I was going to hold it right here until he made his next move. And then I would follow him again, drawing closer. If I started to move first he could hear me coming, and with that .38 Colt he could draw a nice bead on me.

We played that cat-and-mouse game for three or four minutes, and I remained immobile, still on one knee, my pistol pointing in the direction where I last heard him. I had fired one shot, and that left five bullets in the pistol. There was an extra box of shells in the glove compartment of my car, but that wouldn't do me any good now. I'd have to make those five shots good, particularly if I only wanted to wound him.

Then I heard the snap of a branch directly behind me, and I knew what had happened. He had managed to silently crawl around me so that he was right in back of me now. He might have been a lousy tail man, but he sure as hell knew a lot about jungle guerrilla tactics.

The moment I heard that snap, I hit the ground and did a fast rollover. He fired, and missed. I got up on one knee, my shoulders hunched down, and saw him coming, crashing through the underbrush toward me. His second shot also missed, and I carefully squeezed the trigger. My bullet hit him somewhere in the right hip, and he jerked to a stop and staggered backward a step. But he didn't fall.

"Put your gun down," I shouted at him from my crouched position.

I could see the expression on his face clearly now: pain, indecision, but most importantly, rage. "You fuckin' bastard!" he screamed at me, and he started coming at me again, in a crooked run on that injured hip. He fired, and the bullet hit me in my left shoulder. It spun me with its impact and I fell backwards.

I was lying on my back now, more concerned with getting out of his line of fire than getting off a shot at him. I did a half-roll, and his next shot hit in the dirt, inches from me. He was about six feet away, coming in that hobbled run, trying to get clear aim at me, obviously trying to finish me off.

From my supine position, lying on my back, I steadied my arm by digging my elbow into the ground, and I fired. The trajectory of my bullet was upward in a sharp angle, and the bullet hit him someplace under the chin and must have carried right on up into his brain. He went off the ground a few inches, as if he had suddenly been jerked up by a strong rope. And then with ridiculous grace, like a diver doing a back dive, he seemed to float backward, finally hitting the ground with a soft thud.

I laid my pistol on the ground and pushed myself up to a sitting position. There wouldn't be any more shooting for a while, I knew, because my NFA friend was quite dead.

The first thing I did was to inspect the damage in my shoulder. Pulling off my jacket, I probed at the wound. Blood was running down my arm, staining my shirt, but the wound was not as serious as it looked. The bullet had hit right at the top of my shoulder, but I couldn't feel it lodged in there. It had apparently passed through, and I couldn't feel any broken bones. Pressing a handkerchief against the wound, I tried to stop the flow of blood, and I got up and walked over to inspect the corpse.

He was lying faceup, with that gaping hole under his chin, his eyes still open, staring vacantly out into space. Damn, I thought, I've really screwed this up now. I had wanted to take him alive, but at that last moment with him charging at me, firing, I didn't have time for any fancy shots. He was determined that it was a fight to the finish. And I recalled that disturbing note of fanaticism in General Camillo's voice on the phone. I was sure that this young man wasn't Camillo, but he seemed to be infected with the same brand of thinking.

I have little compunction about killing a man who is trying to kill me, but I was sorry as hell that this one died before I had an opportunity to pound information out of him. And I was really in a bind now. If Ellen Rankin was truly being held by kidnappers—and I simply had to work on that assumption for her safety—then when they learned that I'd killed one of their men they could really go on a rampage, perhaps even killing Ellen Rankin in retaliation. I had created a mammoth problem, I thought ruefully.

My clever little plan had backfired brutally. If I had been able to take this guy alive, I'm sure I would have had it all out of him by now. If the kidnapping was genuine, then he would have told me where the girl was being held and we could have gone and gotten her out of there.

But now ...

I sat down on the ground, beside the corpse, and began to go through his pockets, hoping I could get a lead. But this young fellow knew one other thing about guerrilla tactics: he had absolutely no identification of any kind on his person, only a handkerchief and the keys to the car. That's another old guerrilla trick: Don't carry any identification in case you are captured.

However, he made one mistake, and I found it in the upper pocket of the bush jacket, a small note-sized slip of paper with some words scrawled on it in pencil. I held it up, angling it so I could capture some illumination from the moon and read it:

Lieutenant Timothy Bronson—use the blue Chevrolet today. Liberation to the people!

General Camillo

I could also notice a small pinhole at the top of the note, as if it had been attached to a bulletin board of some kind. That seemed to square with some type of funky operation where these guys were trying to play little tin soldiers with all sorts of military discipline. Apparently the NFA had a number of cars at their disposal, and Camillo assigned the cars to each of the members. This Timothy Bronson had seen the notice for his car on the bulletin board, removed it, and placed it in his pocket unthinkingly.

At least I knew his name. That was something. And if we were able to do a regular investigation we could lift his prints, and get a fix on him in a number of hours. Then we'd have a real lead. But we couldn't do it that way.

The only plan I could figure now was to somehow conceal from the NFA the fact that I had killed one of their members. But how? Maybe I could make it appear that this Timothy Bronson had just deserted the NFA, perhaps gotten frightened and run away, taking the Chevrolet with him. Suppose he just disappears, leaving no trace of himself. Would they think he had deserted? I didn't know, but it was worth a chance.

In fact, it was the only chance I had.

The next step, then, was to get rid of Bronson's body. I didn't relish the idea of driving around with a corpse, trying to find someplace to hide it, and so I decided to plant him right there where he had fallen. I remembered that I had a shovel in the trunk of my car, one of those collapsible Army ones, which I kept there in case I had to dig myself out of a snowstorm, and I trudged back to the road to get it. I counted my steps carefully out to the road, not only because I wanted to be able to retrace my steps to the corpse that night, but also because I wanted to be able to make a map later of where the body was buried for possible future use.

It took me a number of sweaty hours to dig the grave, and my fatigue was increased by the throbbing pain from the wound in my shoulder. I wasn't concerned about a neat symmetrical grave, because I planned to stuff the body down in the smallest space possible, but I did want to make it deep enough so that the body wouldn't be clawed out by animals. I lifted Bronson's corpse by the armpits, and dragged it over to the lip of the small grave, and then I slowly lowered him into it feet first. When I felt his feet touch the bottom, I let him go, giving him a little push forward so that he doubled over at the bottom of the grave.

Furiously I began to throw the dirt back into the hole, covering the body. There was enough dirt left for a little mound, not high enough to attract attention, but enough to prevent an obvious mark of a hole in the ground when the earth began to settle after a rainstorm. Then I pulled branches from a small tree and placed them over the grave a few feet around it. It looked pretty good, and at least it wasn't immediately obvious that a hole had recently been dug there. I knew that the grave would be discovered eventually, but all I wanted was a few days before someone stumbled on it.

I returned to the road again, and did a second count on the number of paces from the gravesite to the road. There was a large oak tree near the spot where my car was parked, and I hit it a number of times with the edge of my shovel, cutting a deep gash which could be used for identification.

Bronson's car was a problem, and I was considering various ways of getting rid of it. I went over the car carefully, but as I expected, I couldn't find anything of value to me in it. I was quite sure that the car was stolen and that different stolen plates had been used on it, and therefore I didn't feel that there was anything to be gained by trying to do a check on it. I placed the car key which I had taken from Bronson's pocket under the front seat, and then I locked the car. I didn't think anybody would bother about the locked car in the country lane for the next few hours, but I had to get it out of there fairly early tomorrow.

I watched my speedometer closely on the drive back to the secondary road, noting the exact distance from the road to the marked oak tree, and then I did the same thing on the drive back to River Road. Before I turned out onto River Poad, I stopped for a minute and made a notation of all the calculations. Now I could accurately direct anyone to the only member of the NFA I knew, young Timothy Bronson lying back there in a fresh grave.

It was after midnight when I arrived back in Virginia, and I made my first stop at Kevin Lynch's house in Alexandria. Kevin was an old friend of mine, a pediatrician, and he has his office in an annex he built next to his house. There were still lights on in the downstairs section, and thus I didn't feel too bad about barging in on him in the middle of the night. Kevin was up, alone and reading, and when he answered the door and took one look at me he knew what I wanted. He has had to patch me up a number of times over the years, and I used to give him some cock-and-bull story about the cause of my injury to prevent him from reporting a gun wound to the police. He knew the story was patently fictitious of course, and now he only shakes his head and doesn't even bother to ask. Which is what he did that night. He examined the wound, probed to make sure there was no foreign matter, patched it up, and gave me a tetanus shot.

As I was leaving, he said: "If that was a bullet wound, Brian—which of course you'll deny—but if that was a bullet wound, it was only about five or six inches from that precious skull of yours."

"I've got a thick skull, Kevin."

"Not thick enough to withstand that," he said, tapping his finger on the shoulder where the bullet had struck me.

It was about one-thirty in the morning when I finally arrived home, and the first thing I did was go down to the bar and pour myself a stiff glass of scotch. I didn't even bother to add my customary piece of lime. As I sipped the drink at the bar, I pulled the telephone toward me and dialed a number. It was answered on the first ring.

"I'm glad I didn't get you up, Calvin," I said.

"I'm in bed, but I react to that phone like a fire alarm. Wait a minute, let me go downstairs and take this so I won't wake up my wife."

I lifted the glass and gulped another big draught of scotch while I waited. Calvin Johnson was another old friend of mine whom I now had to call on in the middle of the night because he had resources I needed immediately. He worked in the ghetto area over on Georgia Avenue, the part of the city they don't show the tourists, and he had founded a job-training school for young blacks. Calvin, a black himself, was a graduate of Harvard Business, and he brought a lot of professionalism and competence to his operation. Zach had even managed to get him a number of government grants during the years he was in the Senate, and through Zach I had come to know and like Calvin Johnson.

"You in trouble again, Brian?" he was saying to me now.

"I sure as hell am. Big trouble."

"Seems like all you do is get in trouble these days. Can I help?"

"That's why I'm calling, Calvin. There's an old automobile parked on a quiet country lane out in Maryland past Potomac, and I've got to get rid of that car right away."

"What do you mean, get rid of it?"

"Get it out of the area completely, destroy it, anything, as long as there's no trace of the car around these parts."

"Is it hot?"

"Probably. But that's not the real problem. I don't think you'd really want to know the true problem, Calvin. But if I don't get rid of that car there's a good possibility some innocent person might get hurt."

There was silence at the other end of the line for a few seconds, and then he said: "I guess I could get rid of it for you. If it's an old car and not much good, maybe we could break it down in our shop and use it for training. I could send a couple of my boys out there first thing in the morning. Where'd you say this car was?"

I gave him the directions, and then cited the mileage distances from River Road, using the computations I had written down. "The door's locked, but the ignition key is under the seat. But I guess you can get in the car somehow."

"Yeah, we can get in. Some of my boys did a little time for doing just that."

I thanked him, and we chatted some more, but before I hung up I asked him one last question, on a hunch: "Calvin, did you ever hear of an organization called the National Federation Army?"

He repeated the name slowly before he said: "That rings a bell someplace ..."

"It does?" I asked excitedly.

"But I can't make the connection right now. There are so many organizations around town, street groups, clubs, societies. I could be wrong, but I think I heard of that cat someplace."

"Could you ask around?"

"I'll ask the dudes."

After the phone conversation, I stretched out in a large over-stuffed chair, closing my eyes while I continued to sip my drink. It might work, I thought. Bronson disappears, and his car disappears, and then the NFA concludes that he's suddenly skipped. For a while I thought I'd go out to Rankin's in the morning and tell him what had happened, but eventually I dismissed that idea. He would be upset—rightfully—that I had screwed this up, and I couldn't afford to have him come unglued on me now. Furthermore, we were going to have to play it that we never heard of any Timothy Bronson and we certainly didn't know what happened to him, and the easiest way to pull that off convincingly was to leave Rankin completely in the dark about the demise of Timothy Bronson.

I remembered the note from Camillo to Bronson, and I pulled it out of my pocket to examine it again. A message from the commander-in-chief to one of his soldier boys. Then I noticed something I had not seen out in the dark woods, a thin line drawing in the corner of the note of a clenched fist holding a streak of lightning. The NFA symbol. Damn them.

CHAPTER EIGHT

A nd so for the next five days we continued to make preparations to hand over the ransom money of three hundred thousand dollars to the NFA.

On the morning following my confrontation with Bronson, I arrived at the Riggs Bank and went right to the desk of Carlton Jones, a vice-president and an acquaintance of mine. I handed him the number of my checking account and asked him to ascertain my present balance. He dialed a number, listened for a moment, and then raised his eyebrows in surprise. "Three hundred and five thousand and fifty-two dollars. And some change."

"Times have been good. Keep the change."

"They certainly seem so for you, Brian."

"I'd like to take out three hundred thousand of that right now. In cash. You can give it to me any way you want, old bills, new bills, small denominations, big denominations, I don't care. That wouldn't cause any problem, or make you want to notify anybody, would it?"

He studied me intently through small beady eyes, and then he shook his head slowly. "I guess not, Brian. But I don't know if we can gather that much cash at a moment's notice. Here, let me check." He made another phone call, and when he hung up he told me: "You're in luck. We just got a large shipment of new bills from the Treasury. Will denominations of hundreds be all right?"

"Perfectly."

He got some papers for me to sign, and then we went into a back room where a teller, accompanied by a bank guard, was waiting for me. On the table were the mounds of hundred-dollar bills, and Jones asked me to count them to verify it. I told him, no thanks, I trusted Riggs, and I proceeded to stuff the bills into a diplomat's briefcase I had brought with me. They asked me if I wanted a guard to accompany me, and I said no again. The briefcase had one of those wrist chains and I fastened it to my wrist, placing the keys in my pants pocket. I was also still carrying the .32, of course, now freshly oiled and reloaded after last night's use.

I took a cab over to McFarland's office on Pennsylvania Avenue, and I was able to get in to see Big Dan almost immediately. Wordlessly, I put the briefcase on the desk, and opened it. He looked at the piles of bills sullenly, as if he were now regretting he had agreed to launder it for me.

He shook his head. "I don't know why I'm letting myself get involved in this," he said.

"You're just a great humanitarian, Dan."

When I arrived at my office I asked Annie to get her steno pad because I had some more notes to make about the Rankin affair. I usually try to conceal some of the more violent aspects of these assignments from Annie, because I know it upsets her, but the death of Timothy Bronson was essential to the case now, and I wanted it on my records. Even at that, I omitted the more gory details of my fight in the Maryland countryside last night, but nevertheless Annie's eyebrows arched and I saw her biting her lip. She's always thinking that I'm going to get myself killed one of these days, and maybe she's right.

When I had finished dictating, she closed her notebook and rose from her chair rather abruptly, saying that she would type up the notes right away. There was a frown on her face, and I knew that last night's adventure was distressing her. A few minutes later she buzzed me to tell me that Tom Breyer was on the phone from Chicago.

"I don't think your Cathy Morrison is around these parts," he said.

"Are you sure?"

"I went out to that address in Winnetka you gave me, and met her aunt. I played the bit that I was a credit investigator, and the girl had opened a charge account in Washington, giving her aunt as a reference. The aunt's a voluble old dame, not too bright, but friendly and lonely and eager to talk to someone. Seems that this Cathy was orphaned at a fairly young age, and the aunt brought her up. So that's really her home, and I got the aunt to concede that if Cathy were in the area she'd certainly be staying there. But she hasn't seen Cathy in over a year."

"Any line on what Cathy is like?"

"Oh, the usual stuff. The aunt thinks she's a wonderful girl, and she hopes she meets a nice man and has a flock of kids. But Cathy apparently had to do a little bit of career work first. Seems that about a year and a half ago she decided to go to Washington for a while. The aunt says that she had all that stuff in her head about wanting to overthrow the system and all, but that's young people's talk and she'll get over that."

"I wonder," I said quietly into the phone.

After I hung up, I mulled over that phrase which had been attributed to Cathy Morrison. It was almost a cliché, I realized, but I wondered if the girl perhaps took it seriously. Seriously enough to join an organization like the NFA?

I then got a call from Steve Harrison at the *Post* and he told me that he had checked here and in Chicago, but no one had ever heard of anything called the National Federation Army.

"You're not earning that lunch I promised you," I told him.

"Then I'll just have to keep working on it, old buddy."

Annie returned a little while later with the typed notes and placed them on the desk in front of me. I took a slip of paper from my pocket, and clipped it to the top page of this section of my notes about the Rankin affair.

"What's that?" she asked.

"The directions how to get to the spot where I buried that boy last night."

"Do you really think that the kidnappers will believe that he just disappeared?"

"They might. Annie, I want you to remember this set of directions attached here. If anything happens to me, or if this whole Rankin affair blows up in our face, I want you to give this to the police. Then they can exhume that body and start checking fingerprints and maybe they'll get a direct lead to the NFA."

"Oh, Brian, don't you think the police should be doing that now?"

"Of course they should. But, damnit, Annie, we've got to play this Rankin's way and go along with the kidnappers."

Later that afternoon I got a call from Tom Walsh at the Press Club, and he told me that if he could meet me he could give the very little he had picked up on that matter we discussed yesterday. That was Tom's cagey way of talking over the phone. He is an old Washington hand, and he has the veteran's fear of the phone tap. And he's right—this city is wired like the inside of a stereo set.

We had a drink down at the end of the long bar in the Press Club, and Tom gave me the information he had been able to pick up about Ellen Rankin from some casual conversations with his friends. There was nothing particularly new about most of it, and nothing which seemed helpful to me, but then he mentioned the ugly rumor he had picked up about the Senator's daughter.

"Ugly rumor?" I asked.

"It's only a rumor, Bri, and you know this town thrives on rumors, true or false. But according to the story, Ellen Rankin had an illegitimate child about a year or two ago, and put it up for adoption. The whole episode caused quite a fight between herself and her father, so much so that she finally moved out and got her own apartment. But it's only a rumor."

"It's an ugly one, though."

So, I thought: maybe the relationship between Ellen Rankin and her father was not as rosy as we had been led to believe.

I had dinner alone at home that night, but in the early evening I drove over to John Lollard's house in McLean. John was in his late 70's now, a former high official in the FBI from the J. Edgar Hoover era, and I thought that maybe I could edge him into a conversation about the kidnapping problem and thus learn some of the techniques the Bureau had perfected over the years. God knows, I needed all the help I could get.

John answered the door himself, and his face lit up when he saw me. His wife had died a few years ago, and he now lived alone here in suburban Virginia, and I suppose he was delighted to have someone drop in. Despite his advanced years, he still carried himself with almost military bearing, a tall erect man, with thin strands of grey hair plastered carefully across an almost bald head. It appeared as if he were having trouble with his eyesight, because he squinted uncertainly when he talked to me, but his mind was as sharp as a tack.

We settled in his living room where he poured some drinks, scotch for me and bourbon for him, while I carefully engineered him into a conversation about the old days in the Bureau.

He reminisced enthusiastically, occasionally pointing to pictures on the wall, most of them featuring Hoover himself. Then I edged toward the crime of kidnapping.

"I think our handling of the kidnapping problem is one of the brightest pages in the Bureau's history," he said at one point. "The Director was determined that kidnapping would be stamped out at a time in the 30's when it threatened to become a national menace. And we did it."

"But, John, kidnapping continues, and maybe more than ever."

"Ah, yes, Brian, but don't you see, in practically every case we've made it an unsuccessful crime. The kidnapper doesn't get away with it. That's the biggest deterrent to any crime. And then during the 30's we were able to enforce the death penalty for kidnapping, and a kidnapper had to know that we'd get him within a short while and he would be executed. Brian, they should really restore that death penalty for kidnapping."

"What made you so sure that you'd always get the kidnapper?"

"I said *almost* always. But you see, in a kidnapping we had one major advantage going for us that we didn't have in other types of crimes—the criminal had to come back; he had to surface to pick up the money sometime, someplace. The drop. Yes, the delicious drop. That was the crucial moment in any kidnapping case."

"And how would you get him at the drop?"

"In the early days our efforts were a bit crude, large-area stakeouts and that sort of thing. But as the years went on we were presented with an astonishing amount of sophisticated technology. Tracking devices, trailers, helicopters which could fly high in the clouds out of sight and still follow the kidnapper with extremely sensitive sensor devices."

"But what about the victim, the child who was kidnapped?"

"Yes, of course, that was our primary concern. But even that gave us an advantage we didn't have in other crimes. We had something the kidnapper wanted, the money. And he had something we wanted, the child. That gave us leverage. And we tried to use that leverage, as a bargaining tactic."

"How?"

"A number of ways. One of the things we always tried first was to get the kidnapper to release the child at the place of the drop in exchange for the money."

"But, John, would a kidnapper go along with that? It seems pretty risky for him."

"Of course it's risky, and most of the times it wouldn't work. The kidnapper usually wants you to drop the money one place and he promises to release the child some other place. We tried to avoid that if we could, because we diminish our control over the release of the child. But sometimes if the kidnapper is particularly amateurish or particularly frightened, we could have the parents talk him into it, especially if they could convey the impression that it's the only way the kidnapper is going to get the ransom money. So, first of all we always tried to make the stab for the direct exchange: you give me the child and we'll give you the money. You've got nothing to lose by asking for the direct exchange, because the kidnapper can only refuse. But it's always better if you can work the drop and the exchange at the same spot. At least, you're sure of seeing the child again. But that's only the first ploy. If that didn't work, we tried all sorts of other things, using the ransom money as our leverage. We could delay the drop, saying it was taking us time to gather the money, or we could engineer the location of the drop to our advantage, or sometimes we even dusted the ransom money with invisible ink which adhered to the kidnappers' hands for months and months. Since we had the money he wanted there were all sorts of tricks.

Remember, there comes a time when the kidnapper has to pick up the money someplace."

We continued to talk for almost two hours, as I probed gently away at John Lollard, digging into his great fund of knowledge about kidnapping cases. But after a while I noticed that John was squinting at me with even greater intensity, and I knew then that I wasn't fooling him, that he realized I just wasn't asking casual questions. With his sharp intelligence and his long experience he knew that I was somehow involved in a kidnapping situation.

Finally, he took a long sip of his bourbon and laid the glass on a marble-top table in front of him. "Brian," he said softly. "If anybody's been kidnapped the very best thing you can do is go to the Bureau directly."

"I suppose so."

"They've got that fantastic record in kidnapping cases. And all that technology."

"But, John, it's not a hundred percent, you said so yourself. Look at that Greenlease case in Kansas City." God, I was beginning to sound like Rankin.

"Nevertheless, the percentages are far in the Bureau's favor."

"John, percentages don't count when your own child is concerned unless it's one hundred percent. Suppose your child was kidnapped and the kidnappers told you they would kill her if you went to the police. What would you do? Play along with them, or go to the police?"

He didn't answer for a long time. "My immediate answer, of course, Brian, would be to go to the police. But who can say what any of us would do in a given situation until it actually happens to us."

That was pretty much the end of our conversation, but as John Lollard escorted me to the door he paused, and placed his hand on my arm. "Remember, Brian, the drop, that's the crucial moment."

Driving home, I mulled over the many useful things Lollard had told me about a kidnap situation, and I considered how I could use some of them. However, there was one thing he didn't have to tell me: the importance of the drop. Although Lester Rankin didn't realize it, I had been planning from the very beginning to be present when that drop was made to the NFA.

CHAPTER NINE

No further word was received from the NFA for the next three days, and I was beginning to think that my ploy had worked and that they had assumed Timothy Bronson had simply deserted. Otherwise, there would have been irate phone calls from General Camillo about a double cross. But then I began to get worried that perhaps the disappearance of Bronson had frightened them and they had simply fled, killing Ellen Rankin before their departure.

Thus, when Lester Rankin phoned me on the day before the drop that he had received another tape in the mail from the NFA, I rushed out to his house with mixed feelings of relief and concern. However, the tape from Camillo made no mention of the missing Timothy Bronson, but I did notice a new strain and agitation in his voice as he went through his Tupamaro rhetoric routine again. Maybe the disappearance of Bronson was working to my advantage, making the NFA unnerved and unsure of what was happening to their membership.

The tape was the same old line about how bad we capitalistic fascists were and how good things were going to be when the NFA freed the people, but there was one new feature on this tape, a longer statement by Ellen Rankin. I turned the volume up and listened attentively with Rankin as she spoke:

Daddy, I'm all right, and these people haven't hurt me. And they're feeding me. They keep me tied up most of the time, and I'm blindfolded, and the only thing I want to do is get out of here. They promise they'll let me go if you pay the ransom. I've just got to believe that they'll do that. Daddy ...

The voice broke off, and Camillo finished up the tape with a statement that he would contact Rankin tomorrow with instructions where to deliver the ransom money so that his daughter could be released. And freedom to the people. Nuts to you, Camillo, I thought.

Rankin turned off the machine and I asked him: "No doubt that it's Ellen's voice?"

"None at all."

"Is that her natural manner of speaking?"

"Yes. Obviously, she sounds tired and under a strain, but that's understandable. But she doesn't sound drugged or in pain, or anything like that."

I lit a cigarette slowly, thinking about Ellen Rankin's voice on the tape. I still couldn't decide if the girl had been really kidnapped or if she was engaged in a paternal rip-off.

Rankin said to me: "Do you have the money yet? I need it by tomorrow."

"I'm gathering the last of it today. I should have it all by late tonight, and I'll bring it out first thing in the morning, seven o'clock." Actually, Dan McFarland had delivered the laundered money to me earlier that day in his office, an almost wordless transaction in which he gave me a briefcase full of old bills, most of them twenties, dirty and crumpled and obviously not in serial sequence. I signed a receipt for the money, and then took it back to my office safe where I intended to keep it until early tomorrow. I didn't want to deliver the money to Rankin today because I wanted some excuse to be around here on the day the drop was arranged. The crucial drop, as John Lollard called it.

"Could you make it six o'clock in the morning?" Rankin asked. "I know it's an imposition, but those maniacs may contact me early."

"Okay, six o'clock. Now listen, Senator, one more thing. I'm sure they'll contact you by phone, and here's what you should do." I proceeded to outline John Lollard's ploy of asking for a direct exchange someplace: the ransom money for the girl.

"But do you think they'll go along with that?"

"You can only try. But make a good pitch for it. It insures our chances of getting your daughter back. You handled Camillo nicely on the phone the other day, and I'm sure you can do it again tomorrow."

"All right, I'll try," he mumbled. Rankin was sitting in the large leather chair, and his chin was slumping down toward his chest. He didn't look like the strong, dominant figure whom I had seen on the Senate floor. I sure hoped he wasn't going to crack.

As I rose to leave he looked up, and I saw the misty look in his eyes. "Petersen, do you think we'll get her back?"

The pleading tone in his voice, so unusual for Rankin, embarrassed me, and I looked away. "I'm sure we will, Senator."

I wasn't sure at all.

I drove directly from Rankin's to Eddie Perkins' shop on Rhode Island Avenue where I was going to make preparations for the next day's ransom drop. I had been looking carefully out of my rear-view window these past few days, trying to see if I could spot another tail, but I never saw another one. Either the NFA had run out of tail men after Bronson's disappearance, or they were now convinced that I wasn't a police officer.

I drove my Olds into the alleyway behind Eddie's shop, and knocked on his metal back door. Eddie opened it himself, peering cautiously out through a crack over the safety chain, and then his face broke into a grin and he opened the door for me.

"Got everything ready for you, Mr. Petersen," he said. "Why don't we start on the car first. I'll get one of my boys."

Eddie Perkins' "boy" turned out to be a thin, little, old man in his early sixties who began carrying boxes of equipment out to my car. I watched for a while as he started to affix two sturdy antennas to the rear bumper of my Olds, and then Eddie placed a piece of electronic equipment on the passenger side of the front seat and he called me over to explain it.

"This here's your receiver," he said, pointing to the heavy square metal box whose surface was covered with dials. "All you got to do is watch those two larger dials on the top."

"Do I have to set them or anything, Eddie?"

"You don't have to do anything. Just read them. Here, Mr. Petersen, let me explain the little system I worked out for you here. What you got, really, is an omni-range directional finder built into your car. Those two antennas my boy is putting on the bumpers are really hollow inside, and they rotate, something like a radar pickup. They'll pick up the signal from the car you're following, and then transmit it into some more equipment we're going to put into the trunk, and then we'll wire that to your little console here in the front seat."

"And what do the two dials tell me, Eddie?"

"This one is distance, and its range is a little over two miles. It's got over two hundred calibrations on it, and each numbered calibration mark means fifty feet. So if you're at the hundred mark you're about a mile behind. Now look at the other dial. That's a directional finder, and the needle will point in whichever direction the other car is from you at the moment."

"And the signal from the other car?"

"This little gadget here," he said, showing me a thin, metal-covered box. "All you got to do is attach this anyplace on the car you're following and it sends out the signal. Believe me, Mr. Petersen, this is high-class equipment. If you stay at least two miles behind that other car you won't lose it."

Eddie's "boy" continued to work on my car, and we went inside to the back room of the radio store. Eddie had a list of the equipment I had asked him to obtain, and he checked it out for me now. "Here's the briefcase," he said, and he placed a brown leather briefcase on the table. "It's no cheap false bottom thing either, Mr. Petersen. Most so-called experts could look that thing over and not find the equipment I got hidden in there. The stuff is in that metal ribbing which runs up the sides of the briefcase. And here is the receiver for this one." He showed me a leather-covered carrying case, about the size of a portable record player with some dials on the top.

"And this works the same way as the equipment in the car?"

"The same principle, the two dials for distance and direction, but this can't be as high-class equipment as the other, because of its size. I don't say you'll get the really accurate reading from this as you will from the car equipment. But if somebody carries this briefcase around and you stay within a mile of it, you'll have a pretty general idea of where they are."

"That's all I need."

"And the last thing. That was the hardest one, Mr. Petersen. You wanted me to bug a man without him knowing it, and you wanted a range of about a mile. That's a big order, but I come up with this." He showed me what appeared to be a thin metal strip about six inches long and a fraction of an inch thick. "This guy you want to bug, you said he'd probably be wearing a jacket, so

I fixed this up. You pin it under the collar of the man's jacket behind the neck, and I don't think he'll even know it's there. And here's the audio receiver for that one."

By the time I drove away from Eddie's shop, the two antennas on my bumper swaying gently in the breeze, my Olds was loaded down with thousands of dollars of highly sophisticated electronic equipment. I now felt I was ready for the drop tomorrow.

I rose about four-thirty that morning, showered, and made myself a pot of coffee. While I was waiting for it to heat, I went into the boiler room and opened the weapons trunk. I took out the Smith and Wesson .38 Police Special, that favorite weapon of law enforcement agencies all over the world. It was a good, heavy pistol, about thirty ounces, with a high degree of accuracy. I checked it, loaded it, and then put an extra box of shells in my trouser pocket. My shell box is oblong and thin, like a cigarette case, and it is made of bullet-resistant metal. A lot of fools have been unnecessarily killed when a bullet strikes an unprotected box of extra shells on a person, causing them to explode like lethal fireworks.

I took the .38 out to my car, and placed it in the hidden section at the back of the glove compartment. The Olds came with that handy little section because the dealer explained that it had been specially made for a foreign diplomat who wanted to carry confidential papers or something, but who was suddenly transferred to another country before the car was delivered. The compartment is practically undetectable, and when I snapped it shut I doubt if anyone would be able to find that pistol in there without a great deal of effort. I was also wearing, of course, the .32 on my belt holster. Armed for the day.

It was still dark, and there was little traffic as I drove across the bridge from Virginia. There were few lights on in the Kenwood area, but Rankin's house was all alight when I drove up. He answered the door for me himself, and he looked pale and drawn, as if he had not slept the entire night. I was carrying the briefcase and he spotted it immediately.

"Is that the money?" he asked.

I told him it was and handed it to him. "It's an old brief-case," I said. "Keep the money in it and give it to the kidnappers." Actually, it was Eddie Perkins' wired briefcase, and I had placed the laundered money from my office safe in it. The electronic equipment in the ribbing was giving off a signal, and with the tracking device I had in my car I would be able to follow its journey all day, wherever it led me.

Rankin led me into his study where he had a pot of coffee laid out for us. I was gratified to see that he was wearing a heavy tweed suit. Eddie Perkins' bug would fit nicely under that collar, and once I got it somehow attached I'd be able to listen to Rankin's conversations throughout the day, as long as I could stay reasonably close behind him.

"Petersen, there's not really any reason for you to stay around if you don't ..."

"That's all right, Senator, I think I'd better wait here to see if this General Camillo actually contacts you as he said."

He seemed relieved that someone was going to sit with him to wait. And waiting is what I did a lot of that long day. We had to wait until almost noon before the call came. Rankin and I were still in the study, and when the phone rang I went into the other room to lift the receiver and listen to the conversation.

Camillo: Do you have the money ready, Rankin?

Rankin: It's all here. Just as you requested, in unmarked and nonserialized bills.

Camillo: You keep it right there. We're going to call you later and tell you where to leave it. And you'll have to deliver it yourself—alone.

Rankin: Now wait a minute, what about my daughter?

Camillo: She'll be released after you deliver the money.

Rankin: That's not good enough.

Camillo: What do you mean, that's not good enough, Rankin?

Rankin: Just what I said. I'm perfectly willing to give you the money, but I want my daughter in exchange. As soon as I see my daughter, I'll give you the money, or I'll leave it wherever you want.

Camillo: What do you take me for, a fool? As soon as we released your daughter, we'd never see the money.

Rankin: All right, we'll do it the other way then. We'll meet someplace, and I don't even have to see your face, and then when you hand over my daughter, I'll give you the money.

(Listening, I again had to admire how adroitly Rankin handled him. Despite his shaken condition, Rankin was summoning resources from someplace and remaining insistently firm. But so, apparently, was Camillo, and I hoped that Rankin wouldn't weaken first.)

Camillo: We promised you we'd release your daughter.

Rankin: I'm afraid I need more than promises from someone I don't know. I need performance.

Camillo: If you want your daughter back—

Rankin: I want my daughter back, and I presume you want the money. Now we can both get what we want if we have a fair exchange. I'm afraid I'm going to have to insist on that. It's the only guarantee I have of seeing my daughter again.

Camillo: You can't insist on anything, Rankin, don't you understand that?

Rankin: You do want the money, don't you?

(There was a pause at the other end of the line, and I knew that Rankin had him. I smiled. John Lollard's analysis was right—you might be able to maneuver them if they were amateurish and frightened.)

Camillo: Well, maybe we can set something up in a place of our choosing. We'll have your daughter there, and when you see her, you toss the money to us.

Rankin: That's fine.

Camillo: But no tricks.

Rankin: No tricks.

Camillo: You stay right by that phone, Rankin, you hear? And we'll call you back with further instructions later today.

The line clicked off, and I hung up the extension phone. Rankin was still holding the phone in his hand when I walked back into the study, and I took it from him and hung it up.

"You did wonderfully, Senator," I said.

He shook his head. "I was getting terrified. I was about to give up and do it his way."

We had to wait until almost three o'clock in the afternoon for the second call from the NFA. Rankin told me I could leave if I wanted, but I told him I would stay with him until he departed for the drop. I used part of the time to wire Rankin's car and his person. On the pretext of taking a brief walk, I slipped out into the garage and fastened Eddie's little electronic box to the underside of Rankin's large black Lincoln. Now, with the omni-range directional finder in my car, I would be able to follow the Lincoln at a safe distance to the drop location.

Putting the bug into his suit jacket was a little harder, since Rankin didn't seem to want to take it off. Shortly after two o'clock I suggested that he stretch out on the leather couch in the study for a few minutes because he was going to need all his strength today. He was reluctant to do so, but he finally agreed to lie down for a few minutes, with the phone at his elbow. I helped him to take off his suit jacket, and when I tiptoed out of the room I took it with me. Eddie's thin bugging device fitted easily under the collar without any bulge or apparent noticeable weight, and I fastened it with some pins. Now, if I stayed close enough, I'd be able to pick up Rankin's conversations.

The phone call from Camillo at three o'clock was short and terse: "Rankin, come alone, and bring the money. Repeat, you are to come alone. There is an outdoor phone booth at the corner of Exeter Street and River Road. Be there in fifteen minutes, and go into the booth. You will receive a phone call directing you where to go next."

I walked with Rankin out to his Lincoln, and held the door open while he threw in the briefcase and then climbed in.

"Good luck, sir," I said.

He looked bleakly at me, an uncharacteristically frightened look in his eyes. "Thanks for everything, Petersen. I'll call you later and let you know how this works out."

I watched the Lincoln pull out of the driveway, and I thought: Don't bother, Senator, I'm going to be right behind you.

When the Lincoln disappeared from sight, I jumped into my Olds, and inched carefully out of the driveway. I couldn't see the Lincoln, but I knew where it was. Eddie's machines were working perfectly, picking up the signals. One of the dials on the omni-range finder told me the Lincoln was 500 feet away, and the other one showed it was directly west. That meant he was on the street heading toward River Road.

I was even getting fine reception from the other machine, the one picking up the signal from the briefcase. And then I heard a cough on the audio machine: it was Rankin's cough, relayed clearly from the bug I had attached to his jacket.

I pulled out of the driveway and drove at moderate speeds, my eyes flicking constantly toward the dials on the tracking device. I allowed Rankin to get about 1200 feet ahead of me, and then I increased the speed a little, reducing the distance to 1,000 feet.

Leaning over, I opened the glove compartment and extracted the .38 Police Special, laying it on the seat beside me. We were now on our way to meet the NFA, and I was rather looking forward to it.

CHAPTER TEN

When we turned on River Road, I allowed Rankin to get way ahead of me because I didn't want to be visible when he entered that phone booth to take the second call from the NFA.

The phone booth was near the intersection of River Road and Western Avenue, and when I pulled over to the side of the road to wait I was almost a mile behind Rankin. The bug in his jacket was still working excellently, and I could even hear the door of his Lincoln slam as he got out. He must have stood in that public phone booth for three or four minutes when I heard the phone ring. Rankin answered and I could hear him being given instructions to proceed to another phone booth in Georgetown near the intersection of M Street and Wisconsin Avenue.

The members of the NFA must have seen a lot of kidnapping movies over the years, because this was the traditional technique for insuring that your drop man is alone and not being followed. If you keep sending the drop man from public phone booth to public phone booth, you can have some of your people staked out casually at each place, and then they can get a very good view of whether the drop man looks clean. If anything appears suspicious, they can immediately contact their headquarters and cancel the whole operation. It was an old-fashioned technique, but it was effective. However, there are now many ways to circumvent it.

When I heard Rankin get back in his car and start the trip to Georgetown, I purposely let him get quite far ahead, almost to the two-mile mark, before I started up again. I wasn't too worried now about following him closely because I knew where he was going. In fact, I could afford to be a little cute. My directional indicator showed me that Rankin was making a sharp turn, and I imagined that he was cutting through Forty-sixth Street to Massachusetts Avenue, the usual route downtown. I decided to take another route entirely, so that there was no chance of anybody's spotting a car following along behind Rankin even at that great distance.

I took a right at Western Avenue, and then over to Westmoreland Circle, moving as fast as I could now. I lost Rankin on my machine for a few minutes, but I picked him up again when I turned on Massachusetts Avenue. Far ahead of me, he was apparently making a right on Wisconsin Avenue, but I turned off at Ward Circle and headed toward Georgetown via New Mexico Avenue. Rankin and I were now proceeding in the same direction over different routes, but there was over a mile between us. Eddie's machines were allowing me to do a perfectly beautiful tail job.

The second phone call in Georgetown directed Rankin to cross the Key Bridge into Virginia and go to a phone booth near a Hot Shoppe in Rosslyn. I had to close the gap now, because I didn't want to get caught too far behind him in the flow of traffic across the bridge. I cruised right by the Hot Shoppe where I saw Rankin's car parked and drove on for a few blocks, listening intently while he waited for the third phone call. This one directed him to a phone booth out on Dolly Madison Boulevard, and I knew he would take Memorial Parkway to where it linked with Dolly Madison. I wheeled around, cutting back to the Parkway, and when I raced out on it my omni-range directional finder told me that Rankin was about a mile and a half ahead. I kept it at that distance. Everything was going smoothly.

My plan for the drop consisted of a dual option. As we neared the scene of the actual drop, I was going to draw closer and closer, and hopefully I could get within a couple of hundred yards of the scene. Then if the scenario was straight, I would simply lie back and allow the drop to take place. If Rankin handed over the money and received his daughter in return, I would lie low until they cleared out of the area safely. Then I would make my move. That tracker in the briefcase was sending out a clear signal, and I was going to follow it to the NFA headquarters. And if it looked simple, I could take them myself. But if there were any complications, we would then be free to call the police and we could mop up the NFA.

But I didn't really think it was going to be that simple. And I had a second option. Now that the drop was about to take place, I could allow my suspicions about the whole kidnapping to surface freely. I felt that there was something entirely bogus about this whole kidnapping, and in that case I would be right behind Rankin, ready to move in and help him if it appeared he was simply being victimized by a fraud of some kind.

At the very least, I surely felt that Ellen Rankin's missing roommate was somehow implicated in this, perhaps the engineer of the whole plot. Maybe she actually did plot the kidnapping of her own roommate. But the more probable explanation, I felt, was that Ellen and her roommate were cohorts, planning together this cruel rip-off of old man Rankin.

But my theories really didn't make much difference now, because in a very short time I would find out which of the two options I would have to exercise.

There was a brisk amount of traffic on Dolly Madison Boulevard, and I shortened the gap to about a mile when Rankin stopped to receive the next phone call. This one was a bit more clever, and I had to admire the NFA technique. The phone call directed Rankin to drive along at fifty miles an hour, and some place in the next two miles he would see a hitchhiker wearing a red wool cap. He was to pick up the hitchhiker and he would then receive directions on where to proceed next. Smart. This would allow them to make sure that Rankin didn't have radio equipment in the car over which he was broadcasting his route to someone behind him. And, if I didn't miss my bet, the hitchhiker would give all driving directions to Rankin manually in case the car was wired.

That was the reason I had Eddie Perkins install the dual system in my Olds, the audio one and rangefinder. It was a bit of trailing insurance I had learned in Intelligence: if they try to defeat one system, you can always rely on the other.

Sure enough, I heard Rankin come to a stop and the door of the car open, and then he said: "Where do you want me ..."

"Quiet!" a male voice broke in, and then I heard the car start up again. The hitchhiker was indeed giving him manual directions.

I was sure that we were close to the drop, and I picked up speed, following about a mile behind now. However, the Lincoln ahead drove on for another four or five miles, and we were getting into fairly open country. Then the needle on my directional dial jumped sharply to the right, and I knew they had taken a turn off the main road. I hit the accelerator, my eyes flicking toward those two dials. They were about three-quarters of a mile away from me and to the right. I was proceeding in a southeasterly direction, but the directional needle was swinging gradually to the north. I had no trouble finding the road where they turned off. As I approached a small, unmarked road, the needle began to move more rapidly, and just about the time I came up on it, the needle was pointing almost due north.

The road was paved and fairly wide, with a few houses on each side along the way. The Lincoln was about a mile ahead of me, moving at about fifty or fifty-five miles an hour. As we continued along, the road narrowed and we were entering some farm territory. I saw the directional needle make another slight flick to the left and I imagined that they had taken a turn-off again. When I came to a fork in the road, the needle swung even more dramatically to the left, and I followed its indication, bouncing along an unpaved dirt road. There were no houses of any kind now, but the road was lined with tall trees, providing a nice cover.

The car ahead was decreasing its speed, and I was following about a half-mile behind. Then Rankin's car stopped abruptly, and I heard a voice say: "Get out."

The drop was taking place.

I have a finely tuned motor, and I didn't think my car made much noise. So I drove even closer. Slowly, quietly. Two thousand feet. They were ahead of me, around a curve in the road up there, and I couldn't see because of the trees and the foliage. At the point where my dial showed that Rankin's car was stopped about 1500 feet ahead, I found a small road leading into the woods, no wider than the width of a car. I backed slowly into it, and then kept moving backwards for about fifteen or twenty yards until I felt I was concealed. But I was now facing out, ready to make any move that was required.

"You have the money?" I heard a voice say over the audio. It sounded like Camillo's voice.

"It's right here," Rankin said. "In the briefcase."

"Give it to me."

"No, not until I see my daughter."

"There."

There was a silence for a number of seconds, and then I heard Rankin say: "No." I didn't know what was going on, but the scenario sounded like it was getting peculiar.

"Give me that money, Rankin," the voice said.

"You're cheating me, you're not returning my daughter as you promised."

I heard a grunt over the audio receiver, and then something which sounded like scuffling. And then I heard Rankin's voice cry out, as if in pain.

It was a fraud, all right, and I already had the Olds in gear and I was rolling down that narrow lane. I did a fast turn on the larger dirt road, pressing the accelerator down, racing toward that bend in the road. I had the car over fifty, the .38 now in my right hand as I came screaming around the turn.

The sudden appearance of my screeching Olds seemed to startle everyone, and they all froze for a second in sudden surprise. It gave me a split second to catch the scene which lay before me. There were two cars parked in an extremely wide stretch in the road. Rankin's Lincoln was nearest me, and Rankin himself was lying on the ground, trying to get up. A few feet away from him a man was standing, holding the briefcase. As he whirled to look at my approaching car, I could see that he was wearing khaki fatigues, but he had a stocking mask over his face, from which I could see a beard protruding. He also had a pistol in his hand, a .45 apparently, and he lifted it to fire at my approaching car. About ten yards ahead another car was parked, and next to it another man in a stocking mask was standing, holding what seemed to be an M-14 automatic rifle, which he started to bring around toward me.

I pressed the accelerator to the floor, and jerked the wheel to the left so that I would miss the outstretched form of Lester Rankin, and then I drove it directly at the man with the .45. He got off one shot, and then another, but they only splintered the windshield. The right side of the windshield at that, because he was firing off-balance, trying to get out of the way of my car which was bearing down on him. But his straight-on shots weren't worrying me—a few years ago after someone had taken a shot at me in this car, I had bulletproof glass inserted in the windshield panel.

The guy with the .45 tried to dive out of the way at the last minute, but I nevertheless caught him with my left fender, sending him spinning high into the air. I was speeding past the other car now, my head ducked down to avoid the fire from the M-14. I didn't have bulletproof glass in the side windows, but even if I had, I still didn't think it could stop the bullets from that powerful military rifle at such close range. The gas-operated rifle was pumping shells against my car, and I heard them hit the side window over my head, sending a spray of shattered glass over me.

I got past that second car, and then hit the brakes, allowing my car to skid to a stop twenty yards or so down the road. At the last minute I yanked the wheel again, so that when I finally got it stopped, the driver's door was facing away from the man with the rifle. I tumbled out of the car and got to my feet behind it, using it as a shield. Rifle bullets were still pounding off the side of my car, and I leaned over the hood and began to return fire. My first shot frightened the man with the rifle, and he ducked behind his car.

Out in the middle of the road I could see Rankin starting to rise to his feet, and I shouted, "Stay down, Rankin!" I don't know if he heard me or not, but he started to crawl back toward his car, and when I last noticed him it appeared as if he were trying to crawl under it for protection. My attention had been diverted by the man whom I had struck with my car. He was getting back to his feet, dazed, but apparently uninjured. When I had spun him into the air he had dropped both his pistol and the briefcase, and he was trying to retrieve them now. He had the pistol in his hand when I fired, but the bullet missed, kicking up dirt at his feet. He dove behind Rankin's car, leaving the briefcase on the ground in the middle of the road.

But he began shooting at me from behind Rankin's car, and then the M-14 started up again. And there was more. I saw another khaki-clad figure scrambling out of the rear seat of the other car, and he had an M-14, too. And from the front seat of that parked car I could see another man's head sticking up, and he was aiming some sort of hand weapon in my direction.

My God, I was overwhelmed by this enormous firepower surrounding me: two automatic rifles, a .45, and another handgun. I bitterly cursed my stupidity for allowing myself to come charging foolishly in here with only two hand weapons, the .38 in my hand, and the .32 in my holster.

I got three shots off with the .38 from behind my car, hoping to keep everybody pinned down. I then took the shell case out of my pocket and laid it on the ground beside me. I was going to have to reload very shortly. I then pulled out the .32, so that I had guns in both hands now. I took one more shot with the .38, and then one with the .32. But I wasn't hitting anybody. And my ammunition wasn't limitless.

The guy with the .45 was really pumping away at me now, and I was looking in that direction, trying to get a clear shot at him, but all I could see was that gun hand reaching around from behind Rankin's car. Then there was some movement over at the other car, and for a moment I thought they were making a charge at me. The back door of the car opened, and someone started to get out. I was taking range on the form when I suddenly held my fire.

The figure was a girl, dressed in jeans and a pullover sweater, and she was having a difficult time getting out of the car because I could see her hands were tied in front of her and she was blindfolded. She got out, took a few hesitant steps, and then she managed to get her hands high enough to rip the blindfold from her eyes. I couldn't get a good look at her face because her long blonde hair had fallen down around her face, but I could sure hear her. She was screaming at the top of her lungs, trying to stumble along in that awkward run with her tied hands. It was Ellen Rankin, and she was trying to excape.

"Get down," I shouted at her. "Hit the ground!"

But she stumbled on, still screaming, looking wildly about. And then one of the guys with the M-14 came out from behind the car, running after her. I tried to get him in range but I couldn't take a shot because the girl was between us and I was afraid I'd hit her. He caught up with her and grabbed her, and started to pull her back. He was holding the rifle in one hand and the girl with the other, but suddenly she wheeled, kicking him sharply in the shins and tearing away.

She started to run away, stumbling, almost falling. The man took a step after her, but then stopped. He lifted the M-14, and brought it up to firing position, aiming it at the fleeing girl. She was about ten feet away from him, and at that close range the automatic weapon would tear her to shreds. But the distance between them gave me an open shot at the man. I had the .38 in my right hand, and I think I only had one bullet left in it. He had the rifle up on his shoulder when I fired, and I got him someplace square in the chest. He dropped the rifle as he started to pitch forward on his face, and just before he hit the ground I could see him clutching at the hole in his chest, as if he were trying to tear the bullet out of there.

At the moment my bullet struck him, the girl stumbled again and fell to the ground. I shouted at her to remain there, and this time she seemed to hear me, because she did lie there, digging her face into the ground. I could see, though, that her body was being racked by giant sobs.

I heard the ping and I hit the ground immediately behind my car. It was the unmistakable sound of a ricochetting bullet near me, the deadliest kind, because its crazy, deflected path can send the bullet in any direction. But I wasn't quite fast enough. I don't know whether the bullet hit off my car, or if perhaps it struck a nearby rock, but it creased me right over the eyebrow. The bullet didn't enter, but I felt the sharp sting, and blood began to trickle down the side of my face. They had drawn first blood, and with all that firepower they had the capability to draw a hell of a lot more.

I laid the .38 on the ground beside me, and swung out the cylinder, trying to reload. I kept pumping off occasional shots with the .32 in my left hand, and clumsily I stuffed six new shells in the .38. But this couldn't go on forever. There was still arrayed against me another M-14 and two hand weapons, and they could keep firing away at me from different angles until one of them finally caught me or I ran out of ammunition.

I surveyed the lines of battle, and they didn't appear very advantageous for me. Up ahead of me was the guy with the .45 behind Rankin's car, and over to my right was the other car with one man inside firing with a hand weapon, while the other man was behind the rear fender with the M-14. If they made a charge at me they could come from different angles, and I couldn't take them all.

The only thing I could do was make a move first, before they had time to realize their advantage and start closing in on me. I fired the last shot from the .32, and then dropped it to the ground. My .38 was fully loaded and it would have to do the job.

About ten yards to my left was a large rock, perhaps three feet tall, and if somehow I could get quickly behind it, I would change the firing angles immediately. However, if I made a dash for it, I would be exposing myself to open fire. On the other hand, if I simply remained crouched here behind my car, they would get me eventually.

I ducked down low, and crawled down to the end of my car. Then I got up on one knee, and got that large rock in range. And I dashed, going out in a zigzag, in a low, crouching run. Bullets splattered around, but my sudden move had caught them by surprise and they didn't have the proper range. A few feet from the rock I took a headlong dive and slid behind it. But I immediately got up on my knees and peered around the other side. It had all happened so fast that the man with the M-14 hadn't had a chance yet to move around his car for protection. He was exposed. I fired twice. The first shot missed, but the second one got him high on the forehead, someplace near the hairline, and I could see part of his scalp fly off as he crumpled to the ground.

I also had a better angle on the man with the .45 now, and I started firing at him. But he had gotten a faster jump, and he was moving now, running from behind Rankin's car over to the other one. He, too, was doing a zigzag, and I couldn't hit him. He ran by the briefcase on the ground, made a grab for it, but couldn't get it. He let it go.

The rear door of the other car was still open after Ellen Rankin's escape, and he went diving in, pulling it closed behind him. Almost as soon as he had thrown himself in the back seat the man in the front seat hit the accelerator and the car began speeding away. The motor had apparently been running, and thus they were able to make that instant start.

I fired once more at the departing car, but it was out of range now, sending up billows of dust as it raced away on the dirt road. I took a step after it, but then stopped. There was no chance of catching up with them. By the time I got back to my car, started it up, and turned it around, they would be too far ahead of me.

I stuck the .38 in my belt and looked around. There were two NFA men on the ground, obviously dead. Rankin had indeed made it under his car, and now he was peering cautiously out after the shooting stopped. And the girl was beginning to sit up and look around, a terrified and bewildered expression on her face. I also noticed that the briefcase with the ransom money inside was still lying on the ground. I was weary and drained, but I felt quite satisfied with myself.

I walked over to the girl who was now sitting up, fumbling with the ropes around her wrists. "Who are you?" she asked, her eyes still filled with frightened tears.

"A friend," I said, reaching down to help her untie the knots. "Are you all right?"

She nodded yes, and I knelt beside her to work on the knots. I heard a footstep behind me and there was Lester Rankin.

"It's okay, Senator," I said. "Your daughter is unhurt."

He looked at me, disbelief in his eyes, and then they narrowed. "Petersen, you fool," he almost spat at me. "That's not my daughter. That's her roommate.

CHAPTER ELEVEN

Rankin was shouting at me now, demanding to know why I had followed him, blaming me for destroying his chances of getting his daughter back. But I was hardly listening to him. I was seeing it all now with terrible clarity, and although I didn't know all the details, I was quite sure of what had happened. And I was filled with inner rage at my own stupidity.

Finally I turned to Rankin, and said: "Shut up, Senator." The bitter harshness in my voice seemed to stun him, and he stopped talking.

I pulled the girl, Cathy Morrison, to her feet and said to her, more as a statement than a question: "You and Ellen Rankin were kidnapped together, weren't you."

"Yes," she said, her voice coming in short gasps.

"Where is Ellen now?"

"She's still at that place they've been keeping us for the past week, I guess."

"Do you have any idea where it is?"

"No. We were kept in a basement, blindfolded most of the time. But I think it was some kind of farmhouse out in the country. I could hear horses and animals outside."

"Is it far from here, do you think?"

"I don't really know. I've been in that car, blindfolded, for almost two hours, but part of the time I think we were riding around in circles. When we stopped and I heard the shooting start, I thought maybe I could break away."

JAMES P. CODY

"But why …?" Rankin started to ask, but I cut him off. "We haven't got time for a lot of questions now, Senator. We've got to get out of here—and fast. But just tell me one thing. What happened when you arrived here a few minutes ago?"

"Well," Rankin said, "I picked up that hitchhiker, as they instructed, and when he directed me here he got out of the car. Then that fellow with the mask approached and told me to give him the money. I stepped out and asked to see my daughter first. He pointed to the other car over there with this girl in it. They were trying to convince me that it was Ellen. And for a moment I was almost fooled. Both the girls are blonde, and they both wear their hair long like that. But then this girl moved her head, and even though she was blindfolded I knew it wasn't Ellen. And then … but I guess you know the rest. But, Petersen, when you barged in here you ruined everything. You …"

"Senator," I interrupted him sharply, "don't you realize? They had no intention of returning your daughter today."

"But …"

"We'll talk later, Senator. We've got to clear out of here. Somebody's bound to have heard all those shots, and in a short while this place will be filled with police. Besides, I think you're going to be getting another phone call from General Camillo within the next few hours."

I told Rankin to return home and I would follow him in my car, bringing Cathy Morrison with me. I watched Rankin drive off, and then I got Cathy into the front seat of my car. But before we departed I walked over to inspect the two NFA corpses which were sprawled on the ground. The one nearest me had on a stocking mask, and I pulled it from his face. Middle twenties, white, no distinguishing facial characteristics. And, again, no pocket identification on his person. The other corpse was wearing large airplane sunglasses and red wool hat, pulled low over the forehead, and I knew that this had been the hitchhiker on the road. There was no identification on him, either.

I certainly wished that one of these two fallen soldiers was General Camillo, but I really doubted that. If Camillo had been here at all, he was probably that bearded fellow with the .45 who had tried to get the briefcase from Rankin.

I picked up the briefcase from the ground, and threw it in the back seat of my car. Before I slipped behind the wheel, I took one last look at the scene: the two corpses, and their rifles lying near them. There was no need to try to conceal them, as I had done some days ago with the first NFA corpse. My war with the NFA was all out in the open now.

On the ride back to Kenwood, I offered Cathy Morrison a cigarette and she smoked it hungrily.

"Feel like talking?" I asked her gently.

"A little." She was a pretty girl, early twenties, blonde, grey eyes; but the strong odor of perspiration hung over her—attributable, I was sure, to the fearful situation she had been in, and also to the fact that she undoubtedly hadn't changed her clothes during the week she was in captivity.

"What was the reason for kidnapping both you and Ellen Rankin together?"

"They didn't want to kidnap *me*. Why would anyone want to kidnap me? I don't have any relatives with money or influence. But Ellen and I had been out together to the movies, and we were walking back home alone and we had just turned the corner into that quiet block near our apartment when a big four-door sedan pulled up alongside us. These fellows wearing those stocking masks over their faces jumped out and they grabbed Ellen. They seemed to know who she was, all right. But she fought them, and I fought them, too. They tried to shove me away and drag Ellen into the car, but I held on, kicking and screaming. I guess they couldn't handle me or they were afraid my screams were going to bring the police, but at any rate when they got Ellen into the car they shoved me in on top of her. They threw a blanket over us and drove us away. I know they didn't have any intention of kidnapping me, because when they got us to that place I could hear a big argument going on about why they had brought me along, too."

"What did you learn about this NFA crowd, Cathy?"

"Not too much. They kept us blindfolded in the basement, but I did hear them talking a lot. My God, did they talk, talk, talk. It was an old house and I could hear them talking far into the night through the floorboards over us. There are probably about a dozen or fifteen of them, and they think they're going to take over the world, or something. Free the people, they keep shouting at each other all the time. From what I could hear, it's apparently a fairly new group, and they're terrified that they're going to get shot up by the police like the Panthers or somebody before they have a chance to really get going. I heard them say they didn't want to go public until they could get more recruits and more financing. They were really counting on that ransom money from Senator Rankin to get them going."

Yeah, it made sense, and it explained all the inconsistencies about this whole affair which had been puzzling me. And I was entirely convinced that Cathy Morrison was telling me the truth. Not only did what she said make sense, but her own personality was entirely credible. Furthermore, that little scene a few minutes ago was absolutely persuasive. The girl was really being held against her will by those guys, and it would have taken one of the great actresses of all time to fake that scene when she was stumbling out of the car trying to escape. And there was no doubt that the guy with the M-14 was actually trying to kill her when I dropped him.

It blew all my neat little theories clear to hell and gone.

And I had no one to blame but myself for allowing those theories to trap me. Maybe it's a sickness you develop when you live in Washington for a long time. You begin to suspect the worst in every person and situation, and you let suspicion and rumor and innuendo rule your appraisal of situations. That's what I had foolishly done here. Cathy Morrison disappears, and I begin to conjure up all kinds of sinister machinations on the part of a girl I had never even met. And then a few stray remarks. One girl is said to be an activist. The other one is supposed to have had a rift with her father. I had built it all into an elaborate fraud scheme.

Damnit, I thought bitterly.

Oh, I had convinced myself that for safety's sake I was going to play this perfectly straight as a valid kidnapping, and I suppose I had taken the minimal precautions. But deep in my heart I was obsessed with this other theory, and I thought I was only fooling around with a bunch of amateur punks who were trying to pull an easy rip-off. And so I had gone dashing into that drop scene with only those two hand weapons, thinking that was all old Brian Petersen needed. But that enormous firepower, and those high caliber rifles. I could have gotten all of us killed. However, if I had been better prepared I might have been able to take one of those guys alive, and then I knew I could make him lead me to the NFA headquarters.

Cathy Morrison was slumped against the door on the other side of the front seat, her eyes closed, and I thought she might be asleep now. But she opened her eyes, and said: "I heard them make Ellen do those statements on a tape machine, but they wouldn't let her say anything about me. I suppose no one even knew I was being held there, did they?"

"No. I should have figured it out, Cathy, but my mind was running in different channels."

"That's the final indignity. I was kidnapped for a week, and no one knew it." Then she closed her eyes again.

I made one brief stop on the way back to Kenwood at a public phone booth where I called Hank Phillips and asked him to join us immediately. He arrived at Rankin's house before we did, and when Cathy and I entered the study the two senators were engaged in a sober conversation. Rankin had apparently gotten himself pretty worked up on his long, solitary drive home, and now there was a furious expression on his face.

"Petersen, why in God's name did you follow me today?" he asked me.

"To protect your interests, Senator."

"But, damnit, Petersen, you've destroyed everything."

"Not at all. They still have your daughter, but I told you they had no intention of turning her over today. But we still have what they want, the money. And we can still bargain with them."

Hank Phillips was looking at the wound over my eye and the blood which was caked down the side of my face. "Do you need a doctor, Brian?" he asked, solicitously.

"No, I'll just clean up in the bathroom. But I think you could give this girl a belt of brandy. She's had a rough time."

I went off to a nearby bathroom, and with a face cloth wiped off the wound. It was still oozing a slight bit of blood, and I held a cold compress against it until it stopped. Pulling the cloth away, I could see that it was an extremely shallow crease wound, only about an inch long. It wasn't serious, but it would leave a nice little scar. A souvenir from the NFA. I found some adhesive plaster in the medicine cabinet and fashioned a small bandage, which I placed over the wound.

Cathy Morrison was sitting in one of the leather lounge chairs, a brandy snifter in her hands, when I returned, and she had apparently been telling the two senators about the abduction and captivity.

"But Ellen's all right, isn't she?" Rankin was asking.

"They didn't harm us at all," Cathy answered. "They kept us tied up most of the time, but they fed us. Oh, it was only hot dogs and hamburgers, but we weren't hungry."

However, as I heard the girl make that statement I noticed a peculiar tone in her voice, and I thought that for the first time she wasn't telling the complete truth for some reason.

At that moment, the phone rang, and I said: "I have a feeling that's your General Camillo. Stay calm, Senator."

Rankin took the call on the phone in the study, while I went out to the living room and listened on an extension. It was Camillo, all right, and he was totally enraged, his voice tumbling out in a furious torrent of words:

Camillo: Rankin, you dirty bastard, you fucking fascist, you've double-crossed us. And now your daughter is going to die. We told you to come alone, and you brought that murdering fascist bastard, Petersen. You're a cheat and a liar and …

Rankin: Now wait a minute, General Camillo, and listen to what I have to say.

Camillo: You're a fascist bastard …

Rankin: Would you listen, please. I had no knowledge that Mr. Petersen would follow me today. He did it entirely without my authorization, and I have upbraided him for it. But while we're talking about double-crossing, you fellows haven't played square with me. You promised to hand over my daughter, and all you produced was her roommate, Cathy Morrison.

Camillo: That was to test you, Rankin, to see if you were being honest. We would have released your daughter later if everything had gone okay. But we were holding her in another place as our insurance policy. And we were right: you weren't being honest. You brought that pig, Petersen, along with you.

Rankin: I tell you he followed me without authorization. He was here when I departed, and he foolishly followed me.

Camillo: He murdered two of our soldiers, and he's going to pay for it.

(Camillo continued talking about me for two or three minutes, an almost hysterical stream of words in which he called me every name in the book and then he swore that the NFA would execute me. I listened indifferently, perhaps even with some amusement. A lot of people have called me names before, and a number of them have threatened to kill me. But I'm still here. Rankin, though, was handling him well again, allowing him to rage on about me, trying to interrupt every so often to gently turn the conversation back to the release of his daughter. However, Camillo continued to rage about me, almost as if he were out of control. It was near the end of his tirade that he made one remark about me, an offhand remark at that, which made my mind snap to attention, wondering if I had heard him correctly. I was still puzzling about the remark while I listened to Rankin start to work him around, trying to arrange for another exchange of ransom money for his daughter's release. I knew from what Cathy Morrison had told me that they desperately wanted that money, and gradually I heard Camillo begin to deal for it.)

Camillo: But next time, Rankin, we make all the arrangements. And it won't be like last time. We'll tell you where to drop the money, and then we'll release your daughter in some place of our choosing.

Rankin: Agreed.

Camillo: And you'll have to pay more money next time, as a retribution for our two comrades who were killed. The price is now four hundred thousand dollars. In small, unmarked bills.

Rankin: That can be arranged. I'll need some more time, though.

Camillo: Your time is running out, Rankin. We're only going to allow you seventy-two more hours. All right, it's eight o'clock Tuesday night right now, and so we'll call you at eight o'clock Friday night. And you'd better have that whole four hundred thousand in small, unmarked bills. That will be your last chance to get your daughter back. But no more double cross. And I don't want Petersen following you, and if we even hear that he's hanging around your house, we'll call the whole thing off. Get rid of him, Rankin. And no police and no media.

Rankin: All right.

Camillo: You tell Petersen that the high tribunal of the National Federation Army has convicted him of murder, and he will be executed. And that Morrison girl will also be executed because she disobeyed our orders about attempting to escape. Freedom to the people.

Camillo hung up abruptly, and I walked back into the study where Rankin was attempting to tell Hank Phillips what went on at the other end of the conversation which he couldn't hear. I bent over to turn on Eddie Perkins' tape recorder beside the phone, and told them that it was easier to play back the whole conversation for Hank. Actually, I wasn't so much concerned about Hank's hearing that conversation as I was about trying to listen again to that strange remark from Camillo.

It was in the middle of his angry tirade about me, and I almost missed it the second time. So I stopped the machine for a moment, and rewound it for a few seconds of playing time and listened again. And I got every one of Camillo's words that time:

> We know all about Petersen. He's a fascist pig, and he's still engaged in that same type of fascist operation as he did at Cambridge.

I saw Hank Phillips looking curiously at me while I replayed that section of the tape, but he didn't say anything. When the tape was over I snapped it off, and Rankin began speaking immediately.

"You can see that my hands are tied, gentlemen," he said. "I simply have to do what they say."

"Lester," said Phillips hesitantly, "don't you think we're getting over our heads in this? Don't you think that maybe we should call in the police now?"

I noticed Cathy Morrison's eyes widen. "You mean the police don't even know about the kidnapping?"

"We decided that it was the surest way to get Ellen back," Rankin said. "I'm sorry, Miss Morrison, but we had no idea that these maniacs had abducted you along with Ellen. I'm glad you've been released, but I must ask you to respect our confidentiality and tell no one about this until we have Ellen back, too."

Hank Phillips looked at me. "What do you think, Brian?"

"You know how I feel. From the outset I've maintained we should call the police." It was still the proper thing to do, I realized, but now I was almost hoping that Rankin would stick to his position. I wanted to find out for myself what was at the bottom of this NFA group.

"I'm sorry, gentlemen," Rankin said. "But it's my daughter, and that's the way I'm going to do it."

"But what about those men Brian killed this evening," Phillips said. "Won't that bring the whole affair out in the open, anyway?"

"I don't think so, Hank," I interjected. "There's no identification on those bodies, and if we merely leave them there and say nothing to anybody, it will just be another crime puzzle for the police."

"That's what you all should do then," Rankin said. "And, Petersen, I know you were well-intentioned tonight, but that's got to be the end, do you understand? I appreciate what you've tried to do, but I simply have to go along with that maniac, Camillo. I want you to stay away from this house, and please do not have any further communication with me until after Ellen is returned. And, Petersen, please take that tape recorder with you when you go. I don't want anything to jeopardize Ellen's return."

"What about the extra hundred thousand dollars, Senator?" I asked. "How are you going to launder that?"

He hadn't thought about that, and he seemed puzzled. Finally, he said: "How did you do it, Petersen? Maybe I can do it myself."

"I got Big Dan McFarland to launder it for me, without using your name."

"My God! McFarland! Do you mean we're dealing with him?"

"Emergencies make for strange bedfellows, Senator."

"I don't like people like McFarland, but I'll just have to swallow my pride and ask him to do it for me. How can I get in contact with him tonight?"

"His home phone is unlisted, but I have it at my house. I'll call you back later and give it to you. In fact, I'll call Big Dan first and tell him to expect your call."

"I appreciate that, Petersen. And I'm sorry that I've gotten you and Miss Morrison so involved in this. Maybe I can arrange some protection for you against those NFA maniacs."

"I don't need protection, Senator. And don't worry about Cathy Morrison. I'll take care of her."

"All right, then, gentlemen, you'll have to excuse me. I want to get on that phone and make some more financial arrangements for the ransom money."

He escorted the three of us to the front door, and as he was holding the door open for us he said to me: "I still don't understand how you were able to follow me out there tonight. They certainly took me on a circuitous route, and I didn't see you behind me."

I reached behind Rankin's neck and extracted the bug from his jacket. "A tracking device, "I said, somewhat inaccurately.

"I'll be damned," he said.

There was no harm, I felt, in telling him about that one device, because I doubted if I could ever get that near to him again to insert another one. But I wasn't telling him about the tracking devices on his car and in the ransom bag. I planned to have them working for me again.

Outside, I put Cathy Morrison in my car, and then I walked over to talk with Hank Phillips for a minute. We were standing beside his Cadillac, and he lowered his voice to almost a whisper as he talked to me.

"He's a stubborn man, isn't he?" Phillips said.

"I guess you can't blame him."

"Brian, you're not really going to leave him to his own devices in this, are you?"

"Not a chance. I'm staying right with it."

126

"That's what I thought you'd do. And I'm relieved. Thanks, Brian."

He started to get into his car, but he paused. "I'm curious, Brian. What was that thing which intrigued you so much in that statement by that Camillo? Something that happened at Cambridge. What was that, some student thing at Harvard?"

"Yeah, Hank, some student thing at Harvard."

There was no sense in telling Hank at this stage, but I knew that Camilllo wasn't referring to Cambridge, Massachusetts. I had never spent any time up there, and I certainly hadn't been engaged in any activities of any kind there. No, he could only be referring to an episode of mine at Cambridge, England. It had slipped out in the midst of his almost uncontrollable tirade about me, but it frightened the hell out of me. Because I knew now that the NFA was not the uncoordinated little group of fanatics it appeared to be. General Camillo's army apparently had some vital connections which reached into powerful areas of the federal government.

CHAPTER TWELVE

Cathy Morrison was slumped against the door on the opposite side of the front seat as we drove away from Rankin's, her eyes closed again, and she seemed almost ready to pass out completely from fatigue and nervous exhaustion.

"I'm taking you home with me," I said.

"No, I'll be okay. Just drop me off at my apartment. All I want to do is sleep for days and days."

"I've got a guest room at my place, and you can sleep there undisturbed. Besides, I've got to keep you out of circulation until we get Camillo and his group. You heard him threaten your life."

"Okay," she mumbled. At that moment I think she would probably have agreed to anything as long as she could just lie down and sleep somewhere.

We drove on in silence until after I had crossed the Fourteenth Street Bridge, and I thought that surely she must be asleep now. But I still had to ask her one more question. "Cathy," I said softly.

"Yes, Mr. Petersen."

"Brian."

"Okay, Brian."

"What were you holding back from Senator Rankin, Cathy?"

Her eyes opened wide now. "What do you mean?"

"When Rankin asked you if his daughter was unharmed."

"She *is* unharmed, but ... Well, I don't know how long she'll remain unharmed. Those crazy kids are trying to brainwash her, make her an adherent of their National Federation Army. They think it'd give them the prestige they need if they could have as one of their members the daughter of a prominent conservative senator. But I didn't want to tell that to Senator Rankin, because it really hasn't happened yet. But it might."

"Have they used drugs on her?"

"Not yet, but they might eventually. Ellen is a real smart girl, and she's got wonderful emotional control. She's been playing them beautifully so far, listening to their endless rhetoric, which they keep spouting at her, and pretending to be slightly convinced for a while. Then she takes them in circles, and makes them start all over again. They think they're making headway with her, but they're not. I think the only reason they haven't used drugs on her yet is because they're so damned convinced of the persuasiveness of their two-bit philosophy. But I wonder how long she can hold out before they finally decide to use drugs on her."

"Did they try to turn you around, too, Cathy?"

"Conversion, is what they call it. Oh, yeah, they made some feeble attempts at me, but they gave up pretty quickly. They weren't interested in me, they were only interested in converting Rankin's daughter. Ha, I was the troublesome baggage in the whole kidnapping. Brian, I don't think they ever really intended to let me go, no matter what happened to Ellen Rankin. That's why I tried to escape from their car today."

"It's okay, Cathy, you're free now."

"But what about Ellen?"

"We just have to get her out of there," I said grimly. "Before they convert her."

And then I remembered that we only had seventy-two hours until the second drop. It didn't allow me much time to operate, and I knew that every hour was going to be precious from this moment on.

❧   ❧   ❧

I put Cathy Morrison in the guest room on the second floor, and showed her the private bathroom adjacent to it. She said she desperately needed a shower, but she felt she wouldn't be able to stand up that long, and so she tumbled on the bed, still dressed in her dirty jeans and sweater. I threw a blanket over her, and snapped out the light.

Time was vital now, but the security of the house was the first order of business. I went around checking all the locks on the doors, and the special security locks I had installed on the windows a few years ago. I also turned on the outside floodlights, the ones in front, and the ones which illuminated the pool area behind the house. Then I flipped on the burglar alarm, which was wired to all the doors and windows. Finally, I reloaded the .38 and placed it on the top of the bar while I mixed myself a scotch.

I had worked out a pretty tight security system for my house about a year and a half ago, and I was quite sure that Camillo and his friends wouldn't be able to break in on me unexpectedly and start shooting it up. No, Cathy and I were quite safe as long as we stayed here. But nevertheless, I wasn't going to allow myself to get walled in here, because I was going to have to move around if I wanted to get those bastards.

I thumbed through my private phone directory until I found Dan McFarland's unlisted home phone. A maid answered and told me that Mr. McFarland was entertaining and couldn't be disturbed, but I pressed the urgency of my call upon her and a few minutes later Big Dan came on the line.

"Yes, what is it, Brian?" he said, a note of annoyance in his voice.

"Sorry to break up your brandy and cigars, Dan. But do you remember that deal you worked for me a few days ago?"

"Yes," he said warily. We would both be very cautious, of course, about mentioning specifics over an open phone line.

"I'm afraid we're going to have to ask you to do it again for us in regard to the same problem. Another one hundred big ones, this time."

"Now, what the hell, Brian. I've done enough."

"But this time the principal himself will be contacting you later tonight. Lester Rankin."

"Rankin," he repeated incredulously. Rankin had never had any dealings with him before, and I knew that Dan would relish having him in his debt. "Why didn't you tell me the last time that Rankin was your principal?"

"I wasn't permitted. But things have changed. For the worse."

There was a pause, and then I heard Big Dan chuckle softly. "Sure, have old Lester contact me. I'm rather looking forward to it."

"One other thing, Dan. This time he'll need that job done in seventy-two hours. I'd like to make sure that it takes the full seventy-two hours."

"My God, Brian, of course it will take me seventy-two hours to launder a hundred big ones. What the hell, do you think I'm an alchemist?"

"But I'd like to make absolutely certain it takes that much time. It's for Rankin's own good." I was trying to insure time for myself, and I wanted to know exactly how much maneuvering space I had before the second drop. I didn't want Rankin to get the extra hundred thousand in the next day or so, and then arrange to make the drop before I had a chance to get mobilized.

"Okay. Seventy-two hours, Brian. Have Rankin contact me." I heard Big Dan chuckle softly again.

I phoned Rankin and gave him Big Dan's number and then I called Eddie Perkins. There was no answer at his store, but I traced him to his home.

"Eddie," I said, "do you remember those little additional devices you put in those phones out in Kenwood last week?"

"Sure do, Mr. Petersen."

"I'd like to activate them now, Eddie."

"A piece of cake. But how do you want it transmitted? You want a tape of them calls?"

"No, I'd like to monitor them live."

"I think we can work that out, Mr. Petersen. Where do you want your monitoring position?"

"Would it be possible to transmit all the way across the river to my home here in Arlington?"

"It's a big order, Mr. Petersen, but I think I can work that part of it out. Let me get busy on setting it up. You want to start right away?"

"No, get some sleep, Eddie. I don't think there's going to be any more action tonight. But I'd like to start sometime tomorrow morning"

"Can do. I'll get out to your place and set up the receiver once I get the operation going." He paused. "One thing, Mr. Petersen. This could be a pretty expensive operation, depending on how long it continues."

"Spend, Eddie. Spend."

That meant I would have a tap on Rankin's phone, and I would be listening and waiting for that next communication from Camillo. And with the seventy-two-hour interim McFarland promised me, I would have time to get set up. My mind was racing along, making preparations. I needed some help in monitoring those calls, and I needed help in guarding the house. I was trying to keep my mind away from that disturbing remark Camillo had made on the phone earlier this evening, because I didn't want it to distract me at the moment. However, I couldn't seem to drive it from my consciousness, and maybe that was a good thing, because it made me think of Bill Holman. Cambridge, England, meant that old Intelligence operation we engineered outside the British university town, and one of the people in that operation was Bill Holman.

I hadn't seen Holman for almost five years, until I bumped into him on a downtown Washington Street about six months ago. He was out of the Army now, retired after twenty-eight years, and I insisted he join me for a drink in a nearby bar for old times' sake. Holman had been a career noncommissioned soldier of high competence, and he had been assigned to Intelligence in London during my rather brief tour of duty there. We had three drinks in a dimly lit bar, reminiscing about old days, and he then told me he was living alone, a widower, out near Fort Belvoir in Maryland. He seemed lonely and rather lost now that he had completed his Army service, and we promised to get together soon again. But we never did.

I looked up his phone number in the public directory, and I had to pause and remind myself of his real given name, William. As long as I had known him everyone always called him Sarge. It was after midnight, but Sarge answered on the second ring.

"Sarge, this is Brian Petersen," I said.

"Oh, Captain. Nice to hear from you again. I really enjoyed meeting you a few months ago."

"Sarge, I was thinking about you tonight. Remember that operation we worked out near Cambridge a few years back?"

"Sure do, Captain. That was a smooth one, wasn't it?"

"Well, I'm involved in something like that again. On a private basis. And I thought if you've got a few free days you might be able to help me."

"Captain, I'd be delighted to help." I heard the sudden rush of enthusiasm in his voice. The old pro was being called back into the game.

"I'd pay you for your services, of course."

"Forget the pay, Captain. I'm itching to do something again. All I'm doing is sitting around and collecting my pension check. I don't like reading, and I get tired of that damned television."

"I'm afraid this would actually take all of your time for the next three or four days."

"Time is what I've got."

"Could you bunk in here with me, Sarge?"

"I can come right over now."

"Excellent. When you get here I can fill you in on the details."

"I'll be there in an hour or so."

"One other thing, Sarge. Do you have any power? I think we may need it on this assignment."

There was a slight pause. "I've got some good pieces, Captain. And make that a half-hour. I'll see you then."

I had just hung up the phone when I heard the scream from the guest bedroom. Grabbing the .38, I raced up the stairs two at a time and flung open the door, the pistol pointed in front of me. But there was no one there except Cathy, who was now sitting upright in bed, tears streaming down her face. The terrors of earlier today had finally caught up with her. I went over and sat on the edge of the bed, holding her in my arms while the sobs subsided. Finally I gently laid her down and went to the bathroom to get some sleeping tablets. I handed them to her and she washed them down with a glass of water. I stood silently by the bed for a few minutes until she closed her eyes. Neither of us had said a word to each other during the entire brief episode.

I returned to the bar and made another drink for myself while waiting for Sarge to arrive, and I began to think again of that Cambridge operation. It had really been no big deal, but as Sarge had stated, it was, by Intelligence standards, a smooth one. The target of the operation was a British scientist at Cambridge University, who was suspected of passing over sensitive information of a scientific nature to a foreign agent. There was also an American businessman in England who was suspected as part of the ring, and thus our people were included in the operation. We worked in cooperation with the English M boys in attempting to apprehend them in an actual transmission of information.

The final scene took place in the English countryside near Cambridge, and we used a series of cars and omni-range tracking devices to box the whole thing in. Army Intelligence had a lot of equipment available in London at that time, and I was put in charge of coordinating the whole tracking operation from a large console in a truck just outside town. As far as the British were concerned, the whole thing worked out perfectly. The British professor and the American businessman were both killed, and the foreign agent allowed to escape. There was a particularly intense détente going on at that time, and they wanted to hush up the whole affair, as long as the ring had been broken. The cause of death of the Englishman and the American was faked, and the agent, who was a staff member in an embassy, was declared *persona non grata*. And the whole case was quietly closed with no publicity or newspaper stories of any kind.

However tonight Camillo had evidently alluded to that episode, and I could understand how it would spring to his mind during his angry tirade. He obviously knew that I hadn't been able to follow Rankin over that long route with any simplistic devices. I might have been able to sell Rankin a bill of goods on that, but these NFA people seemed to know a lot about guerrilla tactics. No, they must have later realized that I was using some tracking devices, and that's when Camillo apparently recalled my earlier use of them at that Cambridge operation.

But how in the hell had he known about it?

Possibly from someone who had been in Intelligence with me at that time? No, that was inconceivable. I remember that all those fellows were an exceptionally tight-lipped crowd, and I certainly couldn't imagine any of them having a connection with an NFA-type group at this later date. And the foreign agent couldn't possibly have communicated the episode to them because I was far removed from the actual scene and he wouldn't even have known that a Brian Petersen existed. And, of course, there was no media awareness of the event. Quite to the contrary, it was painstakingly hushed up.

There was only one logical place that anyone who was not connected with the original operation could have learned about it at this late date—my old promotion jacket at Army Intelligence. I remember that I had received a special and secret commendation for the Cambridge caper, the only one I had ever received during my rather brief tour in Intelligence, and it was duly inserted in that highly confidential jacket. That single commendation would leap out of the pages at anyone who had access to the jacket, and then he would read about my expertise in supervising a tracking operation. And the Cambridge operation did bear some remarkable resemblances to the way I had worked the drop scene earlier tonight.

That led me to the final disturbing realization. Camillo or his allies had access to that unbelievably secret Army Intelligence file. And if you know anything about Intelligence, you would understand that nobody but people with the highest possible security clearance or the biggest clout could gain access to those files.

Then who was Camillo's connection?

The doorbell rang, and I picked up my .38 and went up to the front door. Through the peephole I could see Sarge standing there, a large, battered valise in his hand. I opened the door and pumped his hand.

"Reporting for duty, Captain," he said.

"For God's sake, Sarge, stop calling me captain. I was only in the Army for four years, and that's over with. Call me Brian."

"All right," he said, and then a pause. "Brian." He was uncomfortable using it.

I took him down to the recreation room and offered him a drink. He asked for a cold beer, and as he snapped the top off the can, I looked at him appraisingly. He was probably in his late 50's now, but he looked at least ten years younger, a trim and fit man with a flat stomach and a thick, powerful neck. His hair was now quite grey, but it was closely cropped, and his only new concession to advancing age which I could notice was a pair of steel-rimmed glasses. Sarge had a well-deserved reputation as a tough, spit-and-polish soldier, but I knew from my contacts with him in Intelligence that behind that formidable exterior there was an alert mind and a surprising amount of sensitivity. Tonight he was dressed in a rather inexpensive, conservative suit, and I could see from the tight bulge under his left armpit that he was now wearing a shoulder holster.

"What's the piece, Sarge?" I asked him, pointing toward the bulge.

"A Browning .380 semi-automatic," he said, extracting the pistol from the holster. "A good hand weapon. Rapid fire, six-round magazine. But I've got a more powerful Browning in my suitcase there." He laid his can of beer on the bar and bent over to flip open the suitcase. I watched him as he took out the parts of a disassembled rifle and then laid them carefully on the floor. "It's a converted weapon," he explained, "and I did a lot of the work myself. It operates on automatic fire, and it carries 15 magnum shells, and they're 7mm. That baby can do a hell of a lot of damage."

"Good. We may need it."

"What's the operation, Captain—I mean, Brian?"

I proceeded to tell Sarge every detail of my experiences in the Rankin kidnapping. I wasn't concerned about breaking Rankin's confidentiality to Sarge, because I knew he would maintain the secrecy, but also because it was imperative that he know precisely what was going on now that he was an integral part of the operation. As I recounted the story, Sarge listened intently, but he also began to assemble his automatic rifle while I was talking. I noticed the painstaking care with which he unwrapped every part, and then screwed the barrel to the stock. He also had a scope for the rifle which he attached and then sighted at some object on the other side of the room. By the time I had finished my narrative, Sarge was slowly filling the magazine with 7mm cartridges. He laid it carefully across the bar.

"We're in this alone?" he asked. "No back-up at all?"

"That's the way it's got to be, Sarge. Rankin doesn't want the authorities brought in, and I think we have to respect his feelings."

I could see that Sarge didn't like that, but he was accustomed to working under orders he didn't always particularly like. "How do I fit in the operation?" he asked.

"I think the first thing we have to do is protect that girl upstairs for the next few days. It's not inconceivable that those NFA people may try a rush on the house, and I need you here for protective purposes. I intend to get out on the streets tomorrow and I wouldn't feel right leaving that girl unprotected. Secondly, tomorrow morning I'm going to set up a phone tap on Rankin's phone from here, and I'd like you to monitor the phone calls so we can listen in for Camillo's instructions about the second drop."

"Then we're going to be part of that drop scene?"

"We sure as hell are. We can't make any definite plans yet, because we don't know how the NFA is going to arrange it. So a lot of it will have to be improvisational, sort of spur-of-the-moment thing. However, those boys have some heavy firepower, and I think we should try to match them a little bit. If they want to play army, we can play army, too. Do you have any friends in ordnance in the area who could help us out?"

"Sure, I think so. I've got some good buddies at both Fort Belvoir and Fort Meade, and I'm sure they could sneak some equipment out for us."

We continued to talk about possible weaponry, and Sarge offered some extremely valuable suggestions. He made notes on a piece of paper, and said he would contact some of his buddies in the morning and get them working on it.

Finally I said: "Sarge, let's catch a few hours' sleep, because I don't know how much we're going to get in the next few days."

I escorted Sarge upstairs to the other guest room, and when I entered my own room I glanced at the clock. It was after three in the morning. That meant that it was now early Wednesday morning, perhaps only about fifty hours away from the second drop. Time was running out for somebody.

CHAPTER THIRTEEN

woke to the alarm at seven o'clock that morning, and I immediately smelled the strong aroma of bacon and eggs. It reminded me, forcefully, that I hadn't eaten any dinner the previous day, and so I slipped on a robe and went downstairs. Sarge, fully dressed in slacks and a sport shirt, was standing in front of the stove, his hand on the handle of the frying pan. Incongruously, he was wearing his shoulder holster, from which the butt of his .380 Browning pistol was protruding.

"Sunnyside up, Captain?" he asked.

"For God's sake, Brian, will you."

"Sorry—Brian."

"Sunnyside is fine. How long have you been up?"

"Since five-thirty. Old Army habits. Can't break them."

I went out to the front step and picked up the morning paper to see if there was any story yet about the two men I had killed in Virginia last evening. Fortunately it was a big news day with a presidential press conference downtown and the appointment of a new Secretary of Agriculture, and those stories occupied a large part of the front page. I found my story on page three, a rather short article about the discovery of the bodies of two unidentified men in a rural section of northern Virginia. There were no clues to the killers as yet, but Virginia police suspected that it was some sort of gang slaying by a rival gang. Excellent, I thought. If the NFA people read the story they would realize that Rankin hadn't gone to the police as yet. The kidnapping was still a covert affair.

Sarge and I were finishing breakfast when the doorbell rang. I got my .38 and answered it myself. It was Eddie Perkins, and contrary to my suggestion, it appeared that he hadn't gotten any sleep. His eyes were red and there were dark smudges under them, and he hadn't shaved.

"It's working, Mr. Petersen," he said. "We should be able to pick up that transmission now."

Eddie had a younger man with him who was carrying a large box, and I invited them both in. After introducing him to Sarge, Eddie wanted to know where he could set up his receiving unit, and we decided to place it in the recreation room downstairs. I told Eddie that Sarge would be doing the monitoring, and I left the two of them alone to discuss the procedure while I went upstairs to shower and shave.

I took a peek in Cathy Morrison's room, but she was still asleep. After I dressed, I called Annie at her home and told her that we wouldn't be opening the office for the next few days. I didn't want to do the obvious thing of showing up at my Connecticut Avenue office where those NFA guys could get a clear shot at me. I told Annie as briefly as I could what had happened last evening, and I heard her gasp. She offered to come over to my house to help me take care of Cathy Morrison, and I thought that was a fine idea.

When I came downstairs to the recreation room, Sarge was sitting before a large radio receiver and Eddie was pointing out various dials to him. Eddie turned to me: "What we got here, Mr. Petersen, is really your own little radio network. I've got a small sedan cruising around that Kenwood area with a receiver which is picking up the signal from the Rankin phone. The sedan has another set in it which boosts it and transmits it to a truck

I've got a few miles away. There's a lot of heavy equipment in that truck, and it sends it out on seldom-used high frequency on the citizens' band. And you pick it up here. I've had one of my boys climbing up on your roof to attach a better aerial to that TV antenna you've got. You should get fine reception."

"Won't that sedan in the Kenwood area look suspicious, Eddie?" I asked.

"I'm way ahead of you, Mr. Petersen. The sedan is only a starter. In the next few hours I'm going to add another car, and a delivery truck. They can spell each other on a twenty-four-hour basis. That way the same vehicle won't be cruising all the time."

"Your mind works beautifully, Eddie."

"One more precaution I've taken," he said, looking pleased. "I've given Mr. Holman here a timetable of different frequencies we'll be using. Every three hours we're going to change the sending frequency a few degrees, and he'll have to adjust his receiver here. That way we can prevent someone just happening to catch our frequency, and then stay tuned to us. If anyone hears those occasional phone calls over a three-hour span, they'll probably think that there's a crossed wire or something, and they're picking up a signal from the phone company."

At that moment there was the sound of a phone ringing over the radio receiver, and Eddie said: "There you go." The three of us listened as we heard Lester Rankin himself answer the phone. His voice was clear and distinct, and so was the voice at the other end of the line, a banker from the West Coast who was helping Rankin arrange for the immediate transfer of some additional funds. Rankin was working on the ransom money, but we were right with him now.

Rankin was still talking when I went into the mechanical equipment room, and from that trunk which was bolted to the floor I took out some additional .38 shells and put them in my shell case. I also strapped on a shoulder holster, pulling the two loops over my shoulders. I was wearing a loose-fitting sports jacket that day, and I didn't think the holster with its .38 Police Special showed. But I didn't give a damn if it did, I was armed, and I didn't care who knew it.

The Rankin phone conversation was completed when I returned to the recreation room, and Eddie was explaining something to Sarge about the receiving unit. I heard Sarge say: "Mr. Perkins, you weren't ever in the federal government, were you?"

"Ten years. The Company."

Sarge nodded his head. "It figures."

They were still talking when I left.

My first stop that morning was the Pentagon, that sprawling five-sided labyrinth of military office space on the Virginia side of the Potomac. I wanted to see if I could find out who had been snooping in my file, and I tried to recall any old comrades who might be stationed in Washington now. Bill Benson seemed to fill the bill: he had been stationed with me in Paris, and although I'd hardly call us close friends, we always seemed to get along rather well. Bill was a career officer, now in his late thirties, and he had spent most of his time in Army Intelligence. The last time I met him he told me he missed the field work and regretted being relegated to a desk job in the Intelligence division at the Pentagon.

His secretary told me that Major Benson was very busy, but when she relayed my name to him he asked to have me shown right in. He seemed glad to see me, and apparently he was ready to do some reminiscing about the old days in Paris, but I cut him off.

"This isn't social, Bill," I said. "I've got a beef with Armtel."

He straightened up in his chair, and I could see the instant change come over him: he was a professional soldier faced with a complaint of some kind. "What's your beef, Brian?"

"Somebody's been poking around in my Intelligence jacket sometime in the past few months."

He whistled softly. "You've got a beef. And, boy, do we have a big problem if you're right. Wait right here, Brian. Let me go and check this out."

He left the office, walking in brisk, determined strides, and I had to wait almost a half-hour before he returned. He had a slip of paper in his hand, a frown on his forehead. "You're wrong, Brian. Nobody's been in your file in the last year."

"Are you sure, Bob?"

"The files of former Intelligence officers are under the same tight security as the files of the active ones. They're kept in a vault, and every time anyone even touches one of those files there's a triple screening process with signatures at every step. No one's even touched your file. What makes you think someone might have?"

"A rumor. But I guess it was a bogus one."

"It sure as hell was."

"What about previous to this year? Anyone using my file then?"

"Let me tell you, Brian, we don't let anyone just *use* a file. And those files never leave the building. However, sometimes we extract information from the files, and use it in other documents." He consulted the slip of paper in his hand. "During the past five years your file was only touched once. That was thirteen months ago. We had a request from the Security Division of Justice for data about you. The request was co-signed by the Attorney General, and the purpose was a security check and a competency analysis requested by

Senator Haynes Brickman. Would that be the rumor you're referring to?"

"No, that wouldn't be it. I did a sensitive job for Brickman about that time, and I can understand that he would want to do a security check on me. But, Bob, in my jacket there's a commendation for a little job I did a few years back in England, and it's the only one I ever got. Would that have been included in the report you made to Justice?"

"The report to Justice is now part of your file, Brian, and I just read it a few minutes ago. And, yes, the details of that commendation are included. A good job, I must say, Brian. And I might tell you also that the whole jacket is quite flattering. That's why I'm surprised that a man of your experience should even suspect that our system had broken down someplace."

"Yes, I guess I was just mistaken, Bob."

The cordial atmosphere which had prevailed when I first entered Major Benson's office had now dissipated. I had the temerity to suggest that the system had broken down. And we know the system never breaks down, don't we? Bob seemed to have lost the zest for any reminiscences about the old days, and I left his office a few minutes later.

I drove into Washington, and then down Constitution Avenue, on my way to the Department of Justice. I had learned one thing from Benson, and now I was going to try to follow the trail. A little over a year ago that Cambridge incident had been lifted from my file and reported to people on this side of the Potomac. The Brickman inquiry was a perfectly valid one, but who else had read those reports he requested about me? It could have been anyone. A clerk in his office, an aide in Justice, some disgruntled government worker who then transmitted it to a radical group headed by Camillo. There were innumerable possibilities, but maybe I could pick up a lead.

The area along the Mall between the Washington Monument and the Capitol is a difficult place to find a parking space, and I had to cruise around for almost fifteen minutes before I spotted a tourist who was pulling out of the rows of tightly parked automobiles. I took his place, and then walked over to the Department of Justice. My contact there would be Craig Wright, a high official and a veteran in the Security Division of Justice, although, for cosmetic purposes, that quite sensitive division at Justice is no longer called Security; and you'd have a hell of a time trying to locate it in the Justice Department if you didn't know where to look for it. Craig, who must now be approaching retirement, was in reality Zach's friend, not mine, but I had gotten to know him fairly well during those years when Zach was in town and in the Senate. He didn't owe me any favors, but he always seemed well-disposed toward me, and he might help me now.

I had no trouble getting in to see Craig, and he rose from behind his desk to shake hands with me, a small balding man in his late fifties, with sharp dark eyes which peered intently at you from behind tortoiseshell glasses. We started to talk about Zach, but again I had to interrupt these reminiscences, telling him I was on a tight time schedule and needed some information.

"Okay, Brian, how can I help you?" he asked.

"Let me tell you what I know, and then what I don't know. A little over a year ago Senator Haynes Brickman requested a report on me. You got some data from my Intelligence files at the Pentagon, and I presume from a lot of other places. Then you made up a report and sent it to Brickman. Am I right so far?"

"I remember the episode. Yes, you're right."

"I presume you keep a copy of that report here?"

"Of course."

"How tightly is it secured? Any chance one of your clerks or somebody could get a look at it?"

"Not a chance in the world, Brian. Those security checks are top-priority security. You know, the Security Division has come under a lot of fire the last few years about prying into people's lives, and so we guard those files absolutely."

I stopped and thought about that for a moment, and then I decided to play a hunch. "All right, one more question, Craig. Has anybody else asked to see that report in, say, the last six months?"

Craig Wright ran his hand slowly down the side of his face. "You know, Brian, I couldn't tell you something like that."

He looked uneasy, and suddenly I felt I had hit paydirt.

"Craig, it's very important to me. I wouldn't put you on the spot like this except that it's a matter of the most vital concern."

He stared intently at me for a few moments, those dark eyes boring into me. Then he said: "No, Brian, I couldn't tell you anything about that."

His voice was a bit too loud, and he nodded his head toward the door of his office. "You parked downstairs?" he asked, and when I answered yes, he said he'd walk me down to the car because he wanted to talk to me about Zach.

I understood perfectly well what he was doing, and we went downstairs and walked out on the Mall toward my car. He lit a cigarette and glanced casually around him as we walked along.

"Afraid of a bug in your office, Craig?" I asked.

"Not really. But you can't be too careful. Everybody's jumpy these days."

"About that report?"

"I shouldn't be telling you this, Brian, and ordinarily I wouldn't. But you've impressed me with the urgency of your concern, and I've been hearing that you've been doing some good things around town. However, don't ever use my name, and if you quote me I'll deny it." He paused, and took a deep drag on his cigarette. "Last Wednesday we received a special request for an analysis check about you from Congressman Jason Miller."

"And you gave it to him?"

"After a lot of consultation and soul-searching, we did. I sat in on the meeting which finally agreed to give him a copy of your report. We gave it to him on Thursday."

The day of the request, last Wednesday, would have been the day after Rankin first told me about his daughter's kidnapping. And it would have been at the very time when the NFA was trying to find out who I was, worried that I might be some sort of undercover agent for the police. It all seemed to fit like a glove. But why Congressman Jason Miller? He was only a name to me, an obscure freshman congressman, one of the 435 members of the House, and he didn't have very high visibility in this town. What was his connection with the NFA? Did they run to him when they saw me hanging around Rankin's house, asking him to check me out? And did he then ask for a fast check with Justice's Internal Security? And did he then turn that report over to General Camillo? It sure as hell seemed like it. But why in God's name would a member of the House of Representatives be connected in any way with a wild group like the NFA? That part of it didn't make any sense.

"Do you usually give security documents to obscure congressmen?" I asked Craig.

"Not at all. That's why I asked you to keep your mouth shut about it. But this Miller is some type of young firebrand, and he's been pestering us ever since he arrived in the House, accusing us of being a secret police and all that nonsense. He's made a number of requests before for similar checks about a number of people, and we've always turned him down. He got mad, of course, and threatened us with trying to get a congressional investigation going about us. So, this time when he asked, we decided to humor him. He said he'd been hearing reports about your secret activities around town, and he felt it was his responsibility to the people to find out what was going on in town. All that crap. We knew your file, and we knew that it was harmless, full of laudatory stuff, commendations and all. And so we thought we could get him off our backs by giving him that one."

We had arrived at my Olds now, and Craig Wright crushed out his cigarette on the ground. "That any help to you?" he asked.

"I think so. Thanks, Craig."

I noticed him looking curiously at the left side of my windshield which had been splattered by NFA bullets last evening. "What happened?" he asked.

"Some kids threw rocks at it."

He looked at the windshield again, and then at me. "It appears that those kids had guns, too."

"You couldn't be more right, Craig."

My next stop was at the National Press Building where I took the elevator up to Tom Walsh's tiny office. Again, without amenities, I plunged right into it. "What do you know about Congressman Jason Miller?" I asked Tom.

He swiveled around in his chair. "I wouldn't waste any time even thinking about him, Brian. He won't be around town long. Definitely a one-termer."

"Why?"

"Let me tell you how he got elected, first. This Miller guy is about thirty-five, an academic type, and he taught in a number of colleges and fancies himself some type of advanced liberal or something like that. He comes from the Midwest, and last election he decided to run for the House. The only reason he got the nomination was because nobody wanted it—the seat was occupied by old man Jennings, and Paul the Apostle couldn't have beaten Jennings in that district. So the nomination was up for grabs, and they threw it away at this unknown professor type. But as you remember, Brian, old man Jennings dropped dead three weeks before the election. They quickly got a substitute on the ticket, but about a week before the election some newspaperman dug out the story that the new candidate was picked up on a morals charge years ago when he was in the service. And so this unknown Jason Miller squeaked in. But he'll never get re-elected. He's some type of firebrand, and he doesn't understand the rules of the Club on Capitol Hill. He just gets on everybody's nerves. And he doesn't do anything for the people in his home district, either. He thinks his mission is to be a great statesman in Washington. I heard that his popularity in his home district is down to about ten, and Donald Duck could beat him next time."

"You say, 'advanced liberal', Tom. What does that mean?"

"Oh, Miller is hard to define. He's basically just a professor of political science. And he seems to be a great theorist. But, as I say, he won't be around town long enough to make any difference."

"Tom, I want you to find out for me everything you possibly can about this Jason Miller guy. I'm interested in his background, his affiliations, his memberships, things like that."

"Hard-hitting?"

"Hard-hitting. I don't care now who knows I'm interested in Miller. And, Tom, I'm in a desperate rush. I'll pay you for this, but I'd like you to get right on it. Start feeding me the stuff as soon as you get it, and send it out by special messenger to my home."

Tom Walsh looked at me quizzically. "You think Miller may be involved in something funny?"

"I think he may be involved in something very funny, Tom."

⚜   ⚜   ⚜

I got my car out of the parking garage near the Press Building, and headed back toward Virginia, hoping to find that Cathy Morrison was feeling well enough to be interrogated more thoroughly about her captivity by the NFA. I now felt that Congressman Jason Miller was the number-one candidate on my list for involvement with the NFA, but I still wanted to proceed with an open mind. I had allowed myself to go crashing blindly down the wrong trail earlier in this affair because of my uncritical acceptance of rumor and suspicion, and I didn't want that to happen again. Time was utterly precious now, and if I got started on the wrong trail again, I could miss the whole thing. After all, that citation from my Intelligence jacket had been included in a report over a year ago, and any number of people along the way might have seen it. Furthermore, Craig Wright at Justice had told me that Miller had previously requested a number of other security and analysis reports, and it might have been the purest type of coincidence that he happened to request mine last week while the NFA was trying to find out who I was.

But if that were the case, it would certainly be the weirdest type of coincidence, one which I found difficult to accept at that point.

I was still tossing it around in my mind as I drove along Route 1 on the Virginia side of the Potomac. I took a righthand turn, and pressed the accelerator to drive up the hill toward the plateau on which my house was located. This section of Arlington was an eyesore and didn't at all indicate the caliber of the fine homes up on top of the plateau. You had to drive up the steep road which was lined by a series of massive windowless warehouses on one side, and an unkempt field of scraggly bushes and small trees on the other which would probably also be used someday for commercial purposes.

Halfway up the hill, I saw a car pull out of a small alleyway between two of the warehouses and turn sharply down the hill. It was about twenty-five feet in front of me with plenty of clearance to pass me on the left. But suddenly it veered toward me, and I got a quick and frightening glimpse of the occupants. Two men were in the front seat and two men in the back, all wearing khaki fatigue jackets. And the bearded man in the shotgun seat was aptly described—only in this case he was holding an M-14 automatic rifle, aimed out of the front window at me.

It was the NFA and they were trying to ram me.

You've only got split seconds to react when someone tries to ram your car, and if you make the wrong move, you've had it. The NFA car was speeding down the hill toward me at what you could call, in aeronautical terms, eleven o'clock high. The normal reaction, I suppose, is to pull your car sharply to the right in order to get away from the car which is coming at you from the left. But the car which is trying to ram you will continue turning in toward you, and in that case it would hit you broadside, right against the driver's seat. And that could be the end of Brian Petersen, fulfilling the NFA's threat to execute me.

Instead, I jerked my steering wheel sharply to the left, catching the NFA car by surprise. I almost managed to slip by the right side of the speeding car, but at the last minute the driver was able to wheel back toward me. He sideswiped me on the passenger side, then kept sliding in toward me. Following the impact, the two cars spun around in a dizzy circle, and I fought the wheel to keep from tipping over. I went up over the curb and smashed into a metal post which had a no-parking sign on it.

Almost at the very moment I hit the post I had my hand on the door handle, and I flung open the door, doing a rollout on the pavement. The NFA car was some ten or fifteen feet away, and both rear doors were already open. The bearded guy in the front seat still had the M-14 pointed in my direction, but he wasn't firing. And then I realized why they were holding their fire momentarily. They had hoped to kill me without the noise of gunfire which might bring policemen running—first, by ramming me, and now by some type of rush.

I heard a footstep behind me, and I spun around, the .38 now in my hand. One of them was running at me full speed with a twelve-inch bayonet in his hand. I could have brought him down easily with my pistol, but I wanted one of them alive. As he made his lunge at me, I feinted to my left, then dove back toward him. His bayonet slashed through the sleeve of my jacket, but it only caught the fabric. My shoulder hit him under the chest, and then I jerked him in the air. The momentum of his rush and my counter-hit caused him to go flying in a wild somersault, and he slammed to the ground some five feet away.

Another one was coming around the other side of the car, but he had a pistol and he was firing. Then the M-14 from the car started to pump away. Their silent rush had failed and now they were going to try to finish me off quickly with gunfire. The first shot from the man with the pistol missed, and I fired twice rapidly at him as he came around the fender of my car. I don't know which shot got him, but one of the bullets hit him on the upper lip just under the nose, and I saw his face explode into a glob of red.

The M-14 was having difficulty getting me in range because I moved behind my own car, and the bullets streamed harmlessly over my head. I went down on one knee, crouching behind the hood of the car, and tried to return fire. But then I heard movement behind me. I swung around as I heard the shot. The fellow with the bayonet had struggled to his knees and drawn a pistol.

My sudden movement had caused him to miss, but the bullet whistled right by my head. I fired instantly, hitting him squarely in the chest, and he pitched forward on his face.

In a crouch, I moved quickly down toward the end of my car, hoping to get a shot at the NFA car from a different angle. Apparently, the guy with the M-14 wasn't going to leave the car. He was being too cautious, and it was a mistake, because if the three of them had rushed me simultaneously with that M-14 blazing I would have been overwhelmed.

I came around the end of my car, looking for an angle at the guy in the front seat with the M-14. And at that very moment he turned toward me, and our eyes caught. It was a split second of frozen tableau, and I got an excellent look at him. Hornrimmed glasses. Small, rather beady eyes. Reddish beard. Incongruously thinning, reddish hair for a young man someplace in his late twenties.

I fired, but my bullet exploded against the metal window post. And then he brought the M-14 around and began firing at me. I ducked behind the car for a few seconds, and then peered cautiously out, hoping to get off more shots. But the car was now pulling away, as the M-14 fired a few times aimlessly in my direction. I fired at the departing car, but it picked up speed quickly and in a matter of seconds it was out of range. I watched it race down the hill, and turn onto Route 1 almost on two wheels. There was no sense in attempting to follow it, because by the time I got in my car and turned it around, the NFA car would be far gone.

The whole scene had occurred with astonishing quickness, and I now still had time to get out of there before people came running to inquire about the gunshots. The two NFA men lying on the ground were both dead, I saw, and their pistols, both snubnose .38's, were lying beside them. I knew it would probably be useless to attempt to search them for identification, and I simply had to get out of here before the police arrived.

I jumped into the Olds, and was gratified to see that I was still able to drive it with the side smashed. I backed off the curb, turned, and drove rapidly up the hill toward my house about a mile away.

Two more NFA men were dead, but I still hadn't been able to take one alive so I could interrogate him. However, one significant thing had happened to me in the last few minutes. Without any truly rational basis for it, I felt quite certainly that I had met General Camillo. I didn't know why, but I was surely convinced that the man who was carefully protecting himself in the shotgun seat with the M-14 was definitely Camillo. And, driving home, I recalled those small, intense eyes. The reddish beard. The receding hairline. The thick glasses. Every detail was being etched indelibly in my mind.

And I knew that I would meet him again.

CHAPTER FOURTEEN

When I entered my house a few minutes later I heard the sound of women's voices upstairs, and I knew that Annie was up there with Cathy Morrison. Sarge was down in the recreation room, sitting in front of the radio receiver, a cigar in his mouth. I asked him if he had heard anything significant on Rankin's phone calls, and he said no. Then he noticed the slash in the sleeve of my sports jacket, and he immediately rose to his feet.

"What happened?" he asked.

"The NFA. They were lying in ambush down the road."

His hand went to the butt of his pistol in the shoulder holster. "They still out there?"

"There are two of them still out there, but they won't ever bother anybody again. Four of them jumped me, but two of them got away."

"Do you think they'll try a rush on the house?"

"I doubt it. The ambush was about a mile away, and I didn't even think they'd try it that close. But when the police discover those two bodies out there, they'll be all over the neighborhood for a couple of days, going from door to door, asking questions. When they come here, we just don't know anything about it. But those policemen all over the area will make a nice little bit of extra protection for us."

"What kind of firepower did they have?"

"Another one of those damned M-14's. But the two guys I killed seemed to have the same kind of gun as that Timothy

Bronson I got the other day—snub-nose .38's. Cheap, five-shot weapons, almost Saturday Night Specials. And I think that's the kind of arsenal we're facing, Sarge. A few sophisticated weapons, and a bunch of cheap handguns."

Annie came downstairs at that moment, and I put my finger to my lips. "How's Cathy Morrison?" I asked Annie.

"Still quite shaky. That girl's been through quite an ordeal, Brian."

"Do you have any doubts about her story?"

"No, that girl is as honest as the day is long. I believe her story one hundred percent."

"Yeah, so do I. Do you think we can get her down here for a little questioning?"

"I think so. Let me go up and get her. I've washed her clothes in your machine, and I think they should be ready now. Oh, you've had two phone calls—one from Steve Harrison, and the other from Calvin Johnson."

When Annie went upstairs to get Cathy Morrison I returned the two phone calls. I reached Harrison at his desk at the *Washington Post*, and he said: "I've been doing some thinking all morning, Brian."

"It helps to exercise those gray cells, Steve."

"Last week you asked me about something called the National Federation Army, which I still don't know what the hell is. Then this morning we have that story on page three of the paper. Two kids killed wearing army khakis, and some high-powered rifles lying there. Could this be some sort of nutty army operation, I asked myself. Could this be Brian's army?"

"Your brain is running away with you, Steve."

"I'm putting two and two together."

"And you're getting five."

"No, my newsman's instinct tells me I'm getting four. But, apparently, you're not willing to talk. Don't forget, you owe me a deep background."

"If anything looks like it's going to break, Steve, I'll give you the story."

Damnit, I thought, as I hung up. That smart son of a gun was getting close to the mark. I then called Calvin Johnson at his training school on Georgia Avenue.

"Think I may have something for you, Brian, on that army thing you asked me about," he said. "It isn't much but it's something."

"Give me what you've got, Calvin."

"I told you I thought I'd heard that expression before, but I couldn't remember where. I kept asking the dudes for the past week, but I couldn't track it down. Then yesterday one of the kids who hangs around here occasionally showed up, and I suddenly remembered that he was the one who had mentioned something called the National Federation Army. This kid does a lot of street floating, and he had heard someplace about a group of honkies out in the Dupont Circle area who were calling themselves by that name. It was kind of a joke, he thought: a group of white middle-class college kids who were going to solve all the problems of the world. We've seen a lot of those groups over the past ten years. Naïve do-gooders."

"Thanks for the tip, Calvin. But don't let your kids misread that group at Dupont Circle. Those honkies aren't too naive, and they're definitely not do-gooders."

A few minutes later Annie brought Cathy Morrison downstairs. Cathy's jeans and sweater had been washed, and she looked much more rested and relaxed than the previous evening. Nevertheless she still showed the emotional strain of her week of captivity.

Annie got her settled in a comfortable club chair, and then went to get coffee for all of us.

"Feeling better?" I asked her.

"Lots. Thanks to you, Brian. Any more word about Ellen?"

"We're working on it."

Annie brought the coffee for the four of us, and I told her she could go home, but she said she had made baby-sitting arrangements at her home today and she could stay. She drew her chair close to Cathy, and flipped open her pad to take notes. Sarge was a few feet away at the radio receiver, not saying anything, but listening intently to our conversation.

"Cathy," I said, "I'd like to go through that whole painful experience with you, step by step. If you get tired, tell me. But I'd like you to give me every detail you can remember, no matter how inconsequential. It may just fit in someplace."

"I'll try," Cathy said.

"Let's start with the kidnapping itself. How far from your apartment were you when they kidnapped you?"

"Oh, a couple of blocks."

"That means they were probably trailing you from the movies. Was anybody else with you at the movies, somebody who might have signalled the kidnappers?"

"No, Ellen and I went alone. It was a last-minute decision. We were both home that night, and neither of us had dates or anything to do, and we suddenly decided to go to the movies. There was nobody who could have even known we were going out."

My interrogation of Cathy Morrison continued for over an hour, and I took her over every step of her kidnapping, up to the moment I saw her break away from the NFA car last evening. Her narrative was complete and colorful, and a lot of it would make extremely interesting reading about the psychological terrors of a kidnap victim. But it didn't give me any additional hard evidence about the NFA or where their hideout might be. Cathy was still convinced that it was in some fairly rural area, and I felt that it was probably someplace in northern Virginia, not too far from the drop scene. But that nevertheless covered a lot of territory.

Finally I rose to my feet, and walked to the end of the room. I lit a cigarette and turned. There was something which had been nagging in the back of my mind ever since I had discovered last night that Cathy Morrison was not implicated in the planning of the kidnapping, and I wanted to try it on her now.

"Cathy, would you consider yourself an activist?" I asked.

"No, I don't think so. I think the system is lousy, but the way to change it today is to try to work in the system somehow. Like the Nader people."

"Judy Powell thinks you're an activist."

A puzzled expression came over her face. "Who's Judy Powell?" She paused. "Oh, that girl down the corridor. Why, she hardly knows me. She probably heard that I worked for that Action for Environment group. That's a misnomer, because that group is about as activist as the Audubon Society." Suddenly she paused again, and looked directly at me, as if she were trying to recall something else.

"What is it, Cathy?"

"That girl, Judy Powell. You asked if anyone had gone to the movies with us. I had forgotten about it until now, but on the way out that evening we bumped into Judy in the corridor, and asked her to come with us. But she told us she had already seen that picture."

Annie lifted her pencil from the paper, and said: "Ha."

Cathy turned toward her. "What does that mean?"

"It means," Annie answered, "that our leader Brian Petersen is not as smart about women as he thinks he is. He thought he was cleverly conning Judy Powell, but it looks like it was the other way around."

"Yes, damnit," I said. "It sure looks like that. Judy Powell. Judy Powell. That name keeps cropping up. When the girls are leaving for the movies, there she is, finding out exactly where they are going. She could have directed the kidnappers to the movie house so they could trail the girls when the picture was over. Then I go breaking into the girls' apartment, and there she is to find out what's going on. And then she carefully tells me that Cathy Morrison is some kind of activist, laying a delicious red herring across the trail. Then the NFA finds out I am involved with Lester Rankin. I thought it was because of the stakeout around his house. That was part of it, I'm sure, but another part could have been Judy Powell. She saw me at the apartment, and she read my ID."

"You think that girl is responsible for our kidnapping?" Cathy asked incredulously.

"I don't know how responsible she is. But it sure as hell seems as if she's involved. Maybe she's a friend of Camillo, or some kind of sympathizer."

Sarge wheeled around in his chair, and for the first time he spoke: "Should we pick her up for interrogation?"

I looked at Sarge, and shook my head slowly. We both knew that he was speaking about an Intelligence interrogation, not the gentle kind we were doing with Cathy Morrison, but the swift and brutal kind where you can twist whatever you want to know out of a person. "No, it's still only suspicion. And I've already made some beautiful mistakes following my suspicions. Suppose we pick her up, and try to twist it out of her, and then find out she's not involved at all. We'd be guilty of kidnapping, the same as the NFA, and I don't want you liable for criminal charges, Sarge. But if I had something more definite to go on, I wouldn't hesitate to pick her up. If, say, we could connect her with that Timothy Bronson."

"Timothy Bronson?" asked Cathy.

"He is a late member of the NFA. Very late." I glanced at the clock. A little more than forty-eight hours until the second drop. Time was running out. "Maybe I can go back to the Dupont Circle area and do some snooping around. Cal Johnson said that the NFA was a group of white kids in the Dupont Circle area. We might find the answers there."

"Let me do it," Annie said.

"Not a chance, Annie. You're not going to get implicated."

"I won't get implicated. I'll be leaving in a few minutes anyway, and I can stop in the Dupont Circle area on my way home. I'll say I'm a social worker or something, and maybe I can get some of those kids to open up. I'm good with kids, Brian. Maybe I can even get to talk with this Judy Powell. You couldn't do that, Brian, because if she is involved she'll either clam up or run away."

"Annie's right," said Sarge.

"I'll be very careful, and I won't take any chances, Brian. Don't worry."

I glanced at that clock again. Damnit, the time problem. "All right, Annie. But, remember, no heroics. If you find yourself getting in deep, just walk away."

Annie departed almost immediately after that, and I later realized her sudden departure was purposeful, because if she had tarried another five minutes I think I would have refused to let her visit the Dupont Circle area to make inquiries about Judy Powell. I told Annie to call me as soon as she got home, but almost four hours passed before I heard from her, an agonizing time for me, during which I continually chided myself for letting her go on this mission.

At one point the doorbell rang, and it was a special messenger with a large manila envelope from Tom Walsh. He had gathered a lot of material on Congressman Jason Miller in the last few hours, and both Sarge and I poured over it. However, despite the amount of material Tom had collected there was nothing in it to indicate any possible connection with groups like the NFA. There was even a newspaper clipping with a large picture of Jason Miller, and I studied the photograph intently. A thin, rather tight-lipped man in his middle thirties. Moderately long hair, full moustache. The mod-professorial type.

Sarge studied the picture, too. "I find it hard to believe that a member of the House of Representatives is connected with a bunch of kids with Saturday Night Specials," he said.

"So do I, Sarge. But strange things have happened in this strange town."

The phone rang shortly after six o'clock, and I got it on the first ring. It was Annie, and I asked her immediately: "Are you all right?"

"Of course I'm all right. But listen carefully, because I have to speak quickly. Judy Powell pulled out this morning, moved suddenly, with no forwarding address. I did find out a little though, about Timothy Bronson, and I'll give you the details later. And I found a friend of Bronson who lives on P Street off the Circle. I went over to P Street, and someone pointed him out. He's in front of his apartment house right now, loading stuff into a Volkswagen bus, and it looks like he's pulling out, too."

It all figured, I thought. The NFA was getting decimated, and they were calling up their reserves and sympathizers. "How long before that guy drives away, do you think, Annie?"

"He's made a number of trips back and forth into the apartment house, carrying clothes and things, and I don't think it could be too much longer."

"Stay right there, Annie. I'm coming over, and I want you to point him out to me. But, whatever you do, don't follow him yourself. I'll meet you at the corner of Dupont Circle and P."

I slammed down the receiver, and ran over to the bar where Sarge had laid the Browning automatic rifle. "Annie's got a lead on one of the NFA people," I shouted to Sarge. I raced up the stairs toward my car, the Browning rifle in my hand.

Annie was standing on the corner when I pulled up, and I told her to get in the car. We drove slowly down P Street until she pointed out the small van to me. It was parked directly in front of the entrance to an apartment house, but there didn't appear to be anybody inside it at the moment. I parked about half a block away, and at that moment a big fellow came out of the apartment house, carrying a cardboard box in his arms. He was about six-four or six-five, perhaps about 250 pounds, and he was wearing a khaki bush jacket.

"That's him," Annie said.

I watched him place the box in the back of the van, and then walk around to the driver's seat. It was the final load, and I had arrived just in time. "Get out," I told Annie. "Go home."

"I'm not going home, I'm going over to your house and wait to see what happens."

"All right, but get out."

She got out of the car, and I immediately pulled away from the curb, following the departing Volkswagen van. It was an extremely easy tail. The van sat high in the traffic, making it quite visible, and I could lie far behind. Furthermore, that big guy who was driving didn't seem concerned about a tail and he wasn't taking any of the usual precautions. That's fine, I thought. If this fellow was actually an NFA type and he was being mustered, he would lead me right to their hideout. I glanced at the Browning rifle on the floor, fully loaded with magnum shells.

The van took me across town, then onto Canal Road. As I expected, he turned over Chain Bridge toward Virginia. The traffic was rather heavy on 123, and I was able to stay fairly close behind him without rousing suspicions. He turned on Route 193, heading toward the Great Falls area, and I was right with him.

We were getting into more rural territory, and I had to do some speed-ups and slow-downs to make my tail less obvious. However, the big fellow driving alone in the van seemed oblivious of me and he hardly varied his rate of speed at all. We passed the village of Great Falls, and then he turned off on a farm road. The road was paved for a while, but soon it turned to dirt and I was able to lie way back because I could see the clouds of dirt kicked up by the van. About eight miles from the main road he took a sharp turn, and drove up a narrow road toward a small farmhouse. The farmland was uncultivated, and there was a forrent sign near the road. It sure looked like an ideal spot for the NFA hideout.

I drove right past the entrance to the farm property, then stopped underneath some trees. Taking the Browning with me, I moved back in a crouch toward the entrance to the farm. I could see the van parked up there by the white frame building. It had been backed up against the door, and the big fellow had opened the rear doors, and was apparently carrying things out of the house and loading them into his van.

There was a row of shrubbery along the road, and it was almost dusk, and so I crept closer to the building. I had to flatten myself against the ground once, when the big guy came out of the house, but when he returned inside, I continued to move toward the house. I waited until the big boy had just deposited a large box in the van and returned inside. Then I made a rush toward the house, flattening myself against the wall. I snapped the safety off the Browning rifle.

Cautiously, I peered around the edge of one window, trying to get a look inside. My heart sank in disappointment. The big fellow was the only person inside, and he was just picking up what appeared to be the last of his load. But I was quite sure that this place had been the NFA headquarters until yesterday. There was large lettering in bright red paint on one wall, reading: *Freedom to the People!* And on another wall I could see a drawing of that NFA emblem, the clenched fist holding the streak of lightning. And I knew what had happened. After we had recovered Cathy Morrison last evening, they probably feared that she might be able to identify this place, and they quickly decided to move to a new hideout. And they left in a hurry. But when they started to call up their reserves today, they asked this fellow to stop by the old place and pick up the last of their stuff in his van.

That meant that he must know where the new hideout was.

I wanted that big boy, and I wanted him now. I wasn't going to take the risk of following him again, because the next time I might lose him. Furthermore, he might have been instructed to take much more diversionary driving tactics when he drove near the real hideout. No, I had him here, and I should take him. Alive. Because there was no way in the world he wouldn't tell me what I wanted to know. I could even get Sarge over here to help, if necessary.

But I didn't need those magnum bullets for this, because if I did have to shoot they could blow him wide open. I laid the rifle on the ground, and took my .38 from the holster. I waited until he came out the front door, a wooden box in his arms, and then I moved quickly behind him.

"Freeze!" I said. He froze, and I said: "Put that box down."

As he lowered the box to the ground, I moved around in front of him, holding the pistol pointed at him. I stood three or four feet away, so he couldn't make a lunge at me. He was starting to straighten up, his eyes trained on me. And then he made his move, an astonishingly adroit one for a man that size, and it caught me flatfooted.

It was a magnificent Kung Fu maneuver—the lightning kick, I believe they call it. At one moment he was starting to straighten up, and it seemed almost a mini-fraction of a second later that his leg was snaking out at me, the heel of his shoe hitting me savagely under the chin. I flew backwards, and he slammed into me before I hit the ground. I still had the pistol in my hand, but he fell right on top of me and the double impact caused the pistol to go flying away. I wrapped my arms around the big fellow, and twisted with all my strength. We rolled over. I was on top for a moment, and then he grappled with me and twisted me on my side. I got my arm free for one short, chopping punch, but it didn't seem to faze him. Then I brought my knee up, hitting him in the groin, and he pushed me away, looking for a little distance to deliver one of those Kung Fu hand-blows.

He chopped with a closed fist, but I rolled away, and managed to scramble to my knees. He was fast. He got up and made a rush at me. I was up on one knee as he charged into me, but I jerked up and drove my shoulder in under his breastbone. I was trying to use the force of his rush to pull him into the air and flip him over my shoulder, but he was too big and powerful and he wouldn't go. He staggered back a few steps, and started at me again, this time approaching me more cautiously, his arms at his side, his fists clenched. I later realized he didn't have a weapon, but he obviously thought those oriental fighting skills were quite adequate. I looked around wildly for my pistol, but I couldn't spot it.

He circled around me, and I extended my arms, palms open, karate style. He made a lunge, but then feinted and pulled back. I made a swipe at him, but missed. He moved around me in a circle, reducing the distance between us. I watched his feet carefully, figuring he would try another of those lightning kicks which had caught me before. I saw him shift his weight slightly toward his left foot, and I got set for the move with the right foot. Even though I was expecting it, the maneuver was unbelievably fast. I was trying to duck at the very moment he started the kick, but it still caught me high on the shoulder, spinning me. However, I allowed myself to go with the force of the spin, and I twirled around, slamming into him. His foot was still off the ground as he was finishing his kick, and I caught him off balance. He stumbled backward, and I moved quickly inside him, catching him in the midsection with a left and following it with a right to the side of the face. But he didn't go down; he threw an overhead punch which hit me high on the forehead. I hit him in midsection again, and I heard him grunt. Then he started punching wildly at me. The oriental skills had been abandoned, and we were in an old-fashioned slugfest.

One of his punches caught me on the cheekbone, and I staggered back a step or two. He moved in, hoping to flatten me, but I caught him coming in with a hard shot across the bridge of the nose. I heard it crunch under the impact of the blow, and blood started to spurt out. He gave a wild yell, and moved in again. This time he got me in the pit of the stomach, and I felt my knees buckle for a moment. God, he was strong. We traded punches, and I tried to aim for that injured nose. I finally hit it with an overhand right, and he yelped in pain. I followed that with a punishing blow to the stomach, and I thought I had him then. His face was smeared with blood, and his legs were wobbling, but he was still standing and trying to fight.

I stepped back, and then moved in, attempting to finish him off with a looping overhand blow. But he must have summoned some last ounce of energy and finally reached back in his mind to those oriental skills in which he had obviously been trained. He intercepted my righthand punch with both hands, clamping his two hands around my wrist, and he jerked me with enormous force, pulling me up in the air over his shoulder. I must have gone flying through the air for six or eight feet before I slammed to the ground.

I was dazed, and I groggily tried to get up and get myself set for the next rush. But I had trouble getting to my feet. And there was no rush. I looked up from my prone position on the ground and saw the big fellow running toward the van. He was staggering, running in an erratic path, but he was going to make it. He had left the engine running in the van, and in a few seconds he'd be able to climb in and speed away from here. My car was way out on the main road, and I'd never be able to catch him. Then I spotted it, a few feet away: the Browning rifle where I had left it on the ground. I crawled over to it, picked it up, and yelled at the fleeing man to stop.

He was about ten yards from the van, and when he heard my shout he looked back over his shoulder at me, but kept running. At that distance I could have riddled him with magnum bullets. But I wanted him alive. I flipped the rifle to single-shot action, and from my sitting position I fired once, well behind him to make him stop. But he kept going. I fired again, but he didn't stop.

He was starting to climb into the cab of the van when I brought the rifle to eye level, trying to get him squarely in the scope. I wanted to hit him in the legs, so I could bring him down without killing him. But at the very moment I squeezed the trigger, he slipped getting into the cab and dropped back down to the ground a few feet. That slip cost him his life. My bullet was aimed at his leg, but when he suddenly slipped down the bullet struck him instead in the side, almost a lethal bullet wound with a magnum shell.

Nevertheless he still somehow managed to pull himself up into the cab, and as I got to my feet the van was pulling away, starting to roll down the hill toward the road. I don't think that the big fellow ever had control of the van. Maybe he keeled over dead after he had released the brake. At any rate, the van careened wildly down the road for only a few yards before it went off the road and headed toward a steep embankment. I saw it go over the embankment, and then roll with frightening speed toward a large rock formation. The van hit the rock formation head-on, and there was a loud crash of metal striking rock. It was perfectly still in that rural setting for about ten seconds, and then the explosion occurred and giant flames began to leap out of the van, engulfing it.

I was bruised and sore from the pounding that big fellow had given me, and I winced in pain as I bent over to pick up my .38 when I finally located it. On the walk back to my car, I looked over at the still-burning Volkswagen van. I deeply regretted that I had killed that big fellow, because he would have been able to lead me to the new NFA hideout. Furthermore, he had fought a good, honest fight, and now he'd never be able to use those oriental fighting skills again.

CHAPTER FIFTEEN

It took me well over an hour to drive home in my battered condition, and when I finally put the key in my front door there was Annie to greet me. She gasped when she saw my face. "What happened, Brian?"

"I had a fight with that big fellow in the van." I paused. "But he got away."

Sarge had come up the stairs behind Annie, and he was standing there, his pistol drawn. I handed him the Browning rifle wordlessly. I glanced in a hallway mirror and saw that my upper lip was beginning to puff up and there was an ugly red welt on my forehead. I remembered the overhand blow which had done that.

"Let me get some cold compresses for your face," Annie said.

"No, what I need is a drink."

We went down to the recreation room, and Annie fixed the drink of scotch for me herself, even remembering to add the piece of lime. She told me that Cathy Morrison had gone to bed, and Sarge reported that Rankin had received no further telephone communications from the NFA yet. I knew that Annie should be getting home to her family, but before she departed I wanted to hear how she had managed to locate the big fellow in the Volkswagen van.

"It was a bit of luck," she said. "I was trying to locate that Judy Powell, but the resident manager of the building told me she had suddenly checked out that morning."

"Had she given any notice that she was moving?"

"None at all. In fact, her rent was paid until the end of the month, but she just took off."

"Yeah, it sure sounds as if that girl is off and running with the NFA. And she did a nice con job on me."

"Then I just walked around the Dupont Circle area, talking to kids. I told them I was a social worker, and they were pretty friendly. I tried to get a lead on Judy Powell, but I didn't meet anybody who knew her. I was talking to this girl, a bright kid in her early twenties, when I got lucky. She didn't know Judy Powell, but she knew Timothy Bronson. She hadn't seen him for quite some time, but she had been on a couple of dates with him last year. According to her, he was a funny kind of person: introverted, angry, always talking about overthrowing the system. She didn't know where he was now, but she remembered that he had a close friend, a big fellow who lived on P Street. That was the person I pointed out to you loading the van. His name is Joseph Riordan."

"Joseph Riordan," I repeated, thinking of the charred corpse in the smoldering van out in Great Falls. "Did this girl give you any details about Timothy Bronson?"

"Not much. I don't think she really cared for him. He comes from Oklahoma, and he was in the Army for a while. He arrived in Washington a little over a year ago. Last January, to be exact. She remembered that because Bronson had just dropped out of the University of Miami after being there for only a few semesters."

"Did this girl ever hear Bronson talking about the NFA?"

"Not explicitly, but she did recall that he used to talk about the necessity of mobilizing the people in some type of citizen's army to overthrow the system."

"Yeah," I said wearily, leaning back in my chair. I plucked a piece of ice from my drink and pressed it against the welt on my forehead.

We talked for a few more minutes, but Annie didn't really have anything significant to add to what she had already told me. Finally I told her to go home, and after she had departed Sarge spoke for the first time. He was still holding the Browning rifle in his hand, and he said: "That fellow you fought really didn't get away, did he?"

"No, Sarge, I killed him."

"I thought so. This weapon has been fired, and I didn't think you'd miss."

"I didn't mean to kill him, but he slipped down just as I was firing and the bullet rose on him. A magnum bullet."

Sarge pulled off the magazine to see how many bullets had been fired, and he said: "Yeah, a magnum will usually do it."

I went over to the bar to replenish my drink, and then as Sarge began adding some more shells to the Browning's magazine, I started to pace the floor. I must have walked back and forth three or four times, a pensive frown on my forehead, before Sarge asked me what was the matter.

"I don't quite know. It's something Annie just said, something which might be important, but I can't put my finger on it." I stopped pacing suddenly, and snapped my fingers. "Of course—that's it. Where'd I put those papers Walsh sent me about Jason Miller?"

Sarge pointed to the end of the bar, and I picked them up and quickly rifled through them. "Yes, here it is. Listen to this. It's part of Miller's bio. A year ago last fall he taught a semester in political science at the University of Miami."

"So?"

"So, that's where Annie said that Timothy Bronson attended school for a while, and he was there the same time that Jason Miller was lecturing."

"It could be a coincidence, of course."

"Sure it could be. A sheer coincidence on a large campus. But, damnit, Sarge, these sheer coincidences are beginning to pile up."

"Can we check it out?"

"We could if we had time. Look at what we've got so far. We know definitely that Bronson was an NFA member, and we know definitely that he was at the University of Miami eighteen months ago, and we know definitely that Miller was also on campus at that time for a single semester. Now, if we could only tie Miller and Bronson together in Miami, we could really pin Miller's tail to the wall."

"Maybe we should take this Congressman Miller, Captain," suggested Sarge quietly.

"No, we can't do that. If we make a move against a U.S. congressman we really should have the goods on him, otherwise if we're wrong the whole thing could come crashing down on our heads and we'll have exposed the kidnapping of Ellen Rankin. I've got this gut feeling about Jason Miller, but it's only based on coincidence and suspicion. I need some hard facts."

I lit a cigarette, and began to pace the floor again. "Miami is the place, Sarge. I just feel it. Maybe it's the place where the whole damned NFA thing got started. Damn. If we only had more time we might be able to expose the whole NFA from top to bottom." I glanced at the clock: it was almost ten o'clock. That was less than forty-eight hours until the second drop, but it still left me some little time in which to maneuver. Tomorrow was Thursday, and I had that whole day, and Dan McFarland had promised me he wouldn't deliver the second batch of laundered ransom money to

Rankin until late Friday afternoon. It was only a two-hour flight to Miami, and I could zip down there in the morning and be back by tomorrow night.

I reached over and grabbed the phone, and Sarge listened while I talked to a clerk at Eastern Airlines, making reservations on an early-morning flight to Miami and a return reservation tomorrow night.

"What do you expect to find in Miami?" Sarge asked.

"I don't know. But it's worth a try. I'll only have a few hours, but if I ask enough questions I might get lucky. Sarge, we want to get Ellen Rankin released. That's the first thing. But if Jason Miller's involved in this, we want him, too. I don't think he's running around with a cheap Saturday Night Special, shouting 'Freedom to the People,' but I sure as hell think he's somehow involved. Maybe he's their guru, or their theoretician, or something."

"And you think you can tie that together in a few hours in Miami?" he asked skeptically.

"I know, you can't do much in a few hours, but a few hours is all we've got. Sarge, I feel this is a hot lead—perhaps the hottest I've had in this whole damn affair—and if I can really pin it down then we'll have a crystal clear picture of the NFA. That's a tremendous advantage for us to have before the second ransom drop. And there's one other thing, too."

"What's that?"

"If we fail, Sarge, and if the NFA wipes us out first, then at least we can leave all this data for someone else to follow up after us."

"We won't fail," he said resolutely.

"Listen, Sarge, tomorrow is Thursday, and nothing's going to happen all day, I'm sure. Friday is going to be our action day. You can hold the fort here by yourself tomorrow, can't you?"

He touched the butt of his Browning .380 pistol. "Sure, Captain—"

"Brian," I said, correcting him.

"Brian. Sure, no problem here. I've got an old buddy coming by tomorrow, and he's going to bring some of that equipment you asked for."

"Fine. You get things ready for the drop, and I'll see if I can't find out how deeply Congressman Jason Miller is involved with that goddamn NFA."

I finished my drink, and then went upstairs, while Sarge remained in the recreation room, saying he was going to sleep there on a rollaway bed near the radio receiver in case Rankin received any interesting calls during the night. I turned out the lights as I went, and when I got to the second floor I saw a figure standing on the small balcony which overlooks the pool. I stopped instantly, flattening myself against the wall, but then I saw it was Cathy Morrison. She was staring out across the pool at a blooming Cherry Blossom tree, and I noticed she was wearing one of my bathrobes which Annie had evidently loaned her.

"Can't sleep?" I asked her.

She apparently hadn't heard me coming up the stairs, and my voice startled her. "Oh," she exclaimed as she turned quickly. "I was asleep, but I woke up. I guess I'm just worried about Ellen."

"Let me do the worrying."

"I feel so helpless, though. I wish there were something I could do."

"The best thing you can do, Cathy, is just lie low here until this is all over."

"That doesn't seem fair, either. I'm just taking up space in your house."

"We've got lots of space here."

For the first time she noticed my bruises, and she said: "Your face."

"It's the result of what they call on the police blotters an altercation."

"Something to do with the kidnapping?"

"Yeah," I answered evasively.

"Are you any closer to getting Ellen back?"

"The ransom date is the day after tomorrow."

She bit her lip. "You know, Brian, the more I think about it, the more I feel that those crazy NFA kids aren't ever going to release Ellen. They seemed so determined to convert her. I don't think they'll give her up, even if Senator Rankin does pay the ransom."

"Maybe, Cathy. But I still think we have to let Rankin pay the ransom money and see if they release his daughter. And then if they don't …" I allowed my voice to trail off.

"What then?" she asked.

"I don't know. We'll have to try some other way to rescue her."

"That girl who lives down the corridor, Judy Powell, did you find out anything more about her?"

"She's NFA connected, and she probably put the kidnappers right on your trail."

I saw her give a slight shudder. "Oh, Brian, it's all so nasty." She clutched the bathrobe tightly around her throat, as if she were experiencing sudden cold tremors. I stepped closer to her and took her into my arms. She came toward me quickly and willingly, allowing me to hold her tightly. We stood like that for perhaps two full minutes, neither of us saying anything. I hadn't experienced any previous romantic feeling for this girl who had lived in my home for the last day or so, but now a sense of overpowering tenderness was coming over me. And it was quickly followed by a fierce need. I pulled her even more closely toward me, and kissed her softly on the lips. She responded, opening her lips, and I inserted my tongue. She was clinging tightly to me now, and we swayed gently together on that small balcony overlooking the pool.

Wordlessly, we broke apart, and with my arm around her I led her into the guest room she was using. She slipped off her bathrobe, and I saw she was only wearing a bra and bikini panties underneath. The jeans she had been wearing gave her a slim boyish figure, but now I could see that she was full and well-rounded. She sat on the edge of the bed, while I kicked off my trousers, and then I sat down beside her, pulling her back on the bed. I slipped off her panties and unfastened the bra, and we embraced, two warm, nude bodies pressed up against each other.

I stroked her breasts gently, and then let my hand glide down her body until I found the warm and now moist spot between her legs. I continued to stroke her, and her breath started to come in a staccato of short gasps. I was fully erected when I rolled over on her, entering her easily and swiftly. We pulsated together, slowly and rhythmically at first, and then more rapidly, and finally furiously toward the crescendo. She gave a low moan as we finished our climax together.

We lay together, embracing, still not saying anything for almost a full five minutes. I didn't want to think about the reasons for this sudden unplanned act. Perhaps in the aftermath of her own kidnapping she had turned to me unthinkingly for comfort. And perhaps I had turned to her for desperate comfort on this night when I was forced to kill a man and when I still faced the uncertainties of confronting that group of terrorists again. At any rate, we had comforted each other.

Finally, I offered her a cigarette, and while I lit it for her she said: "I feel better. Not so scared anymore."

YOUR DAUGHTER WILL DIE!

"That's good."

"Don't you ever get scared, Brian?"

"Sometimes. But I'm not scared now."

"But you are scared about getting Ellen back, aren't you?"

I looked into her eyes which were a misty blue, and now open and wide and honestly inquiring. "Yes, Cathy," I admitted. "I'm scared about that. Scared as hell."

My flight the following morning arrived at Miami shortly after ten o'clock. I rented a car at the airport and drove out into a blazing bright sun on this warm April day in southern Florida. I knew this area quite well and I turned south from the airport on Forty-second Avenue, heading toward Coral Gables and the University of Miami.

If I had a number of days at my disposal and the assistance of some trained investigators, I would have been able to research Jason Miller's semester at the University thoroughly and accurately. And that's the way you have to do it, because contrary to the popular literature, a fruitful investigation is slow, plodding, often dull work, and not that sudden flash of intuition by fictional detectives. But all I could allow myself was a few hours in the Florida sun, and all I could hope for was one or two scraps of hard information, something at least which would help me tie Miller definitely to the NFA.

Even at that, it appeared during my first few hours that I wasn't going to come up with anything at all. When I drove to the campus at Coral Gables I found it strangely quiet, and I soon discovered that there was a spring vacation this week and therefore there were very few people around. Nevertheless, I plugged away at it, asking questions of anyone I could find, trying to locate someone who knew either Jason Miller or Timothy

Bronson during the fall semester eighteen months ago. But I struck out completely.

I visited the office of the chairman of the Department of Political Science, but his secretary told me that he was away for the week, giving a series of lectures in the Far West. Finally, in the early afternoon I was able to locate a young professor in that department who was returning to his office from the library, a pile of books in his arms.

"Professor Jordan?" I asked him, as he came along the corridor toward his office.

He squinted at me through thick glasses. "Well, not really Professor. I'm just an instructor. What can I do for you?"

"I'm a newspaper reporter," I said, and I flipped open my wallet, showing him some bogus press credentials which Steve Harrison at the *Post* had fixed up for me some time ago. "I'm doing a story on Congressman Jason Miller, and we'd like some background about his academic career here at the University."

"I don't think I can help you. I wasn't here then. And, anyway, I don't think it was much of a career. As I understand it, he was only a visiting lecturer for one semester." The books were starting to slip from his arms, and I reached over to help him. Finally one fell to the floor, and I picked it up. "Thanks," he said, and when he pushed open the door to his office I followed him in.

"Did you ever hear anything about his course?" I asked, as he deposited his books on an unbelievably cluttered desk in the small office.

"Let's see, I believe he taught a course in the politics of South American revolution—Che Guevera, Camillo Torres, that sort of thing."

The Camillo in Torres' name struck an immediate responsive chord in my mind, but that again could be one of those damned coincidences which had plagued me throughout this whole thing.

"Was the course well attended?"

"I don't think so. Jason Miller wasn't a congressman then, and I don't think anybody ever had any idea he planned to run for Congress, and it was just one of those small courses we offer periodically in Poly-sci. Maybe there might have been twenty or twenty-five students. But, as I say, I wasn't here then, and you'd have to talk to someone who was."

"That's what I'm interested in. I'd like to talk to some of the students who took his course. For background stuff, you know. We'd like our readers to hear about the students' reaction to Miller in the classroom. Do you know any of the students who might have taken that course?"

"Let me see." He took off his glasses and rubbed his eyes. "Yes, yes, I think I do. I have a student in one of my courses who mentioned it to me some time ago. The student's name is Daniel Potter."

"Do you know where I could locate him?"

"The registrar would probably have his address. No, wait a minute, I might have it here. I know he's not living on campus, and he sent me some assignments a while ago with his home address on it." I watched impatiently while the professor rummaged through a desk drawer, pulling out old envelopes, looking at them for what seemed an interminable time, before he finally found the one he wanted. He gave me the address of a Dan Potter on Douglas Road, just off South Dixie Highway, and I thanked him, getting to my feet immediately.

I thought that the professor was going to start poking his nose immediately into his books, but as I reached the door he said: "There's something that always intrigued me about Jason Miller, even though I never met him."

"What's that?" I asked.

"The way a man can go from the academic life to a life of public service in the Congress."

"Don't even flirt with the idea, Professor. It's much safer in the academic life."

I rode over to Douglas Road in my rented car, the air conditioning purring softly on this day which must now be in the upper 80's. The address I had been given was a small apartment house, and I found the name of Daniel Potter listed over one of the mailboxes, along with three other names for the same apartment, one other male and two female. My knock on the door was answered by a pert young girl dressed in a pair of brief shorts and a halter. When I asked her for Dan Potter, she told me he wasn't there.

"Do you know where I could find him? I have to see him today."

"He's at the beach. Crandon Park."

"That's a big beach."

"If you really have to see him right now, I think you can locate him out there. Dan's on the football team, and he and a number of other fellows are doing some informal spring practice and they work out at the very south end of the beach. You can't miss Dan. He's blond, and a big fellow, about your size."

"Thanks."

"Pleasure," she said, imitating a British accent, and she closed the door.

I crossed over Biscayne Bay on Rickenbacker Causeway, that long bridge which is the only link from the mainland to Key Biscayne, the island playground of winter tourists and the sunny retreat of a former president. Out on the Key I drove along Crandon Boulevard until I came to the Park and turned into the huge parking area. I parked as far south as I could, and then I walked out onto the long stretch of lovely public beach. The beach was fairly crowded in the middle of the afternoon of this warm day, and I felt quite ridiculous as I crunched through the sand in my trousers and jacket, passing outstretched bodies which glistened with oils and suntan lotions.

Near the end of the beach I spotted a group of young men in bathing suits who were lining up to practice football formations. I watched them for a minute while a quarterback called signals and then they broke from the formation, sprinting a few yards straight ahead. They certainly didn't appear to be contenders for a national championship. I walked over to one of the young men who was walking slowly back to a new huddle, and asked him if Dan Potter was here. He was, but he wasn't practicing the formations at the moment. He was pointed out to me as the blond young man who was tossing a frisbee back and forth with another young man at the edge of the water.

He had just caught the frisbee in one hand as I approached him, giving it a quick backhand toss toward his partner. He barely looked at me while I gave him the same routine about doing a newspaper story, and when I showed him my bogus credentials he ignored them completely. He caught the frisbee again, and gave it another flip back.

"So, Jason Miller's gone to Congress," he said. "That shows the bankruptcy of our political system."

"What's wrong with Miller?"

He turned to face me, and he signalled with his hand for his partner to hold the frisbee for a while. "Oh, nothing really, I guess. That's the cynicism you develop in Poly-sci. Miller is as good or as bad as any of them." He smiled, and shrugged his shoulders slightly, a big, blond-haired, healthy kid.

"You were in his course eighteen months ago."

"It was worth two credits to me."

"Is that all it was? Wasn't the course itself any good?"

"It was all right. Political revolution in South America, and you could learn as much from three hours with one good book. But we had a lot of trouble in that course. And I was glad when the damned thing ended."

"Trouble?"

"Oh, not with Miller. He was okay, and he graded easily. But we had some students who were trying to disrupt the thing. They wanted to carry on a private dialogue with Miller in the class-room about how to translate the theories of revolution into the actual practicalities of revolution."

"One of those students wouldn't have been named Timothy Bronson, would he?"

"Bronson," he repeated slowly. "Yeah, that sounds like one of them. A short kid, wasn't he, kind of pugnacious?"

"That's him," I said. I tried to recall the face of the guy I had killed out beyond Potomac, but I couldn't get it clearly.

"Where'd you get that name? That was a long time ago."

"I've been doing some research with former students of the Congressman. For my story, you know. Did those students ever quiet down in class?"

"Not really, but Miller worked out a compromise. He set up a special seminar at his home in the evening for them. There were about six of them, if I remember, and they did all their big talking there. In fact, most of them eventually dropped out of the regular course, and stayed with that pri-vate seminar."

"How often did the seminar meet?"

"I don't know too much about it, but I think it was pretty fre-quent. Two or three times a week."

"Can you remember any other names of people in that seminar?"

"Oh, my, that was a long time ago. Well, there was one chap, he seemed to be the most outspoken one, the leader, if you will. What was his name? Something odd. Oh, yeah, Paul Deserks."

I was going to play a hunch. "I think I know Deserks," I said. "Reddish hair, thinning at the top. Small eyes, hornrimmed glasses. He wears a beard now." I was describing the guy who was shooting the M-14 at me from the front seat of the NFA car.

"That's him. Paul Deserks."

"He was the leader of the group, you say?"

"Maybe that's being too unfair. He was the most outspoken, I'd say, about all that revolutionary business. You know a lot of that course was about Camillo Torres, and we had a joke about this Deserks chap."

"A joke."

"We used to call him Camillo. You know, for Camillo Torres."

"Yeah, I know."

At that moment the frisbee came sailing through the air, and this time I caught it, flipping it back. "Nice heave," he said to me. "You're not really a newspaperman, are you?"

"No."

"Cop?"

"No."

"Well, I hope you find whatever you're looking for."

"I think I have."

"I've got to line up for some football formations now."

"One last question. From what you say, I don't think you liked Jason Miller very much, did you?"

"Oh, I don't think I ever thought of him in those terms at all. I will say this, though. Jason Miller was at the same time one of the smartest men I ever knew and one of the dumbest I ever knew. Do you know what I mean?"

"Yeah, I know what you mean."

A few hours later the giant wide-body jet in which I was flying back to Washington was beginning its descent over Virginia toward National Airport. When the no-smoking sign flashed on, I snuffed out my cigarette in the arm ashtray. My short trip, I thought, had been incredibly successful. I had Camillo's name, and I had now tied Jason Miller, that poor son of a bitch, quite firmly to the NFA.

As the plane descended low over the countryside of northern Virginia, I looked out the window. Someplace down there the NFA was holding Ellen Rankin, trying relentlessly to convert her. She couldn't hear me, of course, but softly I spoke to her from that altitude—hold on, baby, we're getting closer.

CHAPTER SIXTEEN

I t was almost ten o'clock in the evening when I finally retrieved my car from the parking lot at National Airport and drove home to Arlington. The lights in the upstairs section of my house were all extinguished, but the downstairs section was fully illuminated. Sarge's car, a green Dodge, was parked in the carport, and so I parked my Olds in front of the house. I had just inserted the key in the front door and I was in the process of swinging it open, when I spotted the glint of a pistol pointing at me from behind the drapes in the foyer.

I went for the pistol in my shoulder holster instantly, but before I could get it Sarge stepped out and lowered his pistol. "You never would have gotten that pistol out," he said. "I had you in dead aim range."

"You're right on duty, aren't you, Sarge?"

"I heard somebody fumbling with that lock, and I bounced right up here. You can't be too careful."

"Everything okay here?"

"All quiet on this front. Miss Morrison has gone to bed. And we had a quiet day. Rankin didn't get any further communications from the kidnappers, but I did monitor one call from McFarland who called him to tell him that he would have the money ready by five o'clock tomorrow afternoon. And, as you predicted, the Arlington police were around, making a door to-door canvass to see if anybody knew anything about those two NFA people you wasted yesterday. How'd you make out in Miami?"

"I think I've got the goods on Jason Miller. Come on downstairs, and I'll tell you about it."

We went down to the rec room, and while I sipped a scotch and Sarge drank a beer, I proceeded to tell him about my interviews in Miami earlier today. His eyes narrowed as I spoke, and I noticed a tightening around his mouth. I don't think he ever really believed that a U. S. congressman could be mixed up in something as brutal as this, but now he had to face the facts.

"Do we take Miller?" he asked grimly when I had finished.

"I've been thinking about that all during the flight home, and I think that the best plan is to leave him alone, at least until after the second drop."

"Why?"

"Let's review what we know, and let's separate fact from speculation. We know that Miller organized a special seminar group in Miami eighteen months ago to study the practical aspects of revolution. We know that Timothy Bronson, an NFA member, was part of that group. And we know that one Paul Deserks, who evidently now goes by the name of General Camillo and is the leader of the NFA, was also a member of that study group. There's no doubt in my mind that Miller's group was the origin of the NFA, and Miller himself was obviously its ideologue, if not its actual founder. Now, eighteen months later the NFA is here in the D.C. area, and they kidnap Ellen Rankin as the first step in their wild attempt to overthrow the country or something. We don't know what path this group took to come to Washington. Maybe Miller brought them here, or maybe they just followed Miller here. But we do know that Miller is still involved with the group. The fact that Miller requested my security file right after I became active in the kidnapping is, in the light of what we now know, something which simply just can't be ascribed to coincidence."

"So why don't we just take Miller? And interrogate him about the whereabouts of the NFA hideout?" Sarge laid particular stress on the word "interrogate."

"That's just it, Sarge. We're trying to separate fact from speculation. And we don't definitely know if Miller is aware of the location of the hideout."

"But you just said—"

"I just said that Miller was involved with the beginnings of the NFA and he's involved with them now. But I still find it difficult to believe that Miller would have sanctioned such a stupid and ultimately fruitless thing as a kidnapping. There's always the chance that the NFA hasn't told Miller about the kidnapping or the place where they're holding Ellen Rankin."

"It's a pretty slim chance, I think," Sarge said gruffly.

"I know. But I don't think we should even take slim chances when Ellen Rankin's life is involved. You see, if we jump Miller, and it turns out that he doesn't know where the Rankin girl is being held, then we could really jeopardize her life. Suppose the NFA learns that we've taken their guru, or suppose they're watching his house, or even guarding him. Then if we can't find out from Miller where the Rankin girl is being held, they could panic and flee, or they could kill Ellen Rankin in retaliation. Hell, if I were absolutely sure Miller knew the NFA hideout, the new one, I wouldn't hesitate a minute jumping him. But with Ellen Rankin's life at stake, I don't think we should take that chance. Unless something else turns up in the meantime, I think we should let the drop go through first. We owe that to Senator Rankin." I glanced at the wall clock, and noticed it was a few minutes after midnight. "This is the drop day now. Another twenty hours until the NFA contacts Rankin again."

"You mean we're just going to let Miller go scot free?"

"Of course not. We're starting to get some cards dealt our way now, and Miller is one of our aces in the hole. If the Rankin girl is returned tomorrow, then we can go right to the FBI and tell them what we know about Miller. With their resources they can get the names of every student who was in that seminar group in Miami eighteen months ago, and then they can track them down, one by one, until they've got the whole NFA."

"And if they don't return the girl?"

"Then we'll go right at Miller. We'll have nothing to lose then."

"You said that Miller was *one* of your aces?"

"Yes, we've got one more. Timothy Bronson."

"How's that?"

"We are the only ones who know the whereabouts of Timothy Bronson—out in that fresh grave I dug in the woods near Potomac. For all we know, the NFA may still be thinking that he's fled the group and he might turn them over to the police. Sarge, I don't know how we're going to use it, but that card may well turn out to be the ace of trumps."

"I still think we should take Miller."

"We will—eventually. Let's try to get Ellen Rankin back first."

I told Sarge to get some sleep because this could be an extremely big day. When I went upstairs the corridor was darkened, but when I passed Cathy Morrison's door it suddenly opened. Contrary to what Sarge thought, she wasn't asleep. She was awake, and waiting for me. I entered her room, and closed the door softly behind me.

Annie arrived about nine-thirty that morning, and I spent the greater part of the morning dictating to her about the Rankin affair. I started at the very beginning, and reviewed the whole case, and then I carefully outlined all the facts I had discovered, giving the names of Jason Miller and Paul Deserks and Timothy Bronson. There were a lot of gaps in the story, I realized, but I had related a pretty fair outline of the NFA, enough for any competent law enforcement officer to follow up in case anything went wrong at the drop tonight.

There is a small portable typewriter in my den on the second floor, and Annie went right to work on it, transcribing my dictation. She finished in the early afternoon, and she brought the sheaf of papers plus one carbon down to the rec room where Sarge and I were talking. Across the top of the master copy I wrote Craig Wright's name and his office number at the Security Division of Justice.

"Annie, I want you to take this copy home with you. I'll call you in the morning, but if for any reason you don't hear from me or Sarge by nine tomorrow morning, then take this to Craig Wright's office. It's self-explanatory, and he'll know what to do next."

"Oh, Brian," she said, an expression of terror coming over her face.

"It's just a little insurance," I said. "If I don't get Jason Miller, then somebody else will."

Annie wanted to remain at my place so she could see what happened during the second drop tonight, but I told her to go home. "That's part of our insurance plan," I said. "I want you and those papers in some other location entirely."

Reluctantly, Annie departed, and Sarge and I got to work, planning for the evening. The day was exceptionally warm, and I had suggested to Cathy Morrison that she take a swim. And, now, as Sarge and I talked at a small table in the recreation room, I could see her in the pool through the sliding glass doors, making a graceful dive off the board.

"Let's get out the equipment your buddy brought, Sarge," I said.

Sarge placed a small box on the table, and flipped open the cover. Inside were four small black spheroids, each about the size of a gold ball. He picked one of them up and held it out toward me. "Harmless-looking things, aren't they?" he said. "Small, compact, but they pack a hell of a wallop. And they're a lot better than those old pineapple grenades we used to use. They developed this type of hand grenade in Nam. It's actually a fragmentation grenade, and there are about 500 pieces of tiny metal in there. We've got this grenade set for early explosion, about five seconds after you release."

"Do you work it the same way as the old hand grenades?"

"Same way. You put your finger over the spoon here, and then you release the pin. Everything's okay as long as you keep your finger on that spoon, but when you take your finger off you'd better heave it, because you only have five seconds. And if you're not going to throw it very far, I'd hit the deck, because it not only explodes but it throws those metal fragments in all directions."

"Fine, Sarge. And what about carrying them?"

"You can carry them in a hip pouch, of course, but we thought you'd like to carry them concealed, and so we fixed this up."

He showed me a type of grenade holster he and his old Army buddy had devised. There were two small pouches which fitted under each armpit, and they were held in place by leather thongs which looped over the shoulders and then ran across the back in much the same manner as the traditional shoulder holster for pistols. "That might be a bit snug under the armpits," Sarge said, "but it's good concealment. And you can still wear your pistol holster with it."

He put one grenade in each pouch, and I tried the whole contraption on for size. It wasn't very comfortable, but it worked.

I was carrying what was equivalent to a golf ball under each armpit, and I couldn't press my arms firmly against my sides. However, comfort was not going to be my concern when I met the NFA later tonight. I took off the grenade holster, and laid it on the table. Sarge looked at it admiringly, and he said: "I wish you'd let me go with you. Two guns are better than one."

"No, Sarge, I have plenty of firepower this time. I'll take those grenades, and your Browning rifle, and my own .38."

"You can't operate them all at once."

"I don't plan to. No, if we're going to stalk down the NFA I think it's better if we keep separated, and try and come at them from different angles. Besides, I need you here to work the communications."

I could see that Sarge didn't like being away from the front line of action, but he didn't argue it any further with me. "Let's go through it then," he said simply.

"Okay, here's the plan for the evening. In a short while Eddie Perkins is coming out to install a phone in my car. And I'm also having him install a phone in your car, in case we need it later. About seven o'clock I'm going to drive out to the Kenwood area near Rankin's house, and I'll call you from my car. We'll keep an open line, and I'll be able to hear the phone call from the NFA as you monitor on the audio receiver here. Then when Rankin takes off for the drop I'll trail him with those electronic devices we used last time. That omni-directional beam is still being sent out from Rankin's car, and I can follow that. And I'm sure he'll undoubtedly use the same briefcase, and I've got a tracker in there."

"Are you going to try to break up the drop?"

"No, not at all. I'm going to lie way back, and give Rankin the chance to deliver the ransom money. Then when my tracking devices show that Rankin's car and the briefcase have split and are going in different directions, I'm going to follow the briefcase to wherever it leads me."

"And then what?"

"We've got to play it by ear. When I call you I'm going to keep an open line to you, so that I'll be talking to you all the time and you'll know exactly what I'm doing. You'll also be monitoring Rankin's phone. If it appears that Ellen Rankin is really going to be released, I'll lie back until we're sure she's safe. And then we can move in on them."

"And if she's not released?"

"Then I'll be following that tracker in the briefcase, and I'll move right in on them."

"That's when you might need help."

I smiled. "Okay, Sarge, if it comes to that, we'll break off the communications part of the operation, and you can join me."

I heard a loud splash, and looked out toward the pool. Cathy Morrison had just taken another dive, and I watched her as she swam across the pool and then hoisted herself over the edge nearest me. She pulled back her hair, squeezing the water out of it, and I could see the firm roundness of her uplifted breasts. Almost immediately I could begin to feel the first faint stirrings of desire for her. But I shook my head impatiently. It was hardly the time to let my mind run in that direction. I picked up one of the fragmentation grenades, and turned it over in my hand. Sarge had said that there were 500 metal fragments in there, waiting to be shot out when the pin was released.

Eddie Perkins arrived a short while later, and he went right to work, outfitting our two cars with mobile telephones. It took him about an hour, and when he returned to the recreation room he said: "All set, Mr. Petersen. You can talk from car to car with them two phones, and of course I've got you hooked into the public phone system."

"Thanks a lot, Eddie," I said.

"And them calls won't cost you a nickel. I've got a way of tapping into the phone system without Ma Bell even knowing it."

"The less Ma Bell knows, the better."

Later in the afternoon we heard the phone ring on the monitor to Rankin's phone, and Sarge and I both huddled over the set as we listened. It was Dan McFarland calling:

McFarland: I've got that item you wanted cleansed, Senator. And I've got two Pinkerton guards here, and they're going to bring it right out to your house. It should be there in a half-hour.

Rankin: I appreciate that, Mr. McFarland. I hope I can express my gratitude some day.

McFarland: Maybe you can, Senator, maybe you can.

I chuckled softly at that. McFarland sure as hell would think of some way that Senator Lester Rankin could express his gratitude. The phone conversation was a brief one, and after I heard the phone click off I started to make preparations to leave for the Kenwood area. We were getting close to the second drop.

Cathy had come in from the pool, and she went upstairs to take a shower. I changed into an old pair of jeans, and then I pulled on a pair of black leather boots, stuffing the jeans into them. I wore an open-necked sports shirt but I left it unbuttoned when I went downstairs. I slipped it off while Sarge helped me put on the grenade holster. After he had tightened it securely, I put on the shirt again, leaving the top three buttons open so that I could get to those two grenades in a hurry. I then strapped on the shoulder holster with the .38 over my shirt, and finally I slipped into a lightweight nylon golf jacket.

Then I picked up the Browning rifle and the box with the other two grenades. My God, I was armed.

It was now shortly after six o'clock, and it was time to leave. Sarge and I went over our plan once again, and he was just starting to wish me good luck when we heard Rankin's phone ring on the monitor. I didn't pay much attention to it until I heard that unmistakable voice. It was Camillo. Sarge and I both dashed over to the monitor and listened:

Camillo: Do you have the money, Rankin?

Rankin: Yes, I have it all. It's right here. And I'll bring it anyplace you want.

Camillo: There's been a change in plan. That's why we're calling you early.

Rankin: You promised you'd release my daughter.

Camillo: We don't want a double cross like last time, so we decided to change things this time.

Rankin: I'll do anything you want.

Camillo: Here's what we want. We want that bastard Petersen to deliver the money.

(Sarge and I exchanged glances, because we both understood what that meant—they were going to try to set me up in an ambush.)

Rankin: I don't know if I can get Mr. Petersen to do that.

Camillo: He was pretty anxious to be there last time. And this time we want to keep him in plain view and make sure he isn't following you.

Rankin: I don't know …

Camillo: This is a nonnegotiable demand. You get ahold of Petersen, and you have him deliver the money. That's final. You have until eight o'clock, and that's all. There's a phone booth where I want that Petersen to be at exactly eight o'clock tonight with the money, and he'll get further instructions from there. Now listen carefully, Rankin. Tell him to drive out Route 50 in Virginia, and as soon as he passes through the city limits of Fairfax to stop at the first Gulf station on the right. There's a public phone booth on the curb there, and have Petersen in it. Got that?

Rankin: Yes, but …

Camillo: Eight o'clock, and Petersen. No one else.

The phone clicked off and Sarge slammed his fist against the table. "Goddamnit, they're trying to set you up in a trap," he said furiously.

"Of course they are."

"You're not going, are you?"

"Sure I am. They want to isolate me alone someplace of their choosing, take the money from me, and then fulfill their threat of killing me. But I'm not going to walk into that trap blindly. I'll be ready for it, and I'll be armed for it."

The phone rang, and I knew it would be Rankin, asking me to make the drop for him. I didn't have time to play cutesy with him, and so I said quickly before he had a chance to speak: "Okay, Senator, I'll make the drop for you. Get the money over here as soon as you can."

"But how …" he spluttered.

"I have your phone tapped, and I heard the whole thing."

"My God. I'll bring the money right over."

"No, you stay there by the phone. Can you get someone to deliver it immediately? We don't have much time."

"I'm sure I can get some of the Montgomery County police to bring it right over. I appreciate this, Petersen. But, please, no heroics. Just deliver the money as they direct. I want my daughter back."

"That's my prime concern, too, Senator."

As I hung up, I wondered if Rankin realized they were trying to set me up in an ambush. Maybe he did, and maybe he didn't care. I couldn't blame him for that, though. He had to follow the kidnappers' demands if he wanted to retain any chance of releasing his daughter, and Brian Petersen types were expendable, while daughters weren't.

Sarge put his hand on my arm. "Let me go with you."

"No, there's no sense in two of us walking into a trap, if that's what it is. I'll keep in phone contact with you all the time, and if I find myself in a trap, I'll try to blow my way out and capture one of them to lead me to Ellen Rankin. Of course, if it's no trap, I'll just leave the money, and pull back and hope to follow the tracking device later."

I heard a step on the stairway, and I saw Cathy Morrison enter the room. She had changed back into her jeans and pullover sweater, and she now seated herself on one of the bar stools, listening to our conversation, her eyes wide with apprehension.

"Captain," said Sarge in a low voice. "Do you really think they intend to release the Rankin girl?"

I glanced over at Cathy and our eyes met. I knew that she had always felt that the NFA never had any intention of releasing Ellen Rankin. Angrily, I lit a cigarette, blowing out the smoke fiercely, and I started to pace the floor. I walked up and down three or four times, and neither Cathy nor Sarge said anything. Suddenly I stopped, and whirled to face Sarge: "Damnit, no, I don't think they have any intention of releasing her. They want that money, and they want to waste me."

"Maybe we should call up reserves," Sarge suggested.

"No, we still have to allow Rankin that one chance to get his daughter back by paying the ransom. But, okay, Sarge, if the NFA is changing plans, maybe we can change ours, too. We won't do anything to jeopardize Ellen Rankin, but it's the eleventh hour and we don't have much to lose. We're either going to get Ellen Rankin back tonight, or we're never going to get her back. Maybe it's time to start hedging our bet."

"How?"

"Let's use all our cards. And let's play our two aces."

CHAPTER SEVENTEEN

asked Cathy if she was willing to help, and she readily agreed. Sarge, of course, was grinning contentedly, now that he was going to be a closer part of the action. However, it was almost six-thirty, and we had to move quickly.

"The first thing we have to do is see if we can locate Jason Miller at this moment," I said.

I called his office at the Rayburn Building, but a secretary told me he had already departed. I found his home phone number in the papers Tom Walsh had been given about the freshman congressman—Miller, a bachelor, lived in a modest townhouse on Prospect Street in Georgetown. While the phone was ringing at Miller's house, I stuffed a piece of paper inside my mouth, pushing it up against the roof of my mouth. It was a crude, fast, improvised version of the voice alterators used by the boys at CIA. When the phone was answered by a man, I spoke in a high-pitched voice, in order to change the sound of my voice even more.

"John Miller?" I asked.

"No, you've got the wrong number. This is Jason Miller."

"Oh, I'm sorry," I said, as I hung up.

I turned to Sarge and Cathy. "Okay, we know that he's at home right now. Sarge, you get over there and park in front of his house, and I'm going to see if I can flush him out and get him running toward the NFA headquarters, and then you follow him."

"How are you going to do that?"

"I haven't got time to explain. We're still not sure that he knows where the NFA headquarters is, and we may accomplish nothing. But if he does, then I may be able to send him out there tonight. I'm working on the premise that the NFA is someplace in Virginia, probably in some other farmhouse. But no matter where they are, they've only been there for seventy-two hours now, and they certainly wouldn't be able to get phone service established in that short a time. No, if Miller knows where they are, he'll have to go there himself without previously contacting them by phone."

"And I follow him?" Sarge asked.

"That's all you do. Just follow him. We'll stay in constant contact on the two phones in our cars. Don't try to take him, or make any move on the NFA. Just try to get him to lead you to the headquarters. In that way, we'll have two chances of getting to the NFA headquarters tonight. I may fight my way through the drop scene, or you may trail Miller there. Either way, one of us should get through. We'll be tracking from opposite angles. Okay, get going. You'd better take that picture of Miller from the news clipping so you can recognize him if this works."

Sarge was pulling on his jacket, adjusting it over his shoulder holster. "I don't need it," he said grimly. "I've been studying that picture for days, and I'd know him anyplace."

"Call me, Sarge, as soon as you get to his place, and then I'll see if I can give him a push from here."

After Sarge had departed, I explained the mechanics of the radio receiver, which was transmitting the tap on Rankin's phone, to Cathy, and I asked her to monitor it while Sarge and I were gone. When the doorbell rang I answered it; it was a uniformed police officer who handed me a briefcase from Senator

Rankin, asking me to sign a receipt for it. I was gratified to see that it was the same briefcase with Eddie Perkins' tracking devices in it.

The phone was ringing when I returned downstairs, and it was Sarge, telling me from his car that he was parked down the street from Miller's house on Prospect Street in Georgetown. I depressed the receiver, and then picked it up again, dialing Miller's number. "Let's hope this works," I said to Cathy, while I waited for the phone to be answered. I shoved the piece of paper into my mouth again.

The same man's voice answered, and I lowered my voice this time. "Congressman Miller, I have a message for you."

"Yes," he said.

"It's a message from a young man named Timothy Bronson."

There was a short pause at the other end of the line, and then Miller said: "I'm afraid you must be mistaken, I don't know any Timothy Bronson."

"I'm just delivering a message."

"Who is this?"

"I'm a man of the cloth, and I work with troubled young people. Timothy Bronson came to me today with his problem, and I told him the best thing for his soul would be to confess. Repentance is the Lord's will, you know."

"You must have the wrong party, I simply don't know what you're talking about."

"As I say, I'm only a messenger. Timothy told me he first met you at the University of Miami eighteen months ago when he was in a seminar with Paul Deserks and other people. Then there was something he called the National Federation Army you were involved with. And now he says there's something about a kidnapping, too." I heard a slight gasp at the other end of the line, but I continued on. "I told Timothy he should go to the police or the newspapers and tell them everything he knows. But he said he wanted to speak to you first."

"I've told you I don't know any person named Bronson."

"Well, if you don't, then Timothy has been dishonest with me. But he seemed pretty sincere when he told me his story. At any rate, let me give you his message. He says he wants to speak with you and Deserks tonight at nine o'clock, and maybe you can tell him what to do. He said for you to meet him at the new army headquarters, and he said you'd know where that was. Nine o'clock."

"This is preposterous. It is some kind of joke?"

"I'm just telling you what this boy told me. He's a very frightened boy. Well, anyway, I gave you the message. God bless you."

When I hung up, Cathy looked inquiringly at me. "Did he bite?"

"I don't know. If he doesn't bite, I don't think it's going to harm us at this late stage of the game, but if he does, he might lead Sarge right to Ellen Rankin."

It was after seven o'clock now, and time to get out to the phone booth on Route 50 to receive the first NFA instructions for dropping the ransom money. I told Cathy to keep the doors locked, and not to admit anybody under any circumstances. Then I had one more idea. I found the carbon of the notes Annie had typed up for me earlier today, and I gave it to Cathy.

"There's a man named John Lollard in Alexandria and his number's in the book. If you don't hear from Sarge or me by midnight, phone Lollard and read that statement. He's an old FBI type, and he'll know what to do immediately."

Cathy stared at me, and I thought I could almost see the beginnings of tears. She knew what I was trying to tell her. "Yeah," I said. "Tonight it's going to be either me or General Camillo."

❧   ❧   ❧

I drove slowly out Shirley Highway toward Fairfax, and on the way I dialed Sarge's phone from the equipment Eddie Perkins had installed in my car that afternoon. "Any action there, Sarge?" I asked when he answered.

"None at all," he said. "Nobody's come out of that house since I've arrived. Did you try to flush him?"

"I did, but maybe he's too smart for us. But stay right there. He may be beginning to sweat a bit and think he has to get out to NFA headquarters to protect his ass from exposure. I'm going to hang up now for a few minutes, but call me if anything happens. From now on, I'll be Beacon One, and you're Beacon Two. In case anybody starts intercepting our calls. Out."

At Annandale I took a left and proceeded toward Fairfax on Little River Turnpike. I was nearing the outskirts of Fairfax when the phone rang. It was Sarge, speaking in an excited voice. "Beacon Two to Beacon One. Our subject has just left his house. He entered a late-model Ford, and I'm following. I think we're proceeding toward Key Bridge."

"Keep this line open, Beacon Two."

I drove with my left hand, while I held the phone against my ear with the other. I could hear Sarge breathing heavily, but there was no sound for another minute or two until Sarge told me that Miller's car was now on Key Bridge, heading toward Virginia. Maybe it was working; maybe Miller bought my story and was rushing out to NFA headquarters for a conference with Timothy Bronson.

"Beacon Two," I said into the phone. "For God's sake, don't lose him."

"I've never lost a tail yet, Beacon One, and I'm sure as hell not going to lose this bastard."

"You're beautiful, Beacon Two."

"Oh, by the way, Beacon One, thanks for including me in the action." There was a pause. "It's kinda like old times, isn't it?"

"Yeah, like old times."

I drove into the center of Fairfax, and then followed Route 50 out of the city. It was a few minutes before eight when I spotted the first Gulf station outside the city limits. I pulled up beside the public phone booth, and told Sarge I was going to get out of the car to wait for the call. "Where are you now, Beacon Two?" I asked him.

"We're on Lee Highway, skirting Arlington, and starting to head west. It's an easy tail."

I went into the phone booth, and lit a cigarette while waiting for the call. Eight o'clock came and passed, and for a minute or two I thought that maybe the NFA was playing some clever trick on us. Then the phone rang, and I picked it up.

"Petersen?" a voice said. It wasn't Camillo.

"Brian Petersen here."

"Do you have the money?"

"Yes."

"All right, get back in your car and proceed along Route 50 until you get near Centerville. There's a large Mobil station at the edge of town. Go into the phone booth, and wait for the next call." The phone clicked dead.

As I walked back toward my car, I looked around, trying to see if I could spot anybody observing me, but I couldn't. I started the engine and continued along Route 50, and with one hand I dialed Sarge. "Beacon One is proceeding to the next phone booth near Centerville. Where are you?"

"Still on Lee Highway proceeding west. But, wait a minute, we seem to be slowing down." There was no sound for almost a minute, and then Sarge said: "We're just turning onto 495, and we are now proceeding north."

I didn't like the sound of that, because it meant that Sarge and I were now driving in different directions. Maybe Miller wasn't heading toward the hideout, after all. But then a few minutes later Sarge spoke again: "Beacon Two is now slowing again, and we're turning off at 1-66. And proceeding west."

"Very good, Beacon Two," I said. Both Sarge and I were now traveling in the same direction, westward, although we were using different roads a few miles apart. Miller had obviously chosen to use the faster 1-66, while the NFA was directing me along this more populated Route 50. However, I now felt quite sure that Miller was going to NFA headquarters.

I stopped at the Mobil station at the edge of Centerville, and entered the phone booth to wait for the second call. A few minutes later the phone rang, and the same voice directed me to turn south on Route 28 and proceed to a phone outside a grocery store in Yorkshire. Back in the car, I dialed Sarge again, and he said: "Beacon Two moving rapidly now along 1-66. I can see the Manassas Battlefield Park on my right."

That meant that Sarge was now ahead of me: he had picked up the time both because of the delays I encountered waiting for the phone calls and because of the faster road Miller was traveling. But as I proceeded south on Route 28, Sarge was still heading westward. I felt that in a short while he would be turning south, too, because I had a hunch that the NFA hideout and the drop area would not be far apart this time.

As I neared Yorkshire, Sarge said: "Beacon Two slowing. And ... we ... are ... now ... turning. Driving south on 234."

Good, I thought. We were both heading south now, and we were probably no more than ten miles apart. I slowed down in Yorkshire, found the next phone booth, and waited for the call. This time the voice said: "Get back in your car, Petersen, and check your speedometer. Exactly 1.5 miles south you will find a small country lane, about wide enough for one car. Take a left there, and drive exactly 1.8 miles. You'll see a small birch tree on the right with a white rag nailed to it. Look beyond it to the open field and you will see in the middle of the field a short tree stump. The stump is hollow. Deposit the money in it, and leave. Have you got that?"

I repeated the instructions, and the voice said: "And no tricks this time, Petersen."

Back in the car I dialed Sarge, and said: "Okay, Beacon Two, I'm coming up to the drop. Let's keep this line open from now on. Where are you?"

"Beacon Two is still going south on 234, and looking out my lefthand window I can see a small airplane taking off from somewhere."

I looked out my righthand window and saw the same airplane. I pulled a Virginia map out of the glove compartment, and laid it on the seat beside me, studying it in the dim light from my dashboard. "That figures, Beacon Two," I said into the phone. "There's a small field there, Manassas Airport. We're probably about five or six miles apart now, and the hideout must be someplace between us."

I watched my speedometer carefully, and when it registered 1.5 miles from the last phone booth I saw the small lane to the left. I turned, easing the car gradually in. Indeed, it was barely wide enough for one car. I was driving with my right hand now, holding the phone to my ear with the left.

Sarge spoke: "Beacon Two is now turning left on a narrow road off 234. The Ford is about a quarter of a mile ahead of me, and slowing down."

"Beacon Two. Do not attempt to take the Ford. Repeat, do not attempt to take. All we want is the location of headquarters. This may be a legitimate drop, and we want to protect the girl."

"Okay, Beacon One. I'll just follow until I see the car stop, and then I'll lie back."

When I had driven the 1.8 miles along the narrow lane, I spotted the birch tree with the white rag nailed to it. Beyond it was an open field, and in the middle the small tree stump. The area looked perfectly clean, wide open with no place to set up an ambush. I stopped the car, and sat there a minute. Nothing happened.

"Beacon Two," I said into the phone. "I am at the drop area, and it looks clean. I am about to drop the money. I am going to lay this phone receiver on the front seat to keep the line open, and if all goes well I should be talking to you again in about two or three minutes."

"For Christ's sake, be careful, Beacon One."

I placed the phone receiver on the front seat beside me, and then I reached into my shirt and extracted the small fragmentation grenade from the pouch under my left armpit. I held it carefully in my left hand while I picked up the briefcase from the floor and shoved it up under my left arm. Then, slowly and carefully, I pulled the pin from the grenade, immediately depressing the spoon to keep it from exploding. But it was activated now, and it would go off five seconds after I released my thumb from that spoon.

As I stepped out of the car, I extracted the .38 from my shoulder holster, flicking off the safety. And that's the way I started out across that open field: the activated grenade in my left hand, the briefcase under my arm, and the loaded .38 in my right hand. It was perfectly still in the open field, and I couldn't spot any movement at all. The only place where anybody could possibly be hiding was one small clump of three or four bushes, about twenty yards away from the tree stump. But even at that, it was only large enough to conceal one person at the most. Nevertheless, I kept it firmly in view as I neared the tree stump.

When I was about twenty-five yards from the tree stump I stopped, and raised my pistol, pointing it directly at the stump. There was always the possibility that they had booby-trapped the stump and it would explode as I got near it. I fired once, hitting the stump squarely. Nothing. I fired again. And again there was nothing except the loud report of my pistol. Maybe I had misjudged the NFA, and I was going to have to toss the activated grenade harmlessly toward the end of the open field.

That meant I would have to leave the briefcase here, and lie back and hope to follow the tracker in it when they picked it up. And, of course, I was hoping that Sarge had followed Miller to the NFA hideout by this time. We now had two chances, I felt, to track them down.

I approached the tree stump slowly, and peered into it. Yes, it was hollow, all right. I was just starting to bend over to insert the briefcase when I heard the rustle from that clump of bushes. I dropped the briefcase on the ground, and whirled toward the bushes at the moment I heard the shot which went whistling over my head.

There was a man coming out of that clump of bushes, running toward me, a pistol in his hand. Clenching the grenade tightly in my left hand, I went down into a crouch and took careful aim with the pistol. He took another shot which missed, and I steadied my hand. I wanted him alive, and so I aimed my pistol down, trying to get him in the legs. I squeezed the trigger and I got him, hitting him somewhere in the upper thigh. He pitched forward on his face.

And at that moment all hell broke lose. Gunfire began to explode all around me, and I hit the ground immediately. It seemed that shots were coming at me from every direction. As I looked up from my prone position I could see two men running toward me, automatic rifles in their hands, firing. And then over to my left I could now see another man who almost appeared as if he were rising up out of the ground in the open field.

And I realized what a clever ambush I had walked into.

They must have dug some kind of slit trenches in the field, and in the darkness I couldn't see them hiding there, waiting for me. The man in the clump of bushes was meant to be the first, diversionary attack, drawing my fire that way while they scrambled out of the trenches. I counted three automatic rifles, and they were smartly coming at me from different directions, trying to get me in a crossfire.

However, the first two that I had spotted were only about ten yards apart as they charged me. Bullets were splattering all around me. I reached back with my left hand, and I aimed for a spot directly between the first two charging men. When they were about fifteen yards away, I brought my arm up in one of those overhand grenade tosses they used to teach in the infantry.

I released the spoon even before it left my hand, and there was less than five seconds' detonation time. It was a classic pitch, hitting almost directly between them, and I buried my face in the ground as I heard the violent explosion. I think I even felt some of those metal fragments whistling over my head. When I looked up, the two mangled bodies were lying grotesquely on the ground.

But the other automatic rifle was coming at me from the other direction. However, he was farther away, and I crawled around and got off two quick shots with my .38. They missed, but they forced him into a low crouched, zigzag run toward me. With my left hand I reached across my chest to the other grenade under my right armpit. I took one more shot with the .38, and then dropped it on the ground. I transferred the grenade to my right hand, pulling the pin as I did so. I didn't even hold down the spoon, but I went right up on my knees, and with a regular baseball pitch, I threw it directly in front of the charging gunman.

He was about twenty yards away from me when it hit the ground in front of him, almost at his feet. As I fell forward on my face to avoid the blast, I could see him being exploded into the air, one arm becoming instantly dismembered.

I retrieved my pistol, and waited there, looking around to see if there were any more of them. But everything was quiet now. I didn't even bother to look at the three riflemen, because I knew they would all be dead from those direct hits by a fragmentation grenade. But I was hoping that the first one wasn't too badly injured.

He was lying face down on the ground, his pistol a few feet from him, and when I rolled him over I saw that my shot had been a little higher than I thought. He had taken my bullet in the lower groin, and his trousers were red-stained from the oozing blood. But he was alive, and his eyes were open.

"Get me a doctor, you bastard," he said through clenched teeth.

I didn't answer him, but I shoved the pistol back in my holster, and reached down to pull him up. I got him up over my shoulder, and carried him back toward my car in a fireman's carry. On the way back to the car, I also picked up the briefcase.

I pulled open the lefthand front door, and dropped him on the seat. He groaned, and clutched his abdomen.

"Okay," I said. "Now you're going to take me to NFA headquarters."

"No, I want a doctor."

"Not a chance," I said, and I walked around to the driver's seat. The phone was still off the hook on the front seat, and I picked it up and said: "Beacon One is okay. Where are you, Beacon Two?"

There was no answer.

"Beacon Two, come in." Still no answer. "Goddamnit, Sarge, where are you?"

I hung up the phone, and dialed the number of the phone in Sarge's car. But all I got was a busy signal. The phone was obviously off the hook, and Sarge wasn't there. Or if he was, he couldn't talk. A growing feeling of dread was coming over me, as I replaced the phone on the hook.

I turned to the young man in the front seat beside me. He was middle twenties, wearing a khaki bush jacket, and the blood from his wound was spilling out on my front seat. I grabbed the front of his bush jacket, and pulled him closer to me. "Now, damn you, tell me where the NFA hideout is."

"I can't. I want a doctor."

"You're not going to get any doctor until after you take me to the NFA."

"They'd kill me if I told."

"Okay, take your choice of deaths." I pulled the .38 out of my holster, and with my left hand I grabbed him under the chin, forcing open his mouth. I shoved the barrel of the pistol into his open mouth, slamming it up against the roof of his mouth. His eyes opened wide in terror, and his hands came off the wound and clutched at my left hand, trying to pull it away from his throat.

"I'll give you ten seconds, and then I'm going to pull the trigger and a .38 shell will go shooting up into your brain."

I pushed the gun even further into his mouth, and a drool of saliva began to run out of the corner of his mouth. His eyes bulged, and he tried to speak, but he could only make indecipherable, guttural sounds. I pulled the gun back slightly, and he was able to mutter indistinctly: "All right, all right."

I pulled the pistol out, and shoved him up against the door. "Where is it?"

"Off Route 234, south of Manassas Airport."

That was the area where I had last heard from Sarge. I gunned the engine, moved ahead a few feet until I found an open spot where I could back in the car and turn it around, and then I hit the accelerator, bouncing down the narrow country lane. The kid beside me moaned, but I ignored him.

As I was bouncing down the road, I leaned over to the glove compartment and reached back into that hidden section and extracted two boxes. One contained extra shells for my .38, and the other held the last two fragmentation grenades. I switched hands on the steering wheel, as I picked up the grenades, one by one, and carefully inserted them into the two now-empty pouches under my armpits.

CHAPTER EIGHTEEN

As we drove along Route 234, the bleeding man next to me began whimpering. "Get me a doctor. I'm dying."

"Shut up, and tell me where this turnoff is."

About a mile south of the entrance to the airport, he pointed to a narrow road leading off to the right. I was able to maintain pretty good speed along the paved road, but when it turned to dirt I had to slow down somewhat. We were in farm country now, and the only signs of life I could see were occasional farmhouses set far back from the road. About three miles in from the main road, the NFA man next to me pointed off to the right and said: "There."

I couldn't see anything, only a low stone wall and behind it a long hill, sloping upwards. There was no house of any kind visible. "Where?" I asked.

"It's a farmhouse. You can't see it from here. It's up over that knoll about a half-mile away. You drive through that opening in the stone wall, and follow the road up over the hill."

I didn't have time to park the car here and walk that half-mile, and so I decided to drive through the gate and up closer to the farmhouse. I was slowing down, preparing to turn in through the gate, when I slammed on the brake. I had seen a car just inside the gate, pulled off the road. There didn't appear to be anyone in it, but I knew that car: it was Sarge's green Dodge. It was empty, and suspiciously abandoned. I glanced over at the NFA man beside me, and I saw that his eyes were expectantly trained on the small entrance gate through the stone wall.

I pulled out the .38 and jammed it violently into his lower abdomen, right about the area of his wound. He groaned and made gurgling noises in his throat. "Okay, tell me about that gate. What have you got set up there?"

He didn't answer, and I jammed the pistol into him again, and this time he pitched toward me, and I thought he was going to pass out. I pushed him back against the door seat, and his eyes opened. I pulled the pistol back, ready to plunge it in again when he said, his voice almost a whisper: "There's a guard just inside the gate. He's crouched in a small toolshed with a rifle, and you can't see it from this side of the stone wall."

"And what else?"

"There's a trap just inside the gate."

I turned off the ignition, and put the keys in my pocket, and I got out of the car and moved down the side of that stone wall in a crouch. The wall was about four feet high, and I lifted myself easily over it. Ahead of me, near the gate, I could see the small, low, wooden shed. There was a door on the side facing me, but it was closed. There was probably some type of aperture on the other side, facing the entrance, where the guard aimed his gun at incoming cars. I had my .38 in my hand as I crept up to the door. With my left hand, I jerked it open, and said: "Don't move."

There was a young man in there with his back to me, and he was holding a rifle pointed out through a hole which faced the entrance.

"Drop it," I said. "And back out."

He dropped the rifle and clumsily began to back out of the exceedingly cramped quarters of the small toolshed. As he came out, he turned toward me. And then he made a lunge, going for my gun. It was an extremely foolish move on his part, because I could have shot him easily before he got within inches of my gun. But I couldn't risk the noise of a shot. The report of a .38 could certainly be heard a half-mile away in this open country, and it might bring the rest of them running before I had time to set up my move against them.

So, instead of firing when he made his lunge at me, I punched him once with my left, hitting him in the middle of the chest, and then I brought my pistol around, slapping it off the side of his head. He slammed backward, banging his head against the stone wall, and then slumping to the ground. When his head hit that wall I heard the dull crack, and I knew what had happened. Leaning over, I saw the blood running out of his nose, and when I pulled his head away from the base of the wall I could see where the jagged edge of one of the stones had entered. He was dead.

I walked over and inspected Sarge's car. It was empty, and there were no signs of violence inside. Then I walked back to the gate, and I discovered how they had probably trapped Sarge. A trench had been dug just inside the gate about three feet wide and two or three feet deep, and it was covered over by branches. You could avoid the trench if you knew it was there and you drove carefully around it. But if you didn't, and you came through that gate in an ordinary manner, your front wheels would hit that ditch and your car would go down, immobilizing it. That's what probably happened to Sarge. Miller came through the gate, avoided the trap, and then Sarge followed after him. When his car got stuck in the trap, then the rifleman in the shed jumped out and captured him. But where was Sarge now?

I got back in the car, and drove carefully through the gate, avoiding the trap. I drove slowly and quietly up the road until I reached the top of the knoll. Then I stopped and turned off the ignition. I looked over at my bleeding friend in the front seat and thought about tying him up. But I saw it wasn't necessary because he was almost unconscious. I had the Browning automatic rifle in the trunk, and now I went around and got it out.

As I came over the knoll, the rifle in my hands, I could see a large, white, frame building about fifty yards ahead. It was fully lighted inside, and a number of cars were parked outside. I moved toward it in a crouch, until I was able to reach one of the cars. I paused and looked around, but I couldn't see anybody else outside the house. I did notice that one of the cars was a late-model Ford, undoubtedly Miller's.

There was some shrubbery near the house, and I ran toward it, and got down behind it. It was four or five feet from a window, and I could hear voices inside. I snapped off the safety on the Browning rifle, made sure it was on automatic fire, and stealthily moved closer to that window. I flattened myself against the frame building, and then cautiously edged toward the window, so I could peer in.

The first person I saw was Sarge, standing on the opposite side of the room. He was holding his hands clasped on top of his head, and I could see that his glasses had been broken and there was blood running out of his nose and another little trickle coming out of the corner of his mouth. He was being interrogated by a short man standing in front of him who now slapped Sarge viciously across the mouth. And I recognized the interrogator: reddish, thinning hair, beard, thick glasses. Paul Deserks, alias General Camillo.

And then I saw the rest of them in that large room. The whole damned crowd of them. Congressman Jason Miller, standing behind Camillo, watching the interrogation. And there was Judy Powell, the little neighbor from down the corridor who had conned me so nicely, but now she was wearing two cartridge belts strapped across her chest and she was holding a pistol. And I counted eight others: one other girl, and seven men, all wearing

different types of khaki fatigues or bush jackets. But I couldn't
see anybody who resembled Ellen Rankin.

The first thing was to get Sarge out of there. I saw a lot of
handguns, and a few rifles being held around the room, but I had
the advantage of surprise and initial attack. And my angle of fire
would be good. I could pick off Camillo, without hitting Sarge,
and then I could sweep back across the room, getting Miller and
most of the others. Sarge, of course, would be smart enough to
hit the floor and grab one of the weapons and finish off whom-
ever I didn't get.

I took a step back from the window, and lifted the butt of my
rifle, resting it lightly against my shoulder. I brought the scope
around, and peering through it, I had Camillo nearly in it, the
crossbars dissecting his body evenly. But I never got a chance to
pull the trigger.

I was just ready to squeeze the trigger when I was hit savagely
across the back of the neck with a rifle butt, and I went sprawling
forward on my face.

There had apparently been some other guard out there whom
I hadn't seen, and he had come creeping up behind me, slugging
me as I was about to fire. I managed to hold on to my rifle, but the
person behind me immediately put the barrel of his rifle against
the back of my neck, and he said: "If you move an inch, I'll fire."

I was contemplating a rollover in an attempt to grab his leg,
but at that moment a lot of other people came running out of
the house, shouting, after they had apparently heard the noise
outside. The Browning rifle was pulled away from me, and I was
yanked to my feet. They told me to put my hands on top of my
head, and one of them expertly frisked me, removing the .38
from my shoulder holster. However, he missed the two grenades
in the pouches under my armpits. Sarge's concealment holster
had worked perfectly, because those grenades were tiny, golf-ball

size, and no one would ordinarily think of frisking under a person's armpits for a weapon of any kind. But that wasn't going to do me much good now. The grenades were in the pouches under my shirt, and there was no possible way I could pull my hands down off my head and reach those grenades before they plugged me full of bullets with all those guns.

They marched me inside, my hands on my head, and the first one to speak was Judy Powell. "That's him, that's Brian Petersen," she said to Camillo.

"So at last I meet the fascist pig," Camillo said.

"Hello, Paul Deserks," I answered.

"My name is General Camillo, my new name in the movement."

"Your name will always be Paul Deserks. That's the name they'll use on the bottom of the photograph when they book you before they throw you into prison for life."

Camillo reached over and slapped me across the face. "Pig," he almost spat at me. He picked up an M-14 rifle from a table, and he poked me in the ribs with it. "Over there, next to the other one."

I moved over and stood next to Sarge, who was squinting at me through his broken glasses. "I'm sorry, Captain. I failed in the assignment," he said.

Sarge looked pathetic. Blood was now streaming freely out of his nose, and I knew he had been physically abused. But I don't think the physical hurt was bothering him at all; he was agonized that he had failed the assignment and had allowed himself to be captured. I told him: "It's okay, Sarge, I almost fell in that trap at the gate myself."

Camillo was standing directly in front of me now, the M-14 pointed at my stomach. He was wearing a khaki fatigue jacket, and he had two cartridge belts crisscrossed over his chest. He was a pretty stupid soldier to wear all those exposed shells across his chest. "Where's the ransom money?" he asked me.

"Where's Ellen Rankin?"

"She's all right. She's in the basement tied up."

I forced myself to grin sardonically. "So you're still working on her. You couldn't get her to convert and join your dumb army."

Camillo brought the rifle up and smashed it against the side of my head. "She's still under instruction. But I asked you a question—where's the ransom money?"

"There's not going to be any ransom money, Deserks. But we might arrange an exchange of prisoners."

"What do you mean?"

"You release Ellen Rankin, and we release Timothy Bronson."

For the first time, Jason Miller, who had been standing back, now stepped forward and spoke. "See, I told you Bronson was alive. That phone call I received."

"Well, our distinguished freshman congressman," I said.

Camillo turned to him. "It's bluff. He probably killed Bronson like he killed all the others."

"But that phone call ..." Miller said.

"Yeah, you should be worried, Miller," I said. "Your little army is coming apart at the seams, and all of you are going to jail for kidnapping."

"I had no idea they would kidnap somebody," he said to me.

"You started this whole thing, Miller. You started the NFA in Miami eighteen months ago, and you are responsible."

"My God," Miller said. "That was a seminar. I had no idea it would come to this."

"Are you trying to tell me that you just got these kids all stirred up in a classroom, and then they ran wild without your knowledge?"

"That's it."

"Bullshit."

"You've got to believe me. I haven't talked to any of these people since Miami, until three or four months ago. I didn't even know they were in Washington. But they told me they were founding a cell or a study club or something, and they were calling it the National Federation Army. But then they contacted me and told me they had kidnapped Ellen Rankin, and I couldn't believe it."

"Why didn't you call the police?"

"I thought that the best way to get them to release the girl was to try to reason with them, to tell them to let her go. I came out here any number of times in the last week to try to convince them to do just that."

"But you were helping them. You did that research on me for them."

"That was harmless. They just wanted to know if you were police connected. And, my God, so did I. Believe me, I was trying to get Ellen Rankin released."

Camillo had been watching Miller, a deep scowl on his face. "Our once-eloquent professor who spoke so gloriously about the necessity of revolution has now become a revisionist, you see."

I looked back at Jason Miller, who had an anguished expression on his face. "I don't care what you call him," I said. "He's guilty. He got this whole thing started. And he knew about the people who were holding a kidnap victim, and he didn't report it to the police. In legal terms that's called misprision of a crime. And he's going to go to jail for that. Furthermore, I don't believe he gave a damn about releasing Ellen Rankin: he was just concerned that his connection with the NFA would be revealed and his whole career ruined."

JAMES P. CODY

Camillo now stepped closer, and jabbed me with the rifle again. "There's too much talk. I told you I want the ransom money."

"And I told you I'd arrange an exchange of prisoners."

"I don't believe you. Bronson's dead. You've killed him."

"Believe what you want. But Bronson's very much alive, and first thing tomorrow morning, he's going to start talking to the police."

I saw a frown of uncertainty come over Camillo's forehead, and he glanced around, looking for support. Judy Powell stepped forward, and said: "Don't listen to Petersen, the pig. He's lying."

"Talk about lies," I said. "You lied to me pretty good last week."

She wheeled around toward me. "You're so stupid you couldn't tell a lie from the truth."

"How'd you ever get mixed up with this bunch of weirdos, Judy?"

"It's the wave of the future," she said defiantly.

"Their future is over. They've had it."

Camillo stepped up to me, and shifting the rifle to his left hand, he punched me brutally in the nose with his right. He didn't break it, but blood began spurting out my nose and running down my chin. "Shut up!" he shouted at me.

"Don't let pig Petersen confuse you," Judy Powell said. "Bronson must be dead, and he can't harm us. And neither can Petersen harm us anymore."

"What should we do with him?" Camillo asked.

"Kill him. And the other one, too." Judy Powell answered.

"But what about the ransom?" Camillo asked her.

"If Petersen hasn't got it, then we can still deal directly with old man Rankin. We still have his precious daughter."

222

They continued to talk about my fate, discussing the details of how they would kill both Sarge and me and then dispose of our bodies. I looked around the room, trying to calculate my chances, and I had to admit they weren't very good. There were eleven people aligned against us, and most of them had guns of one kind or another. Eight of the NFA people were standing behind Camillo, spread out in a large circle. Camillo, Judy Powell, and Jason Miller were standing in front of the circle facing us.

There wasn't much furniture in the room, nothing I could grab. On a table, about eight feet away from me, was the Browning automatic rifle they had taken from me, but it was too far away to reach. To our left was a huge overstuffed couch which would make a nice barricade if we could ever get behind it. And, of course, I had those two grenades under my armpits, but there was no way to get my hands down from my head before one of those many guns got me.

My hands still on my head, I glanced over at Sarge next to me. He was squinting furiously at me now, trying to catch my eyes. I caught his glance, and I saw it shift toward my left armpit, and then it crossed to my right armpit. Almost imperceptibly, I nodded my head, telling him that I had the grenades.

The discussion about our execution was coming to an end, and I interjected: "Just think, Bronson knows the names of every person here."

That got Miller upset, because he stepped forward and said to Camillo: "Do you think there's a chance they may have Bronson?"

Camillo whirled toward him angrily. "I told you ..." he started to say.

But at that moment Sarge shouted, "Captain, go!" and he lunged at Camillo. It was a totally hopeless move, a sacrifice, and a diversion to give me time to move during the confusion.

Camillo brought the M-14 quickly around, and fired before Sarge had taken two steps, hitting him point-blank in the chest with a stream of automatic bullets. And the blood began to spurt out of Sarge's chest as he crumpled to the floor.

In the split second of confusion while Camillo was firing, I took a running leap toward that overstuffed couch, hitting the floor behind it and sliding up against the wall. Bullets started to thump into the couch, and the wall plaster above me began to shower as other bullets hit against it. My hand was reaching inside my shirt as I was flying through the air, and by the time I hit that wall I had one of the grenades out. I pulled the pin, and didn't even aim. I lobbed it in the air across to the other side of the room. And then I pressed my face against the floor.

The explosion was deafening in the room, and I heard screams and the shattering of glass. Some metal fragments from the grenade shot into the wall above my head. But apparently my grenade hadn't gotten them all, because a few more shots rang out. I got to my knees and peered over the couch. One corner of the room where the grenade had apparently landed was totally demolished. I could see a tangle of blood-splattered bodies, and a gaping hole in the wall which had been torn out by the grenade. But there were people still moving around in the other corner, and I could dimly make them out in the smoke and falling plaster. Then I saw Camillo, the rifle in his hand, and he was standing at the bottom of a staircase leading upstairs. He made a quick move, and started racing up the stairs. And then another man followed him, and raced up the stairs behind him.

A shot rang out, and whizzed over my head. I had the second grenade in my hand now, and I pulled the pin, tossing it toward the corner from which the shots were emanating. I watched it arch gracefully through the air, and just before it hit, the smoke cleared a bit and I could see Jason Miller standing there, a terrified expression on his face. The grenade struck near him, and when it exploded he was thrown violently into the air and slammed against the wall.

And then there was utter silence in the room.

I crawled out from behind the couch, and the first thing I found was Sarge's Browning automatic rifle lying on the floor. I picked it up, and scanned the room, but none of the fallen bodies was moving. First, I rolled Sarge over, and I saw that Camillo's bullets, fired at that close range, had killed him instantly. I moved among the lifeless bodies on the other side of the room, and I found Judy Powell's body. She was lying on her back, her eyes open and vacant. Jason Miller's body was slumped against the wall, and for a moment it appeared that he was just sitting there, waiting casually for something to happen. But when I got closer I could see that the metal fragments from the grenade had riddled his body, and they had fatally pierced his face and skull, making it seem that his face had been cut by dozens of tiny knives.

But then I heard some movement upstairs, and I realized that Camillo and at least one other must have managed to get up those stairs before the blast went off. I checked my rifle, and started up the stairs after them.

CHAPTER NINETEEN

As I began to climb the stairs, I heard Camillo's voice somewhere above me yell out: "He's coming up. Goddamnit, kill him!"

I was half-way up the stairs, holding the Browning rifle on my hip, pointed ahead of me in combat fashion, when one of them suddenly appeared at the top of the landing. He had a pistol in his hand, and he began firing down at me. I returned fire instantly. The first bullets hit him in the stomach, and I raised the rifle, bringing the stream of automatic magnum bullets right up through his chest and face. He pitched forward, and tumbled down the stairs toward me. I pressed against the wall of the stairway as the body bounced past me.

I paused and waited, listening for more sounds above me. I could hear someone running along the upstairs corridor, but that was the only sound I heard. I decided that no more than two of them could have possibly gotten up there before the second grenade explosion, and that meant Camillo was alone up there now.

"Deserks!" I shouted. "I'm coming up after you."

There was no sound for a moment, and then he shouted back. "My name is Camillo. General Camillo of the National Federation Army. And I'm going to kill you, Petersen." His voice trailed off, and there was silence again.

I went up the steps on the balls of my feet, but when I was almost at the upper landing a board creaked under my feet, and three fast shots rang out from someplace down at the end of the corridor. He must have positioned himself down there with his M-14, waiting for me to poke my head out on the landing.

"Deserks!" I shouted again. "Last chance. Throw your rifle down."

Two more shots rang out from the M-14.

Holding my rifle erect now, I attempted to peek around the corner at the top of the landing. He fired, and I ducked back, but I got a good look at him down there at the end of the corridor, some twenty feet away. He was down on one knee, the rifle poised and aimed to fire when I appeared around that corner.

I brought my rifle back to that combat position on my hip, and then I took a deep breath, steadying myself for my move. When I made that dash out into the upstairs corridor, I was at that moment perhaps thinking more of Sarge's bullet-punctured body downstairs than anything else. I came around the corner in a low crouch, my rifle blazing, sending bullets streaming down toward the end of the corridor. But Camillo had moved. He was standing now, pressed against the wall, and as I came charging down the corridor he fired.

One bullet got me in the leg, slightly above the knee, and I stumbled. I thought I was going to fall, but I managed to keep my rifle up. Camillo was moving backwards now, apparently trying to find a room he could run into. My finger was still on the trigger, sending out a steady stream of magnums, and I moved the rifle horizontally. The stream cut right across Camillo's midsection. I don't know how many of the bullets actually hit him. One would have been enough, because one of the magnums struck those cartridges which Camillo had crisscrossed on the belts across his chest. And they went off like fireworks.

Camillo screamed as the bullets began to explode, and he went up on one leg and pirouetted, like a mad ballet dancer performing a macabre dance to the accompaniment of exploding bullets. When he hit the floor the bullets on the cartridge belts were still exploding. I waited a minute until they had stopped, and then I walked down the corridor and kicked his body over with my boot. The cartridge belts were still strapped on, but there was a giant red cavity where Camillo's chest used to be.

Taps had just blown for General Camillo and his National Federation Army.

I laid the Browning on the floor, and pulled up my trouser leg to inspect the bullet wound. It was bleeding freely, running down my leg, but it was only a flesh wound, and the bullet had not entered.

I went back downstairs, and I shuddered as I saw the mass of lifeless bodies again. The air was filled with the acrid odor of explosives, and I could also smell that unmistakable metallic odor of flowing blood. I stepped over one of the bodies, and pulled open a door which led to the cellar downstairs. I flicked on the light, and went down the wooden stairs slowly, and then I saw her.

Ellen Rankin, gagged and tied to a heavy pipe, her eyes wide and almost frozen with terror.

I released the gag first, but she seemed unable to speak. And then I realized she must have thought I was one of the NFA. "You're free," I said. "I've come to release you and take you home."

She looked at me as if she could hardly believe it, and then she said: "Oh, thank God." While I was releasing her wrists, which had been tied around the pipe, her body began to shake until finally sobs broke from her throat. She didn't appear to be able to stand too well, and so I held her until the sobs subsided. Finally she said: "What about Cathy?"

"She's all right. She got away a few days ago. Can you walk?"

"I don't know, I've been tied up so long."

"Here," I said, and I hoisted her up over my shoulder. She was light, probably no more than 110 pounds, and I was easily able to carry her up the stairs on my shoulder, like some great ragdoll which had lost its sawdust. When we got to the first floor, I told her to keep her eyes closed and not look.

On the lawn outside the house I deposited her gently on the grass. "Just sit here for a minute," I told her. "I'm going to get the car over that rise, and I'll be right back."

When I reached my car, I looked in the front seat for the other NFA man I had left there. He had fallen over and was lying stretched out on the front seat. And he had been right about one thing he kept protesting: he had indeed been dying. My bullet to his groin had apparently torn him up inside, and he had bled to death internally. I pulled the corpse out of the car, and laid it on the lawn. Before I drove back to pick up Ellen Rankin I wiped as much of the blood as I could from the front seat with an old rag.

Ellen was still sitting on the lawn, taking deep breaths of fresh air. Shakily, she got to her feet, and I guided her into the car. I asked her to wait for another minute, because I had one more important thing to do.

I went back into the farmhouse, and stepped over bodies until I found Sarge. I got him in a fireman's hold, and lifted him up over my shoulder. Camillo's bullets had ripped open his chest savagely, and when I carried him out to the car his blood began to course down my shoulder and side. I opened the trunk and deposited him carefully inside.

On the ride back to Rankin's house in Kenwood, Ellen said very little. She laid her head back on the front seat, her eyes closed, and she seemed mainly interested in drawing in great draughts of fresh spring air. I picked up the phone on the dash, and dialed Rankin's home.

"I've got your daughter, Senator," I said when he came on the line. "She's all right, and I'm bringing her right home."

"Oh, thank God, Petersen. Does she need a doctor, or anything?"

"That might not be a bad idea. And why don't you get Hank Phillips over there, too? We have some things to discuss."

And then I remembered that Cathy Morrison should be listening to this conversation, monitoring it from my house. "Cathy," I said. "You can stop monitoring now. It's all over. And you can tear up those papers I left with you."

When I pulled in the driveway in Kenwood, Rankin was waiting outside. And I could see Hank Phillips there, too, and another man, a rotund fellow with a thin moustache, obviously the doctor. I had barely stopped when Ellen Rankin hopped out and ran toward her father, embracing him. He led her into the house, and the rotund fellow followed after them. Wearily, I got out of the car, and Hank Phillips came over to assist me. "My God!" he exclaimed when he saw me.

Indeed, I must have been a horrendous sight. I was drenched with blood—the blood from Sarge's body; the blood from my leg wound; the blood which was caked on my face from the punch Camillo had given me. And my face still bore all those bruises from my earlier fights with the NFA.

"I'll get that doctor to look after you," Hank said.

"No, I'm all right," I said. "As the saying goes, bloodied but unbowed."

We went into the house, and in Rankin's study Hank fetched me a brandy. I sipped it, my eyes closed, waiting till Rankin returned before I started to tell my story.

When Rankin came into the study he walked over and shook my hand. "I don't know how to thank you, Petersen. My daughter's pretty shaken, but she's all right, the doctor says."

I handed Rankin the briefcase with the ransom money in it. "Here's a bonus," I said. "All the ransom money."

"But how ...?" Rankin started to ask, and I proceeded to tell them the whole story about the kidnapping, the NFA, and the final shootout tonight. I gave all the names, and omitted no pertinent details.

"That's incredible," Rankin said when I finished.

"Brian, I think we owe you a debt of immense gratitude," Phillips said. "God knows what might have happened next if you hadn't stopped this National Federation Army thing. I ... I suppose the only thing left now is to inform the authorities. Now that Ellen's been released."

"That's what I wanted to talk to you about," I said. "I was all for going to the authorities originally, but now I don't think we should."

"You don't?" Rankin asked.

"What's to be gained? There's nothing left of the NFA. They're all dead. And Jason Miller is dead. It's finished. But I don't relish the idea of spending the next few months appearing at inquests, and telling my story, and all that newspaper publicity. Let's just write finis to it."

"Well, I can see your point," Rankin said uncertainly.

"It's to your advantage, too, Senator. When the police discover all those bodies out in the farmhouse near Manassas, there's going to be a gigantic amount of publicity. And don't forget, one of the bodies is a United States congressman. Now, if we tell our story, your name is going to be dragged through it, and so will Ellen's, as a kidnap victim."

"Yes, I see," Rankin said.

JAMES P. CODY

"And one other thing about Ellen. If the newspapers ever learn that you were able and willing to get four hundred thousand to ransom your daughter, any nut who reads the story might decide to try what the NFA tried."

"Yes, my daughter's safety from future attempts," Rankin said. He turned to Phillips. "What do you think?"

"I tend to agree with Brian," he said.

"All right," I said, rising to my feet. "The episode is closed."

"And, of course," Rankin said, "I want you to bill me for your services, as we agreed."

"Oh, you'll get a bill, all right, Senator. A big one."

Driving home, I inspected the wound in my leg again. The bleeding had stopped, but I was beginning to ache all over. However, I was probably more wounded in spirit than in body, and a peculiar mood was beginning to descend over me. I was horribly depressed, of course, by Sarge's death, and I felt responsible for it. He was dead now because I had asked him to help me on this case. And he had sacrificed himself for me, throwing himself hopelessly at Camillo in order to give me time to get the grenades out. Goddamnit.

But I was also becoming depressed now about all those NFA kids I had to kill. They shouldn't have had to die so young. Sure, they were all screwed up in their minds, but Jason Miller had done it to them, filling them up with a lot of impossible revolutionary ideas. That irresponsible professor was an actual seducer of the young. He deserved to die, all right, but now that it was over, I wasn't too proud of myself that I was forced to kill all of those misguided kids.

I had an additional problem about the disposal of Sarge's blood-splattered body. He had no family to whom I could deliver it, and if I walked into an undertaker's with a corpse riddled with bullets, they would certainly call the police. And then Brian Petersen would have to answer a lot of embarrassing questions, and quite possibly the whole NFA kidnapping would become exposed. No, I didn't think we could afford that.

I crossed Memorial Bridge into Virginia, and I had just turned left on Washington Boulevard, when I saw the Pentagon ahead of me. And I knew then what I would do with Sarge's body: I would return him to the Army he loved.

I drove into one of the large parking lots at the Pentagon, now practically deserted at this late hour, and I cruised around until I found an Army vehicle, a four-door sedan. I stopped, tested the door of the Army car, and when I discovered it was unlocked, I went around to the trunk of my car and lifted Sarge's body out. I carried him over to the Army sedan, and sat him in the front seat behind the steering wheel. I took off his broken glasses and put them in his pocket, and then with a handkerchief I wiped the blood off his face. I found his wallet and flipped through it until I found his ID which identified him as retired military. I put the ID in the handkerchief pocket of his jacket, leaving enough of it exposed that it would be spotted immediately.

The Army would find him, and the Army would take care of its own.

Shortly before I reached my house in Arlington, I made one more phone call from the car. I dialed the Pentagon, and when the operator answered I told her there was a man in the parking lot apparently sick in a car. And I identified the location of the Army sedan with Sarge's body in it. Then I hung up immediately without giving my name. They would find him quickly now, and they would give him the military funeral he deserved.

Cathy Morrison met me at the door, and she gasped, her hand flying to her mouth, when she saw my battered condition. "Here, let me help you," she said.

"No, I'm all right."

Then she saw my eyes, and I think she recognized immediately the strange and distant mood which had come over me.

"Ellen is safe," I said, and briefly I told her some of the things which had happened tonight. I saw tears come to her eyes when I told her about Sarge's death. Finally, I said: "So it's over. I can take you home now."

"Right now?" she asked, puzzled. "Don't you want me to stay tonight?"

"No, I don't want you to stay," I said, averting my eyes from her. I didn't want to speak to Cathy, I didn't want to speak to anybody. I desperately wanted to be alone with my grim thoughts.

Cathy nodded wordlessly, then she bit her lip and went upstairs to get her things. I was waiting for her in the car when she came down. On the drive back to the District we hardly spoke. I did tell her, though, that Senator Rankin had decided that we should remain silent about the whole kidnapping plot, and she agreed. When I pulled up in front of her apartment building near Dupont Circle, I leaned over and opened the door for her. She stepped out, and then she turned.

"I really haven't thanked you for saving my life. And Ellen's life, too," she said, somewhat stiffly. Cathy seemed ready to walk away, but there was apparently something else on her mind. She looked at me, her eyes running over my blood-caked face and my stained clothes. "Why do you get involved in things like this?"

"I don't really know," I said sadly, and I watched her walk into the apartment building.

Now, after midnight, I was driving through the almost deserted section of downtown Washington. I cruised down

Fourteenth Street, and I was about to take the bridge back to Virginia when I noticed there were still a number of cars parked around the Tidal Basin on the Washington side of the Potomac. It was Cherry Blossom Time in Washington, and people would come out here until the early hours of the morning to look at those graceful trees which blossom for only a few short days each spring.

I pulled over at the Tidal Basin, found a parking place, and stepped out to get a breath of fresh air. I stood near my car, far away from any of the people who were looking at the blossoms, because I certainly didn't want anyone to see me in my present horrible condition. But I was able to view the blossoms from this distance, and then I looked across the Basin and saw the Jefferson Memorial, and then further across the Potomac I could see the Pentagon.

And I thought of Sarge over there, hoping they had him inside the building by now. Suddenly, my eyes began to mist. And then I did a strange thing, a very strange thing for me. Slowly I brought myself to attention and I gradually drew my hand up into a military salute.

"Good job, Sarge," I muttered.